The PECULIAR PEGGS of RIDDLING WOODS

The PECULIAR PEGGS of RIDDLING WOODS

SAMUEL J. HALPIN

USBORNE

A MOST PECULIAR MAP OF SUDS

RIDDLING WOODS SCHOOL

SUDS STATION

SUDS STATION SUDS SUDS

THE HELLIGAN MILLS

KEEP OUT

MARLEY'S BARGE

SUDS RIVER

N

S

ST. MARGARETS PARISH HALL

THE SUDS CEMETERY

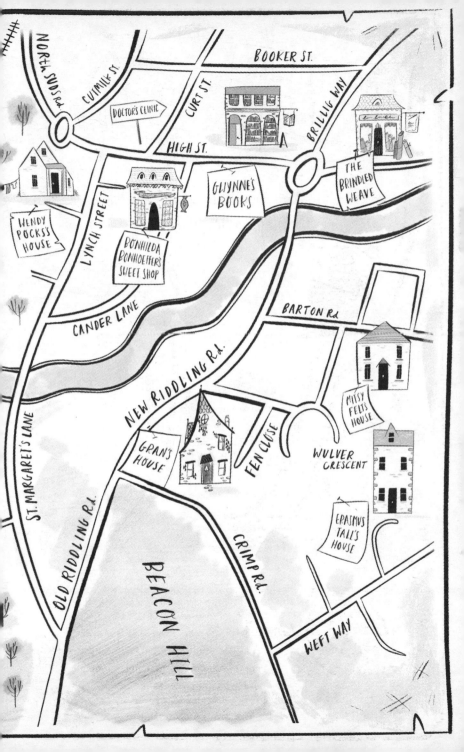

To Mum, Dad, Georgina, Julian, Michaela,
Camilla, Xavier and Remi

First published in the UK in 2019 by Usborne Publishing Ltd., Usborne House,
83-85 Saffron Hill, London EC1N 8RT, England. www.usborne.com

Text copyright © Samuel J. Halpin, 2019

The right of Samuel J. Halpin to be identified as the author of this work has been
asserted by him in accordance with the Copyright, Designs and Patents Act, 1988.

Cover and inside artwork by Hannah Peck © Usborne Publishing, Ltd, 2019

Type by Leo Nickolls © Usborne Publishing, Ltd, 2019

Dirt frame overlay © Thinkstock / jakkapan21

The name Usborne and the devices ♀ ⊕ are Trade Marks of
Usborne Publishing Ltd.

A CIP catalogue record for this book is available from the British Library.

ISBN 9781474945660 04824/1 JFMAMJJASO D/18

Printed in the UK.

Prologue
WORRIED

Poppy had been worried for a long time.

Stretching her neck, she pressed her flushed cheek and the side of her nose against the cold glass of the train window and tried to focus her eyes on the little stones and tracks hurtling past below.

Breathe, she said to herself, *breathe*.

That was what she knew to do whenever her heart began to play that little game where it thought Poppy was galloping up a mountain when she really wasn't.

I'm not worried, she told her reflection firmly. Her reflection had slate-blue eyes and short, inquisitive hair the colour of rust and bricks, just like she did. Although she didn't think her actual arms were as pointy at the elbows, or as skinny as the ones she could see in the window. Wrestling her jacket out of her backpack, she hauled it on over the top of her bottle-green cardie to hide the enormously pointy elbows. The cardie was something of her own creation, and it hung over her favourite tangerine-coloured corduroy dress like a bit of moss on an old tree. The dress had two wonderfully big pockets at the front, which were large enough to secrete away all manner of useful things, and Poppy liked to wear it when she was in a creative mood or travelling long distances.

LOOKOUT 4 MUMBLING MARLEY

read a wonky line of graffiti on the wall of the carriage. She wondered spitefully if whoever had spent half an hour gouging it into the plastic was aware that *lookout*, when employed as a verb, was two separate words.

Stop being so boring, she thought.

Poppy had only brought one backpack with her to Gran's. After all, she was only staying in Suds for two weeks of the summer holidays while Dad was away, so she hadn't packed a whole lot of stuff. She'd had that backpack since, well, since a very long time ago. She wasn't the kind of person who needed new things. After all, who wanted new things? Everyone except Poppy.

To Poppy, new things meant new smells. New shoes meant new blisters. A new backpack meant lodging the sharp end of your drawing compass beneath your fingernail as you fumbled around trying to find your ruler. She didn't like "new". In order for something to be new, something else had to be old, and that in turn meant that the old thing might very well be forgotten.

As with most train journeys that are northbound, the countryside became wilder and greener. The busy patchwork of fields ebbed away into quiet, untamed brushstrokes of leaves and wood, peppered with white flashes from where the chalk seams that ran through this part of the country raised their powdery heads above the surface.

She tried to phone Gran as the train pulled out of the next station to remind her of when to come and collect her. But Gran didn't answer. Gran hardly ever answered. Poppy wasn't worried though. She said so to herself again, *I'm not worried.* Because amongst all the things Gran never did, was forgetting. Gran never forgot.

The train rounded a bend and up ahead Poppy watched as the caterpillar-like succession of carriages vanished into a tunnel up ahead. Poppy's carriage soon flickered to black. She held her breath and counted eight seconds before the train shot out at the other end. She and Mum would do that in the car when they went through tunnels in London. The longest they'd managed was forty-three seconds.

Poppy's heart chugged in time to the train's engine.

Stop it, you stupid thing, she said to the spot on her chest where she imagined her heart must be.

Glancing down the long swaying carriage she noticed, perhaps for the first time, a tall woman at the other end beside the sliding doors. She was looking straight ahead out of the window, her hands clasped around a thin silver cane.

She doesn't look as if she needs a cane, Poppy thought to herself, quietly.

If people did need support getting about, they would use a walking frame nowadays, or one of those nippy little mobility scooters, or those chairlifts that old people sometimes have on the stairs.

The lady was wearing a velvet jacket with an assortment of glittering pins. On her head was a silver cap, and from it poked a feather so curled that it almost vanished against the dark rings of hair spiralling out from underneath. The lady was smiling. A smile that said she knew Poppy was watching her.

Without looking away from the window, the lady removed one of her green gloves and dipped her hand into her pocket, just long enough for Poppy to see her knobbly fingers. Poppy's heart gave a thump in her chest. The lady's hands weren't like her face at all. Her face was like glass, but her hands were like speckled paper.

Poppy turned away for a moment, but only so far that she could still see what was happening. From her pocket the lady pulled a small purse that was the same colour as her jacket. Opening the purse, she found a compact mirror and adjusted one of her curls a little with a hooked finger.

To either side of the train the black trees of the woods which surrounded Suds rose above them like twisted chimneys.

Poppy hadn't noticed the second tunnel approaching, and before she knew it they were plunged into darkness. She held her breath again and counted.

1, 2, 3…

She heard a sharp tap on the carriage floor.

4, 5, 6…

She closed her eyes.

7, 8, 9…

Daylight flooded back in and Poppy could see the rusty eaves of Suds station up ahead. She looked around the carriage. The lady was gone.

How could she be? The train had only been in the tunnel for nine seconds. Perhaps she'd just moved along to the next carriage. But Poppy hadn't heard the doors sliding open.

The voice over the train's speaker garbled something about "Taking all belongings with you" and "This train terminates here".

She heaved her backpack onto her narrow shoulders and positioned herself beside the doors. Then she noticed the lady's purse lying forgotten on a seat. It was almost the exact same colour as the quiet green fabric of the carriage upholstery. Poppy wouldn't have noticed it if she hadn't been spinning in circles as she struggled to squeeze her arm through the strap of her bulging backpack. The doors opened, a sharp gust of autumn wind plunged into the carriage, and instead of thinking, like she always did, Poppy snatched the purse and stuffed it into one of her wonderfully big pockets.

One
CLOTH

"Take the key from around my wrist," Gran told Poppy when they arrived back at her house. Poppy had visited Gran just once before, when she was three or four and Mum had driven her up for the day. After that, Gran took the train down to visit them a handful of times, but otherwise Poppy only really got to talk to her on the phone. It didn't matter though, because Gran's house smelled the same way that she remembered Gran did: of dark wood, musk and sugar. "Go to the cabinet by the fireside and open it just a little."

Poppy did as she was told.

"Now, using only one hand, lift the lid from the jar wrapped in cheesecloth."

Poppy obeyed. Churchill, Gran's miniature pig, sniffed anxiously around the kitchen and then charged through the door towards his basket, where he curled up cosily by the hearth. A fat log of wood surrounded by bundles of dry twigs blazed silently. Mum always said she could never remember Gran's house without a fire chattering away in the lounge room. "Suds was always seven degrees colder than anywhere else," she would say. "And if you didn't like the weather, all you had to do was look in a different direction, because the temperature in Suds was as changeable as the wind."

"Find the tweezers in the cabinet and take two lumps of sugar." Grandma squinted across the room over the top of her glasses. "Bravo," she said. "Now hold the sugar lumps in your hand as tight as you can without crushing them. Lock the cabinet. Bring me back the key."

Poppy did *exactly* as Gran instructed.

"Put the sugar lumps in my tea, as carefully as you can without making a splash."

When she had done this, Poppy stirred the tea.

"Scrummy!" Gran whispered, slurping her tea noisily. "Ahhhh!" She smacked her lips.

Poppy was not impressed.

"You'll soon find that I'm not a proper lady, Poppy," Gran told her, noticing Poppy's quiet disapproval. "I don't mean I'm not a girl. I'm very definitely a girl. I mean I talk with my mouth full. I put my elbows on the table. I *like* interrupting people." Gran winked at her with one little eye.

Poppy didn't know what to say, so she changed the subject. "Why do you hide the sugar, Gran?"

Gran drank some more tea and arranged herself more comfortably. She was wearing a crushed silk robe in a colour she called Burnt Brandy, topped with a hat that was dappled like a sun-drunk avocado. Poppy's eyes liked the colour. Burnt Brandy was a colour that made her think of black coffee, amber and chestnuts. The hat was similar to a fez and had a tassel that danced around Gran's blossomy hair. Perched on her nose was a pair of brass pince-nez, framing her glistening sea-green eyes.

Poppy liked looking at her grandma's armchair. It was furrowed and patched, and dotted with hundreds of glistening pins. Gran always said she got all her best ideas while sitting in that chair. She called it the Seat of Wisdom.

Gran was a seamstress and could make any wearable thing you wanted. Think of a costume now; she could make it. A scaled sea monster, the robes of a golden sultan, a goblin made of nothing but leaves and wind. She worked through the night, her long fingers stitching and milling like a spider. Although Gran wasn't famous, her costumes were. You could always tell if she'd made something by the tiny initials she'd embroider into the lining: T.H.

"The sugar *must* be kept locked up," Gran said simply, which was no real answer at all. Then she changed the subject with insect-like speed. "I moved to Suds forty-six years ago when I was twenty-two. The people here aren't any kinder or meaner than any other town. The library doesn't have better books. The post doesn't come any faster, and the mutton pies are just as delicious as the ones two towns over. I didn't come here for any of that. I came to Suds for the *cloth*."

Gran took another sip from her cup, and when her pursed lips pulled away they created a little ripple in her tea.

"There is no better cloth in the whole, wide, wonderful *world* than the cloth they make in Suds."

Poppy cradled her cocoa and nestled up beside Gran's velvet slippers.

"I've seen cloth that changes colour like a cuttlefish, and fabric that crumbles like ancient stones but stitches like new satin."

"Where do they make the cloth?" Poppy asked.

"At the Helligan Mills, just out of town on the river. Miss Crink at the fabric shop says that once a week, on a Tuesday morning, bolts of the most exquisite cloth float down the river in a crate which stops at the brook beside her shop. There is never any left over, because the perfect amount is always made. Not an inch more or less."

"Who makes it?"

"That", her grandmother said, "remains a mystery." She thought for a bit. "Your mum wouldn't like me telling you this, but since she isn't with us any more I make those decisions now, so I'm going to tell you."

Gran cleared her throat and opened a tin of syrupy peaches sat beside her.

"Many years ago, before there were street lamps and car horns, there opened a famous fabric mill in Suds. Merchants came from all over the world to buy their fabric. Nothing was impossible, no colour too specific, no texture too complex. You could take them a toadstool and they'd weave you a red and white spotted fabric with an underside of pleated bone muslin that was so fine you'd think they'd plucked it from a witch's supply cupboard. They made a voile so light, you could drape it on a ghost."

"How did they make it?" Poppy wondered if perhaps Gran was exaggerating a little.

Gran finished off the last peach and drank the juice

from the tin. "Some say they made it with the web of the Whistling Spider, others say they used silk threads from the Chinese Devil Worm softened in the stomach of the Skipping Camel. But I say otherwise."

The old woman narrowed her briny eyes and leaned towards Poppy.

"I say magic," she said, and picked her teeth with a needle.

Poppy's neck was suddenly aware of the tiny hairs on the back of it.

"You can't expect me to believe that, Gran."

"Then how else do you explain it?"

Poppy thought for a moment and considered biting her nail absent-mindedly.

"Well, no one can ever really prove they've seen a ghost or what it looks like inside a witch's supply cupboard. So no one could ever prove the materials really ever were that special, could they?"

Gran smiled. "You must be careful not to be too clever, my little button. Overthinking clogs the brain like soggy cereal clogs the sink."

Poppy narrowed her eyes. Gran held out her cup.

"Make me another tea and fetch me a biscuit, would you, pet?"

Poppy put the kettle on the stove.

"Where did we leave off? Oh, that's right," Gran said, unpicking a few of the scales from a pair of beetle wings she was making. "The fabric became even more famous. The town of Suds prospered and grew...until something odd began to happen."

The kettle whistled as it began to boil and Poppy poured the hot water over the fragrant tea leaves.

"One by one, like the birds of summer, children began to vanish."

Poppy put the kettle down and brought Grandma her tea.

"What do you mean? How did they vanish? When did this happen?"

Churchill the pig rested his snout on the edge of his basket, as if listening to the story too.

"I mean just what I say: children began to vanish. One here, one there. They faded away. I remember I was twenty-three when Wilma Norbles disappeared. Wilma was a swimming champion. Every day before school she would swim up and down the river like a seal, until one morning something peculiar began to happen. It started with Wilma's eyes. Very slowly, little by little, their colour began to fade. Before she knew it, the colour from her hair began to drain away too. The last time Wilma climbed into the river, despite being ten years old, she was as grey as an old woman. People watching from the shore said that she took a deep breath, sunk beneath the water and dissolved like a blob of paint. Some said she was eaten by the old fish rumoured to live in the River Suds. But even I'm not superstitious enough to think *that's* likely."

Poppy nodded politely. She didn't quite know if she believed her wily old gran. She was twelve after all, and twelve is the age when one truly starts reasoning what is real and what is fabricated.

"I can see you don't believe me, but let me tell you this: ever since, and ever so slowly, the children of Suds have been dwindling away."

"Where did they go?" Poppy asked. "When was the last time it happened?"

Gran looked at Poppy and answered only one of her questions. "No one knows. Sugar, my button. Two lumps."

Poppy retrieved the sugar, heeding Grandma's instructions.

"And what's happened to the Mills now?"

"They're still there," said Gran, sipping her tea. "Somewhere in the woods outside of town. Riddling Woods. Neglected, ruined and overgrown. Whether the fabric which floats down the river comes from the Mills or not is anybody's guess. People in the village like to say they are haunted."

"Haunted?"

"Haunted," said Gran. "By the ghost of a washerwoman who crouches beside the river's edge, washing the stains from a grey cloth."

"That's not real," muttered Poppy, her chest swimming with unease.

"It might not be real, but it's a fact that people have seen her," said Gran wryly. "Now, while your dad is away for the next few weeks and you're staying with me here in Suds, I want you to follow four simple rules. No one else seems to bother with them these days, but I'm a bit old-fashioned sometimes, Poppy, and I like to stick to them."

Poppy fetched her notepad from her backpack and wrote down what Grandma said. With each line she wrote, her fingers stiffened and her heart began to dance its familiar dance.

RULES:

1) All washing must be done during the day. Bring your clothes in off the washing line (even if they are wet) before six o'clock every night.

2) All sugar cubes are to be kept under lock and key.

3) At night close your window, lock it, draw the curtains.

4) NEVER, DON'T YOU EVER, dust the window sills.

Two
SUGAR

The accident that set Poppy's story in motion was not a happy one at all. In fact, it was a very terrible one. It involved three things. A lorry carrying laundry hampers, a nasty corner and Poppy's mum. Poppy's darling mum.

When Poppy thought about those few months after the accident, she could only remember a great black spot and the little flowers on the silver handle of the coffin which she knew her mum was inside. It had been eleven months since it happened now, but that black spot still blotted the front of her mind.

The day they turned the machine off at the hospital and Poppy's mum's heart stopped beating, Poppy's had started racing. It was almost as if her heart was trying to catch up with something, like a dog chasing a postman.

She didn't know why it happened, but when it did she had the uncanny feeling that something dreadful was rounding the corner again. She hadn't told her dad. He would just say things like "That sounds psychosomatic" or "Go for a cycle, you'll feel loads better". Dad thought that cycling could cure anything, even that drowning, icy numbness that had stung their lives like a winter's frost the day Mum left them.

Dad cycled everywhere and had been on cycling tours in more than thirty different countries. Gran liked to say that he should be given a medal for never failing to make Lycra look revolting in more than thirty different climates. The two weeks Dad was spending cycling in Canada right now meant that Gran could make that number thirty-*one*.

Grandma wasn't like Mum at all. Gran liked her coffee black. Mum liked her tea green. Gran kept a noisy miniature pig. Mum kept herself to herself. Grandma's house was cluttered and flecked with paint. Mum's house was crisp, ironed and wiped. Poppy didn't think one was better than the other. All she knew was that Grandma and Mum had always been different. It wasn't that they didn't like each other either. It was just that Mum always went a bit funny when anyone mentioned going to visit Gran and no one ever seemed to know why.

The next morning, which was a Sunday, Poppy watched from her perch in the lounge room as Gran opened her second box of Bonhilda Bonhoeffer's Sour Strawberry Wheels since nine o'clock. She unfurled them like a serpent's tongue and guzzled them up greedily as she stitched.

Gran ate things that would make Poppy's mum turn in her grave. And Gran would rather eat a jar of leeches than the organic food Mum cooked.

"What is this muck you've made, girl?" Poppy remembered Grandma saying to Mum on one of her rare visits. "I've seen better food in a hog trough. I'd rather eat a set of bowling pins than torture myself with this soo-shee."

"Sushi is healthy, Gran," Poppy had explained. "The nori seaweed that the sushi is wrapped in is full of vitamins and minerals. It's good for you. You can't eat sweets all your life."

"Man cannot live on sweets alone," chimed in Poppy's mum.

"Well I am a *woman*," Gran insisted. "And I'd rather die a delicious death than live a tasteless life. *That* is my motto for both fashion and food."

Poppy spent that morning, and the next few days of the holidays, sorting Grandma's jars and jars of buttons into colours, shapes and sizes, while the rain tickled the windows. There were thousands of them. Gran liked to buy second-hand clothes *just* to pick the buttons off, then donated the clothes back to the store.

There was a sock beside Gran's workstation where she kept loose buttons. Poppy soon learned to empty this into one of the button jars at the end of each day like a rubbish bin. Then she used a wide tray to filter through the contents, like one of the gold sifters she had seen in *National Geographic*. She found all sorts of wonderful things hiding among the buttons: thimbles, ear buds, a tiny model ship, blue marbles, bits of coloured glass, paper clips, and one thing that Poppy found very odd indeed. It was a tiny comb with the face of a woman carved into the handle.

"Made from bone, I should think," Gran told Poppy as she examined the comb underneath her magnifying glass. "Yes, it's definitely made from bone."

"What sort of bone?"

"Whale, I should think," said Grandma wisely, "or maybe rhinoceros. People used to make all sorts of things out of bone. Corsets, flutes, shovels, buttons, even houses."

Poppy shuddered.

"I've collected jars of buttons from all over. Someone must have hidden the comb in that one," said Gran, criss-crossing her brow. "Buttons are very magical things. Buttons close jackets, pockets and purses. They keep things sealed. They keep things both out and in. If I didn't want someone to find something, I'd hide it in a jar of buttons."

"Can I keep it?" Poppy asked, holding up the comb.

"Of course. Wear it in your hair."

Poppy didn't know how she felt about wearing a bit of old bone on her head. But she tried it for Gran.

As the great button-sorting operation progressed, Poppy decided that Grandma needed to dedicate an entire room to her buttons.

"Where does the little door up here lead, Gran?" Poppy called down from the top of the steps to the storage room on the second floor.

"I think it's an old sugar pantry," Gran called up. "I haven't been up those stairs in sixteen years, so I'm not quite sure. Bad leg, you see. All the old houses in Suds have a sugar pantry. It was a council stipulation to have them built in, almost like a miniature attic."

Poppy climbed past the boxes of junk and dusty costumes Gran had collected over the years and tried to open the door. It was locked.

"Is there a key?"

"I've lost it," sighed Gran. "You'll have to use a paper clip or something to pick the lock."

Poppy rummaged through the dusty clutter surrounding her until she found a paper clip holding together a yellow wad of invoices. Ruby Gutts, her best friend from school, had showed her exactly how to pick a lock. Ruby was like a magpie. She could pick her way into anything: Miss Baum's treat box, Mr Gillard's exam papers cabinet. Grandma had promised that Ruby could come and stay for a few days before school started back.

With a few swift movements, the little door was unlocked. It swung open and Poppy squeezed her way through.

Had I been any bigger than I am now, she thought to herself, *I wouldn't have fit through this door.*

Gran was right. It was like a miniature attic. Poppy could only fit in the cupboard-sized room if she lay out on her stomach. It was tucked into the eaves and felt like the inside of a doll's house. She couldn't wait to show Ruby when she came to visit.

The walls were lined with boxes and boxes and boxes of sugar cubes. They looked as if they hadn't been touched in many years.

Poppy heard Grandma open a packet of biscuits in the kitchen.

"Are you going to walk with me to the doctor's?" Grandma called up.

Poppy didn't respond. She had felt something underneath her. Something in her pocket. Easing herself onto her side, she discovered the purse she had found on the train just a few days before. Poppy hadn't worn her tangerine dress since then.

She had meant to look for the lady on the platform or hand it in as lost property at the station, but the excitement of seeing Gran waiting with Churchill had let it slip from her mind.

Using the tips of her fingers, she pulled back the zip and opened it up. Inside the purse were a few things that Poppy didn't want to touch (a crumpled hanky, two waxy earplugs and some Fisherman's Friends). But among them was a tatty old book about the size of a slice of toast, with loose threads dangling from the edges. The book was covered in material: a green material that Poppy was certain she'd seen somewhere before.

"Poppy?"

Poppy wriggled her way out of the pantry and stuffed the purse and the book back into the folds of her dress to examine later. As she slipped down the stairs to the front door she couldn't help but feel the tiniest pinprick of annoyance that Gran's appointment had to be this morning of all mornings. She tried to listen to what Gran was saying as Churchill hurtled on ahead of them down the street, but she was finding it desperately difficult to concentrate and her fingers kept finding the silken binding of the book in her pocket.

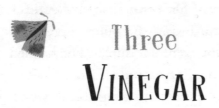

Three
VINEGAR

The waiting room at the doctor's surgery smelled faintly like the hotel Poppy had stayed in with her aunt the night of Mum's accident. The posters were faded, and the laminated signs advising the thorough washing of hands were bubbled and peeling.

Poppy scratched her neck and tried to loosen the itchy collar of her knitted jumper. It was strangely chilly that morning, but she was regretting her choice to combat the cold. The jumper was another one of her own creations. And while at the time she'd thought that combining brown, purple and white wool was a pioneering idea, she had to admit she'd ended up looking like something that was usually flung over a sofa.

Gran's doctor, Dr Yemmen, seemed like a nice man,

but Gran apparently delighted in pretending she hated him.

"Tilda Herisson?" Dr Yemmen called out.

"Alright, alright," said Grandma, getting up and feeling for her appointment slip in her handbag, "I'm not going deaf. There's no need to shout."

"You've got a hearing check-up today, so we'll soon know, won't we, Mrs Herisson?" The doctor smiled.

"A *what?*" bugled Gran.

"And maybe it's time for an eye examination too?" Dr Yemmen suggested, as he noticed Churchill. "Because I don't remember there being a *Vet* sign outside my clinic."

"That's funny," said Gran, "I don't remember there being a *No Pigs Allowed* sign either."

Dr Yemmen rolled his eyes and flicked a prescription slip into a tray on the reception desk.

Gran winked at Poppy. "Stay here until I come out, Button. Look after Churchill. Won't be a minute." As Dr Yemmen ushered her into his examination room, she muttered, "If I come out alive, that is."

Churchill curled himself up beside Poppy's feet. Poppy thought about reading one of the magazines in the waiting room, but Mum had always said that sick children left germs all over them and if Poppy did read them she'd catch typhoid or cholera and be dead before you could say "antibacterial hand sanitizer".

Then she remembered the book in her pocket. To

her disappointment it was blank, except for a tiny M.G. stitched into the back cover. Malicious Gorilla, perhaps? Or Mad Goat?

"Probably some diary that lady never ended up using," Poppy muttered.

"What's that?" came a voice from the opposite side of the surgery.

Poppy looked up. A boy with hair whiter than Poppy had ever seen was watching her from across the room. His eyes were a powerful green and his skin was as pale as a bowl of fresh milk. He was holding a small but thick book entitled *Deciphering Cryptography* by Dr Nial Guntar. On a lanyard around his neck was a clunky looking object which Poppy recognized as a digital video camera. She couldn't remember ever seeing one in the flesh. She'd only ever seen them in movies from the 90's. Beside this peculiar boy was a lady with black hair, black nail polish and black lipstick.

"A pig in a waiting room..." the lady with the black hair muttered to herself.

"What's what?" Poppy asked.

The boy walked over and sat down beside her. "This," he said, sharply tapping the book with his finger.

"It's a...book."

"Which book?"

"I don't know," Poppy explained, flicking through to show him. "It's empty."

Poppy went back to pretending to read her empty book.

The boy sighed, then pinched the book from her to examine it carefully. He held the pages very close to his face and breathed in through his nose. Poppy smiled awkwardly at the woman, who threw what seemed to be a sarcastic smile back.

That must be his mother, Poppy thought. *I don't blame her for wearing so much make-up. I'd probably want to hide too if I had a kid like that.*

The boy gave one of the pages a sniff.

"It isn't empty," he told Poppy.

"What do you mean? Of course it's empty."

"No it's not."

To Poppy's horror, the boy poked out his tongue and gave the page a lick.

Poppy snatched the book back from him and wiped it with her sleeve. Mum was right. Sick children liked to put their germs on everything. She'd probably have scarlet fever before the night was out.

"What do you think you're doing?" she snapped. "This isn't even my book."

"Vinegar," said the boy.

"Vinegar?" asked Poppy.

"That's what I said."

"As in, the stuff you put on chips?"

"You can taste it," said the boy. "There's something written on those pages in vinegar. You need to use a hairdryer to see what's written there."

"Poppy?" came Gran's voice across the waiting room. "Are you ready? Dr Yemmen has finished torturing me, so we can go to the shops."

"Until next time, Mrs Herisson." Dr Yemmen smiled. He turned to the boy with the white hair and showed him into the examination room. Before he vanished behind the door, the boy glanced back at Poppy and said, "Your jumper is really ugly."

"Do you have a hairdryer, Gran?" Poppy asked as they walked down Suds high street. Churchill trotted happily ahead of them on his silver leash.

"No," Gran said, stopping to catch her breath. "Hairdryers are a waste of money. If I need to dry my hair quickly, I use my iron. But because I'm old, I only have one or two hairs left, so I never really bother."

Poppy pinched her fingers at the thought. Gran wasn't renowned for her safety consciousness. She famously told everyone she never used a thimble.

An empty biscuit wrapper glided past them down the street: Jammy Heart Drops. They were Poppy's friend

Ruby's favourite. She had them at school every day at morning break.

Poppy felt something spectacular and empty touch her. She gripped Gran's arm and held it to her cheek.

"Poppy, darling?"

Poppy kept quiet and squeezed Gran's arm even tighter. *She was there. Everything was fine.*

Poppy looked up again. Somehow, Suds high street managed not to feel sleepy. The red-brick shops, dotted with tangles of vacant flower beds and faded *For Sale* signs, spiralled up the slanting road. A large cotton-mill wheel made an attempt at being decorative as it slowly rusted away on the verge in front of the supermarket. At the far end of the street was their destination: Miss Eliza Crink's fabric shop, The Brindled Weave.

A bell tinkled somewhere in the distance as they entered the musty shop. The shelves were stuffed with spools of gilded thread, jewelled buttons, crushed silks, delicate candlewick embroidery, crumpled whorls of Chantilly lace and wads of cotton stuffing.

Eliza Crink slid up behind the counter with an enormous bolt of electric-blue fabric over her shoulder and a hissing steamer in hand. The bolt of fabric was beautifully rolled around a cardboard cylinder that was slightly bent at one end.

"If it isn't my favourite customer, Mrs Herisson!" she chimed huskily.

"She says that to every Tom, Dick and Harry who

walks in the door," Gran whispered to Poppy. "I'm no more her favourite customer than she is a bantam hen."

Poppy was too busy noticing the pencil stuck like a hatpin through Eliza's silver hair, which looked like someone had dolloped a scoop of whiskery marshmallow fluff on her head. She wore a crumpled kaftan in arsenic blue and spectacles fashioned from twists of rusty copper. On her finger was a thimble, which glistened in the dim light as she nipped about the shop like an elf.

"Oh! The latest consignment of fabric from the Helligan Mills must be for you, Mrs Herisson," Eliza realized, tapping her forehead. "How stupid of me. A thousand apologies. Three bolts, I think it was?"

Gran nodded.

"To be sure, to be sure. Follow me, dear Mrs Herisson. Sorry, so sorry."

Eliza cantered down the corridor with her head bowed gingerly, and Grandma and Poppy followed at a distance.

At the back of the cluttered shop was a plain wooden door, which Eliza unlocked with a small key, grinning feebly as she did so.

Poppy peered excitedly over Gran's shoulder, eager to see what lay beyond the door. But she was disappointed. The room was full of shelves, but only three long packages sat in the corner.

Eliza squinted at their labels.

"Six yards of Whiskered Whingecloth, eight of

Rotten Rinse Mink and three of the Brushed-and-Bristled Black Bullthorn."

The fabric was wrapped modestly in bone-coloured paper, so Poppy would have to wait to see how it looked.

Back at the counter, Grandma fished her purse from the bottom of her bag.

"Cash or card?" asked Eliza.

Gran handed Eliza a crumpled note, and Eliza printed her a receipt from the noisiest till Poppy had ever heard.

After business was wrapped up, Eliza's furtive eyes fell to Poppy.

"What's that beneath your arm there, my little gateau?"

Poppy realized Eliza was speaking to her. "It's a book," she said, shifting on the spot.

Eliza tented her fingers and, giving a half-bow to Gran, asked, "Might there be a chance I could take a look at it, dear pretty thing?"

Poppy didn't want Eliza to see the book, but given it wasn't strictly hers she offered it begrudgingly.

For no apparent reason, Poppy's heart began to gather steam.

Eliza gasped and snatched the book from Poppy. Her bottom lip trembled.

"The silk," she whispered in a deep hiss. "*This* book is bound in silk. I haven't seen silk like this in years. This is one of the *old* Helligan silks."

"How can you tell?" asked Gran.

Poppy felt her hands itch as Eliza ran her knobbly fingers over the front of the book.

"There's no cloth that weaves a tale as dark as Helligan silk. I can feel the twisted cunning of its thread."

Poppy felt a muscle in her jaw twitch. Eliza Crink wasn't the only person who had been interested in her book that morning. Perhaps she could smell vinegar too.

Eliza removed her spectacles, her eyes wide. She took Poppy's hand and brushed her fingers against the book.

"Can you feel it? It's as if the fabric breathes in your hand, like skin. This silk was spun in the dark, far from light."

It was then that Poppy had a better chance to look at Eliza's thimble. The truth was, she wasn't really *wearing* it at all. Beneath the silver cusp, Poppy could see the stump of a finger and a clasp which fitted the thimble on top of it.

"How much?" Eliza asked Grandma, closing the book and pulling it closer towards her. She drummed her thimble noisily on the counter. There was something different about her, almost as if she'd grown a few inches in the last minute.

Poppy tried to breathe deeply. Her heart was galloping like a greyhound. "We're not selling it," she interrupted quickly. "It's not for sale."

"Is it your book?" asked Eliza softly.

Poppy shifted again. "Yes." Her heart jumped a hurdle and galloped on.

Eliza turned sharply towards Gran. "Mrs Herisson, I'll give you a very generous eighty-five pounds for this book, and free delivery on your next order of fabric – given your gammy leg and all. Now is that an offer or what?"

Poppy wanted to tell Miss Crink to sling her thimble, but she kept quiet. This was her shop after all.

Grandma looked at Poppy without saying anything and Poppy looked back. Gran's leg *did* look sore when she walked on it.

While Poppy didn't believe in telepathy, at that moment she was sure Gran knew what she was thinking.

"You heard my granddaughter. It's not for sale." Grandma smiled pertly, picked up the book and handed it to Poppy, who tucked it safely into her pocket.

"One hundred and fifty pounds, Mrs Herisson, and free delivery for the rest of the year – think of your poor leg!"

"As I said, Miss Crink," Gran said quietly, "the book is *not* for sale. And I'll have you know my leg is well and truly on the mend. In fact, it feels so chipper, I believe I could kick something."

"But…" Eliza began.

There was a cough from the back of the shop, and Poppy turned to see an older woman with glassy eyes queuing behind them. She was wearing a beige suit and had a small brass trumpet tucked beneath her arm. Eliza seemed to return to her old self in the presence of another customer. She leaned in towards Poppy.

"I'd keep that book *very* close," she whispered with a frail smile. "In fact, if I were you, I'd never put it down."

As they left the shop, Poppy could feel Miss Crink's eyes on the back of her neck. Her hair began to itch, and she willed herself out of that shop as fast as she could. *How odd*, she thought to herself. *How very, very odd.*

Four
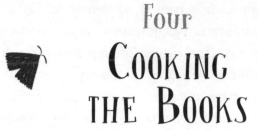
Cooking the Books

At five-thirty, Poppy made sure to bring Gran's washing in for her. Gran didn't have the same type of washing that ordinary grandmothers did. There weren't any doilies, tablecloths and large white knickers. Gran washed caterpillar coats, dragons' tails and astronaut suits.

If she stood in the wheelbarrow that Gran kept beside the garden shed, she could just manage to yank the pegs off the line. The laundry hamper became heavy very quickly, which is where the wheelbarrow came in handy once again. Poppy heard a window open above her.

"Hurry up with that washing, popsicle," Gran called out. "There's been a weather warning on the radio."

Poppy checked the weather forecast on her phone.

Gran was right. She noticed there was also a message waiting from her dad:

Work have asked me to take a look at a few projects and pick up some meetings in Canada while I'm here. I'll be another few weeks. Could you ask your gran if you can stay the rest of the holidays before going back to school? Dad x

Poppy felt a nasty little kick in her stomach, just above her belly button. Why didn't Dad ask Gran himself? Dad seemed to think that putting a kiss on the end of a message meant he was being a good parent.

The first drops of rain began to heckle the windows of the house as she slid the wheelbarrow through the side door and slammed it shut.

Gran was stirring a large pot of cheese sauce with a wooden knitting needle. She added some white wine and began chopping up a clove of garlic with her fabric scissors.

"I once forgot to wash my scissors after making a coleslaw, and I made a Tudor ballgown that made the actress smell like cabbage," Gran told Poppy. "At least it was authentic."

Poppy paused.

"Can I stay with you a little longer, Gran?"

Gran stopped stirring and turned to face her. "Of course you can, poppet. But won't you be wanting to see your dad? He'll be home soon."

"He's staying on in Canada for a bit," she replied coldly as she unloaded the washing. She didn't want to talk about it, and Gran seemed to realize this. Poppy peered into the blackened mouth of the oven. Gran had never cleaned it and never planned to.

"How hot have you set the oven?"

"Not very, I'm just keeping our bread warm. I like it when the butter melts into little puddles. Why?"

Poppy fished around in her bag and produced the silk book. Gran watched as she fumbled around in the cupboard beneath the sink and found a shallow tray. She popped the book in it, intending to shove it in next to the haddock Grandma had prepared earlier.

"Can we put it in the oven? Just for a bit? Seeing as we don't have a hairdryer?"

"Where did you get that book, Poppy?"

Poppy thought for a second, and then she told Gran everything. About the strange lady on the train, and finding the book in her purse, and about what the boy at the doctor's surgery had said.

"Then what are we waiting for?" Grandma cried, fetching her handmade oven mitt, which was really a worm puppet. "Brew it, bake it, boil it, fry it! Let's see what's hiding there."

At first they baked the book neatly wrapped in foil. When that didn't work, they tried taking the foil off and microwaving it. But it still wasn't enough, so Grandma plonked the book in her stovepipe steamer, which she used for painting silk, and gave it a blast for a few minutes.

"I think that boy from the doctor's was a rotten little liar," Grandma huffed, wiping the sweat from her brow. "I'd like to pop *him* in this steamer." She lifted the book out of the steamer with a pair of fireplace tongs and plopped it in front of Poppy.

"Nothing?"

"Nothing," Poppy said with a disappointed little sigh as she opened the book. It had been a disappointing evening.

They ate their dinner in front of the telly on little trays and then Gran fell asleep after her sherry. Poppy cleared the dishes, washed them and put a quilt over Grandma's legs. Churchill tried to climb the stairs up to Poppy's bedroom, but was much too tiny and tumbled backwards at the first step. Poppy filled Churchill's water bowl and tucked him into his basket by the hearth.

When she finally climbed up to her room, she locked her window. The storm was beginning to blow in over Suds and the wind whipped the clouds into a swirling mass of black. Through a chink in the blustery tempest, the moon poked a watchful eye.

She searched under her pillow for the last keepsake her mum had given her. It was a little box of tailor's chalk, used to draw marks on clothing when measuring out the fabric or making alterations. The pieces of chalk were all different colours, shaped like little triangular discs. It was an odd thing for Mum to have given her. A very odd thing. There was a note which Mum had clipped to it using a dodgy wooden peg. Poppy had kept the peg and the note. The note didn't say anything particularly heartfelt, only that the next time Poppy visited Gran she should take the chalk with her to Suds to help Gran cut out her patterns, because that's what Mum used to do herself.

Mum didn't sew, really. At least not the kind of sewing that you needed tailor's chalk for. She could sew a button, or stitch a patch, but Gran's wily skill must have skipped a generation. Poppy could sew like a fiend. She had made her own backpack using a thick stretch of canvas and leather needles.

Poppy began to doze off. She could hear the blood pulsing in her ear, so she turned over on her pillow.

Thump, thump, thump it went. She closed her eyes. And then she heard it. As loud and clear as the night they stood waiting to turn Mum's respirator off.

Thump, thump, thump went Mum's heart.

One of the doctors had whispered to Dad, who'd nodded quietly and gone to the corner of the hospital room to read some forms before signing them. Then Gran had signed them.

If Mum is gone, Poppy remembered thinking, *why is her heart still thumping? Her heart is still awake.*

Before long they had wheeled Mum off, and Poppy never saw her face again. That was it. That was the last time. The last thing she saw was Mum's bruised face, strangled by tubes, whisked past her and out the door at the hospital.

Poppy shook herself awake and sat upright in a cold sweat.

Thump, thump, thump.

"It's nothing," she said out loud. "It's just the wind." That's what Dad would have said.

Thump, thump, clang, twang!

It was definitely something.

Thump! Bang! Tink! Clang!

Poppy's heart began to throw itself against the walls of her ribcage. Sidling out of bed, she edged towards the window and peered out into the garden. The wind was tickling the brambles and little pools of water had begun to collect between the paving stones. Her eye caught something white next to the garden shed.

Something was definitely out there, and it wasn't just the wind. It moved its long pale arms, and the clanging began again.

Poppy remembered Grandma had said not to open the windows at night. She checked the bolt and drew the curtains shut. Even though Grandma was downstairs, Poppy felt unnerved. For a moment her fingers struggled with the mass of cobwebs on her window sill. Because of her rules, Gran didn't dust her window sills, and they had quickly become a home for vast tangles of silky threads. Poppy could see the beauty of the spider, but still didn't class them as the kind of animal whose behaviour she would describe as "winning". Mum had used antibacterial wipes to cleanse her window sills daily.

Don't panic, she thought to herself. *Panicking never did anyone any good.* She carefully released herself from the cobwebs and dusted her hands on her nightgown. From between the threads she saw the lazy leg of the cobweb's inhabitant wave gratefully.

Poppy heard Churchill snort loudly in his sleep downstairs by the fireside. Perhaps he was dreaming? Gran said that pigs dreamed just as much as people did when they slept.

Thump! Thump! Thump!

She peeked out of her bedroom door and down the stairs. Someone was knocking at the front door. Churchill skidded into view from his basket around the corner and snuffled suspiciously underneath the door. Poppy listened; Gran must still be sleeping. She'd noticed she always slept heavily after a sherry.

Poppy's heart began to waltz around her ribcage.

The clanging began again. Poppy shuffled slowly down the stairs, very aware that she could ignore it no longer. Churchill perched his trotters excitedly on her slippers.

"Who's there?" Poppy asked.

"Erasmus," came a voice from the other side of the door.

Poppy picked Churchill up and held him tightly. "Who?" she asked again.

"Erasmus Tall," said the voice.

"Well, I don't know any Erasmus Talls," Poppy told the voice. "So please go."

"We met today."

"I don't think so," Poppy said, trying to retrace her steps in her head.

"Look through the letter box," said the voice.

Poppy thought for a moment. Ignoring her racing heart, she put Churchill down and, kneeling on the rug, lifted the letter flap and peered outside.

Through the rain, she could just see the boy with the white hair and pale skin from the doctor's surgery. He wasn't smiling, but he was waving and dripping wet. Poppy unlocked the door immediately and let him in.

"Why didn't you say it was you?" she demanded, as Churchill watched Erasmus cautiously.

"I did," he shivered, "I told you it was Erasmus Tall."

"Well, how was I supposed to know your name?"

"I thought you might have read it on the collar of my shirt." He turned up his collar to show her.

"No, I didn't. I'm obviously not as good at being nosey as you are," Poppy said, crossing her arms. "Do you mind telling me how you knew where we lived?"

"The house number was written on the form your grandmother was holding as she went into the doctor's room."

Poppy was stunned. She'd never met anyone who pried so much.

"You should know that it's rude to read things that aren't meant for you," Poppy told him.

"What about billboards?"

"What about them?"

"Well if a billboard is advertising men's shaving cream you still read it, don't you? Even though it's not meant for you."

Poppy knew he was right, but she didn't want to agree with him. "I try not to," she said.

Erasmus shivered and hugged himself with cold. "May I have a towel?" he asked after a moment.

"Yes, of course," Poppy apologized, remembering her manners.

She fetched a towel from the hot-water cupboard and made him stand beside the stove in the kitchen.

"Why are you here?" she asked, filling a saucepan with milk. She needed a good strong kick of hot chocolate.

"I wanted to see the book again," Erasmus said, watching Churchill carefully. "Why is your pig so small? He won't make a very good Christmas ham. Hot chocolate would be lovely, by the way. More sugar than cocoa. And more warm than hot."

Churchill was sitting on his stool at the kitchen table, and looked up as if he knew he was being spoken about. Poppy slid the saucepan onto the stove and felt inside the pocket of her dressing gown. The book had been there the whole time. But she didn't want him to see it again. It was hers. She found it.

"He's a miniature pig, I don't think they're edible," Poppy explained, avoiding the subject of the book. "He won't grow much bigger than that. I think he was a runt too, which makes him even smaller."

"I *know* what a runt is," Erasmus said sharply. "Can you show me the book now?"

"I haven't got it," Poppy lied. "I sold it to a man... a man with one leg. You'll have to go ask him."

"No you didn't," Erasmus said, examining Churchill's feeding bowl.

"I beg your pardon?"

"It's in your pocket," Erasmus said calmly.

Poppy was gobsmacked.

"How can you tell?"

"I notice things."

Poppy slowly pulled the book out of her pocket and laid it on the kitchen table. Erasmus sat himself down and examined the silk cover.

"Did you try heating it?"

"Yes," Poppy told him, sitting down opposite. "I tried different temperatures, and different types of heat. Nothing worked."

Erasmus smelled the book, then brought it very close to his eyes, as if it was an insect he was trying to examine.

"I couldn't stop thinking about this book," he told

Poppy. "There's something unique about it."

"What do you think it is?"

"It needs a different type of heat."

"I told you, I tried steaming it, I tried baking it, I tried everything," insisted Poppy.

"But this book isn't made like a normal book. Can't you see?"

Poppy had no idea what he was talking about.

Erasmus explained: "The paper is abnormally thick, and I can't see a join in the binding."

Erasmus was right.

"It needs a different type of heat."

"You already said that," Poppy hissed impatiently.

Erasmus picked an egg whisk off the bench and, putting it over his shoulder, turned the handle as if it were an old movie camera.

"Perhaps you should go," Poppy decided, pulling the book from under his arm. She held it close to her chest.

Erasmus's eyes widened. He had seen something strange. Getting up from the table, he walked round to where Poppy was sitting.

"What are you doing?" Poppy asked, edging her chair away. Churchill snorted at Erasmus like a watchdog. Erasmus said nothing but took the book from Poppy and, opening it to the first page, laid it out on the table. He rubbed his hands together until they were warm, then placed his palm flat on the page.

"What are you—"

"Shh!" Erasmus interrupted. "Put your hand on the other page and hold it there."

Poppy reluctantly did as she was told.

"Nothing's happening," she said.

Erasmus was silent.

At first Poppy thought her mind was playing tricks on her. A thin black line of ink appeared slowly from underneath Erasmus's palm. Soon, ink began to appear beneath Poppy's hand too. Erasmus gestured for her to lift her palm, and he did the same thing.

With a pair of eyes that didn't believe what they were seeing, Poppy read:

The PEGGS

Erasmus's eyes wandered back and forth over the other page, which seemed to have some kind of poem written on it. After a few seconds, the ink faded, leaving the pages blank again.

"May I have a paper and pen?" Erasmus asked.

Poppy looked around the kitchen. She couldn't think. Her mind felt fuzzy and excited all at once.

"There are some pens in the second drawer of the dresser in the hallway. It was ajar," Erasmus instructed Poppy. "And some paper on the bookshelf. I saw it when I came in."

Poppy fetched the pen and paper. Erasmus wrote from memory as Poppy hoisted the bubbling saucepan off the stove and tipped the creamy milk onto generous spoons of cocoa and sugar.

"How can you remember all that?" Poppy asked as he jotted down what he had seen.

"I remember things differently to other people. The doctor calls it eidetic memory. But it isn't really."

"What do you mean?" She added some cold milk to Erasmus's drink and bulldozed it across the table towards him with two fingers.

Erasmus finished writing and Churchill leaped into his lap.

"I don't remember things like a photograph or a camera does. I just give everything a code in my head and put it together into a story."

"I'm still confused as to how you do it," Poppy muttered.

Erasmus sighed impatiently. "There's a cooking book sitting over there beside the sink."

Poppy nodded.

"The barcode number on the back is 9781474945660."

Already Poppy knew better than not to believe him.

"*Nine* little monkeys took the *seven* minutes past *eight* train from platform *fourteen*. *Seven* of the monkeys sat in carriage *four*, beside another monkey who was dressed to the *nines*. When the food trolley came around for them, it had *five* packets of crisps, *six* bottles of cola and *six* drinking straws. But by the time the trolley left there was *none*. 9781474945660."

"That's…enlightened!" Poppy mused.

"*That's* the story of the nine little monkeys," said Erasmus. "Why don't you read what the book says?"

He gave her the piece of paper he'd been working on, and Poppy read aloud:

Don't look up and don't look round,
Close your eyes at night.
Bolt the swinging hatches down,
And tuck yourself in tight.

Be sure your blanket covers up
To just below your nose.
The Peggs, they do delight to sup
On fingers, tongues and toes.

If you can find a night cap,
But not the kind you drink,
Wear it 'fore you catnap,
Else your hair will shrivel and shrink.

Across the sky they fly by night
In airborne wicker hamper.
Once they've got you in their sight,
There's nowhere else to scamper.

If you should wish to play their game,
Then leave your windows wide.
Your fate will always be the same,
When the Peggs come on inside.

So hide the sugar, should you be wise,
Stow away your dreams.
And watch the sky with wary eyes
Lest no one hear your screams.

"Who are the Peggs?" Poppy asked with a shiver, but Erasmus shook his head.

Something in the poem that Poppy couldn't put her finger on had made her think of Wilma Norbles, the girl Gran told her had vanished in the river. Perhaps there were other stories like that floating around Suds?

Churchill had fallen asleep by now and the stove in the kitchen glistened with dying embers as a sense of unease towards the book began to take root in Poppy's head.

Outside the storm raged across the town and thunder rolled recklessly through the sky. If you were about as tall as Poppy and had been standing on the wheelbarrow in Gran's garden, you would have seen a ragged shape floating past the moon. The shape swooped down for a few moments before sailing back up again and vanished between the towering black clouds which gathered over the old Helligan Mills.

Five
PIG

Poppy let Erasmus take the book home with him that night. He didn't seem in the least bit concerned about walking home alone in the storm.

She lent him one of the macs Gran kept in the hall, which was much too big for him. She suspected it had been a lady's mac, given the enormous violets printed all over it, but Erasmus didn't seem too concerned about that either. Poppy had a breathless sort of feeling as she watched the boy dressed in violets vanish into the night. And she found herself standing in the doorway thinking about the silk book: *You'll see it again soon. It will be back soon.*

Gran was up early and made them her Breakfast of Queens. This consisted of croissants stuffed with anchovies and strong black coffee. Gran said she and her old friend Dalia Terce would eat this every morning and do the word games in the newspaper when they worked at a costume shop in London together. Poppy liked the coffee – she was grown up that way – but anchovies were one of her oldest adversaries so she had the croissant by itself instead.

Before they went out, she put her phone on "loud" as she'd been promised a call from Dad that day. She found herself double-checking the volume was up and that she hadn't somehow missed him already.

Despite the storm having blown away in the night, the sky was still grey as they made their way up the bustling high street, with Churchill trotting ahead of them on his silver leash. He'd become an expert at weaving in and out between the mums clutching shopping bags and gasbagging in the street.

It was Saturday, which meant the Suds Market was on. Several of the shops were closed for the weekend and had their aluminium shutters pulled down, and stalls selling everything from jam to junk were set up in front of them on either side of the street. Herds of kids milled aimlessly about, while two boys crouched over the cracked pavement, drawing a picture of some type of monster with green chalk.

The lady with the glassy eyes and beige suit, who Poppy had seen in the fabric shop, stopped on her way past to run her long fingers over Churchill's back.

"What a dear little pig!" she declared in a deep voice, looking Poppy up and down.

"He's a miniature pig," Poppy said.

"A WHAT?" the lady asked loudly. She grabbed a small trumpet from her handbag and held it to her ear. Churchill seemed agitated and began yanking on his leash.

"A *mi-nia-ture pig*," Poppy said clearly into her trumpet, which smelled like brass cleaner.

"That's how I know I'm not going deaf," Gran whispered to Poppy as they walked away. "That's Mrs Gwynne who works at the bookshop. You ask her for *The Pursuit of Love*, and she'll give you a copy of *To Shoot a Dove*."

"Gah!" Mrs Gwynne shrieked, jerking back in fright at the chalk drawing of the monster on the pavement. She sidestepped around it very carefully and the two boys sniggered into their sleeves.

Gran wanted to stop at the sweet shop to pick up "a few" of Bonhilda Bonhoeffer's goodies for the week. Poppy waited outside with Churchill, dreading to think what would happen if they let him inside. Peering through the window, she could just see into the sweet shop past the queue of excited children. Miss Bonhoeffer was using a pair of scales to weigh a mountain of Raspberry Sherbet Scrumps for a smug-looking creature wearing a baseball cap.

A broad-shouldered girl with hair the colour of mustard powder and a carnivorous set of teeth was carefully sliding a few Custard Cusps into her back pocket. Poppy could see quite clearly that she had no intention of paying for them whatsoever. Without warning the girl looked up and caught Poppy's gaze. The girl narrowed her eyes before breaking into a cool smile and swiping a tub of Martian-Mallow, which was actually just normal marshmallow fluff but green.

Poppy looked to see if Gran had noticed, but she had already filled her shopping trolley to the brim with Miss Bonhoeffer's delights and, clever as a fox, and in a few swift moves had successfully made her way to the front of the queue.

As she wondered whether or not she should do

something about the shoplifting she had just witnessed, Poppy's eyes flitted across the street. There was another line of children queuing outside the bookshop across the road, excitedly counting their money and craning their necks to see inside. Kids didn't do that back home – they ordered their stuff online. Standing by himself, separate of the queue, was Erasmus, who was studying the shop window with curiosity. Underneath his arm was Poppy's silk book and a notepad. Behind his ear was a pencil. Poppy crossed the road.

"Hiya!"

Erasmus didn't look away from the window. "There's something unusual about that book," he said softly.

"My book?" she asked, holding out her palm in an invitation for him to return it.

"You said it wasn't your book. And no. *That* book," he said, holding out Poppy's book with one hand while pointing inside the window with the other.

Poppy swiped her book off him and pushed it into her pocket. He was so darned particular.

In the front window of the shop was a pile of violet books embossed with silver writing:

$$Into\ Thin\ Air$$
$$by$$
$$Brooke\ Warden$$

"What's unusual about it?" Poppy asked.

"This is the only shop you can buy it from," Erasmus explained. "It says so on the poster."

Poppy didn't think this was as strange as Erasmus seemed to. She dragged her fingertips up the silk cover of the book in her pocket.

"What's the book about?"

"It's about a boy who has the power to run at the speed of light. All those kids are queuing up to buy a copy."

"Have you read it?"

"No, but I read the synopsis on the poster. His arch-nemesis is a magician who uses an enchanted keyboard to hypnotize people."

"It sounds rubbish."

Churchill perched his trotters on the front window, desperately trying to get a better look. He snuffled the corner of a book poster that had been taped up:

COMING SOON...

BUG EYES

by

Dewy Sponck

One girl's journey to find the Invisibeetle!

"I spent the evening copying out the poem from your book into Edgar and going through it verse by verse," said Erasmus, handing her a thick leather dossier. "The rest of the book was empty, which is probably the oddest thing about it, now I think about it."

"Edgar?"

"Short for Edgar Allen Poe."

"Ah – quoth the boy!" Poppy grinned, feeling clever for one glorious moment.

"There's no point in quoting *The Raven* if you're not going to quote it properly. That's called paraphrasing. And I call my dossier Edgar because it is my Portfolio of Assembled Evidence. P-A-E. Now if you put that backwards it becomes E-A-P, which are the initials of Edgar Allen Poe."

Poppy opened her mouth to say something but closed it again.

"There's something I want to show you. In Riddling Woods," Erasmus said, suddenly snatching his dossier back. "You should see it."

When Poppy didn't react, he crouched down beside Churchill and began to scratch his stomach. Churchill fell onto his back with his hooves in the air, closing his eyes as if he was receiving a deep tissue massage.

Poppy laughed.

"Let me quickly tell my gran where we're going."

Gran was happy Poppy had managed to find a friend, so she only said, "You've got your phone on you, yes?

Not too late, eh? I need you to help me get all the washing in before six."

As Poppy, Erasmus and Churchill walked and cantered back down the high street towards the churchyard, Gran watched them.

"She walks like her mum used to," Gran said to herself. "Always on a mission, chasing after the wind."

Erasmus led them through the churchyard and across the village green. They soon came to the edge of the town, where the coiled woods rose above the tousled heath.

The river flowed between the trees and they followed it along an unmarked path.

Churchill was in his element. Gran didn't often walk him in the woods ("Gammy leg and all, you know") and he nipped back and forth, sniffing the clusters of toadstools and lichen. Poppy liked getting her boots in the mud almost as much as Churchill did. Erasmus was much more careful where he trod, and when they arrived at a clearing his laces were still tied, and his shoes were still clean.

"It was right here," Erasmus thought out loud, lifting a branch.

"What was?" asked Poppy.

"Where the police found Wendy Pocks six months ago."

Something twitched in Poppy's stomach. "Was she dead?" she asked, scratching a fleck of dry mud off her cheek.

Her heart pulsed electrically.

"She was bald."

"Bald?"

"Bald as a boiled egg," Erasmus told her. "She used to have long black hair. She went to my school."

"What happened to her?"

"Nobody knows – she was terribly confused."

"Did the police find anything...you know, odd?" Poppy asked as she watched Churchill rummaging about at the water's edge. A wooden bridge spanned from one bank to the other, half sunk beneath the swollen river.

"The newspaper said that she had insect bites on her arms, but that it was probably from being in the woods during summer."

Poppy dropped to her knees and examined a large fungus that was growing at the base of a nearby tree.

"Why are you telling me this?"

"Don't you see?"

Poppy stared at him blankly.

"Don't you remember the poem I found in your book? The one about the Peggs?"

"Not exactly," said Poppy. "My memory isn't quite as good as yours."

"Obviously," Erasmus added.

"There's no need to be rude."

"Oh," Erasmus murmured, "I didn't mean to be rude. It just seemed obvious that my memory is excellent and yours is…well…not as excellent."

"That was a dreadful apology."

Erasmus looked frustrated. He took his notepad from Poppy and opened it up to the poem for her.

"Third verse: *If you can find a nightcap, but not the kind you drink*," he began.

"*Wear it 'fore you catnap*," Poppy continued, "*else your hair will shrivel and shrink*."

"What happened to Wendy Pocks has something to do with these Peggs in your book. It can't be a coincidence," Erasmus said darkly.

Poppy had a heavy feeling that Erasmus was right. What if Wilma Norbles, the girl who disappeared swimming, was something to do with these Peggs too? And what about all those other kids who had disappeared over the years that her gran had mentioned?

"What are you going to do then?" asked Poppy.

Erasmus put his hand in his pocket and produced the book of ciphers and cryptograms he had been reading at the doctor's surgery.

"Everything has a system and any riddle can be deciphered. There's no such thing as an unbreakable code. If it's unbreakable, then it's not a code. So I'm going to decipher the meaning of this poem and find out what exactly is happening and why."

Poppy thought.

"Was Wendy Pocks your friend or something?"

"Not even a little bit," Erasmus snorted.

"Then it's really nice that you want to find out what happened to her, but I don't understand why."

"I like puzzles. I like problems which bend and tease my brain."

"I like mystery novels – you know, Agatha Christie, G.K. Chesterton and that sort of thing," Poppy added thoughtfully. It wasn't very profound, but she needed something interesting to say.

"Well, in real life you can't turn to the next chapter and hope that what's going to happen will be better," Erasmus said quietly. "All you can do is hope there's a next page to turn to."

Churchill began to grunt loudly.

"What is it, Church?" Poppy cooed, wandering over to him.

"He won't reply in English. He's a pig."

"He's found something!" Poppy cried out, kneeling down in the mud beside the water.

"Is it a truffle or something? I saw a truffle selling for ninety-two pounds at that deli in town, Robespierres'. Mum was applying for a job there."

Erasmus crouched beside her. Sprinkled over the mud and floating on the surface of the water was a bluish powder. Erasmus fished an empty matchbox out of his pocket and, using a leaf, expertly funnelled some of the powder into it.

Something watched them from between the roots of the tallest trees as they followed the river back to town.

"It's thinking! The boy one is thinking!" the watcher whispered in a voice only the worms and insects understood. "It's thinking, plotting, cunning, scheming! It's too clever by half!"

"And the girl one," said another watcher. "The girl one still has the book. The book that talks. The book that can be followed."

"Watch them closely," said a third voice. "We will eat their sweet hearts yet."

Six
ARTICLE

"What's that in your hair, pet?" Gran asked Poppy at lunch the next day, which was Sunday. Lunch was actually a wheel of cheese and ripped up bits of bread.

Poppy felt the back of her head.

"Oh, it's that comb I found among your buttons."

"No," murmured Gran, spinning her around. "There's something else."

Gran freed the comb from Poppy's hair and placed it on the table beside her cake fork.

"Golly! You're going grey!" she cried out.

"What is?"

"Your hair!" Gran cried out again. "It's gone all whitish!"

"Not all of it?" Poppy asked anxiously, checking her reflection in the window.

"No, it's just a spot," said Gran. "But you're ageing faster than I am! I can dye it for you, if you like? Just don't tell your mu—"

Gran stopped and went back to cutting a pattern from her roll of Whiskered Whingecloth, which was the most glorious pink-grapefruit colour.

Poppy knew what Gran had been about to say. She sometimes forgot too. Before the summer holidays, she had scored highest in her German exam and when she got on the bus she'd sent a text message to Mum. Poppy loved German. Mum had a small collection of old German books from when she was at university. It was only when the little blue line that showed the message was sending reached the other side of the screen that she remembered.

She'd felt stupid.

Gran was *right*. There was a white spot at the back of her head where the comb had been. Poppy didn't like it one bit. It reminded her of the story that Gran had told her about Suds. Was it some kind of mark you got before you vanished? She put the comb in a box and locked it. As she did so, she noticed something curious. The teeth on the comb had changed colour ever so slightly, as if they'd been dipped in a greyish paint.

Poppy stuffed the box with the comb inside it right at the back of her dresser, beneath a dusty orange-and-brown-and-yellow jumper that she'd found wedged behind the wardrobe.

Out of sight, out of mind, she whispered to herself. But she knew that wasn't true. She'd be thinking about it all day.

In the corner of her workshop/sitting room, Gran had an ancient computer on which she checked her emails every two or three weeks. Gran had a business card which said that if you wanted to contact her you ought to do so by *Post, phone call or not at all*. To Gran, a tablet was something you swallowed when you were ill, not something you used to catch up on your favourite shows while riding public transport.

"Oh!" Gran called out. "There's an email from your dad. Maybe he's sent some more pictures of himself in that stomach-turning Lycra."

Poppy listened from the kitchen, where she was washing the plates from lunch. Dad hadn't phoned during the week. He knew Gran hardly ever checked her emails. Why couldn't he just call? He was never this distant before Mum died. He would have called. He would have sent Poppy a picture of a squirrel trying to hijack his bike or something.

"How*ever* did I manage to change my computer so that everything is in ruddy French?"

Poppy made a note to herself to show Gran where

the language settings were.

"Oh," murmured Gran again in a more concerned tone. "Oh, Poppy, he's not coming back for another *two months*...more work stuff apparently. And that's not all."

"What is it?"

"He wants you to enrol in a new school...here."

Poppy gave a snort that said "das ist *typical*".

"But I already go to another school. A school where my friends are."

Gran finished reading the email. "He says that your next school term will already have started by the time he returns from Canada and he doesn't want you to miss out." Gran must have thought Poppy couldn't hear her because she muttered, "Useless nitwit..."

Poppy didn't like it when Dad and Gran bickered. Gran would say, "You're a pointless cretin who needs to pull his socks up and take a good hard look at his parenting style."

Dad would yell, "That's rich coming from a woman whose daughter only visited her once every two years!"

Poppy never took sides, because both of these things, no matter how awful, were true. Dad had become vacant and disinterested ever since Mum died, and when Mum was alive she almost never visited Gran. Mum didn't like Suds.

The phone rang.

"Gran?"

"Poppy?"

"The phone's ringing."

"Yes, I know."

"Shall I get it?"

"Only if you feel up to it, pet. Don't strain yourself."

Poppy dried her hands on one of Gran's souvenir tea towels and picked up the phone in the hallway.

"Poppy speaking."

"This is Erasmus Tall calling. Is this the same Poppy with the white spot in her hair and the ugly jumper?"

"How on *earth* did you get this number? It's not even listed in the phonebook. And why didn't you say something about that white spot if you saw it? I can't have white hair at my age!"

"Firstly, *I* have white hair, and the number was written on the—"

"The form from the doctor's, of course," Poppy interrupted, smiling to herself. "Stupid of me. Did you find something else about the Peggs or that poem?"

"It's a newspaper clipping from the archives at the library I think you should read."

"What's it about?"

"A piano recital."

"A piano recital?"

"That's what I said. Why repeat me?"

"Why don't you just read it to me, or – better still – paraphrase it for me?"

"There's a picture too."

"Email it to me then."

"I'm not allowed on the internet. Mum says it makes me aggressive."

Poppy took an involuntary step back.

"Why does it make you aggressive? Should I be turning the data off on my phone whenever I see you?"

"Because there are so many sensible things you can use the internet for, and yet people mostly seem to use it to look at pictures of cats in bonnets or to say spiteful things to each other. And, as I'm sure you'll agree, *nothing* is as peevish as people's judgements of one another."

"And what does your dad have to say about all this?"

"He can't say anything. He's dead."

"Oh," said Poppy softly. "I'm sorry."

"Why are you sorry?"

"It's what people say when they wish they could do something to help…but can't."

Erasmus was silent, but only for a moment. It was strange. No matter how much he spoke, Poppy understood him most when he said nothing.

"I think you should meet me outside the church in one hour and eleven minutes. I need to initiate you into the investigation."

"Why the extra eleven minutes?" Poppy asked, ignoring the investigation comment.

"I'm going to spend fifty minutes in the library pulling up some old articles. It takes me ten minutes to walk from my house to the library and eleven minutes

73

to walk from the library to the church if I wear my walking shoes."

Poppy thought for a second. No one under the age of fifty called them "walking shoes".

"I'll meet you there in one hour and *five* minutes."

"It takes me eleven," Erasmus insisted.

"Then get your A into G and wear running shoes instead."

The tombstones huddled in the churchyard seemed to be hoarding piles of sloppily crushed beer cans and broken glass. Between the plots, the weeds were smeared with the rain-soaked remains of pale silk flowers caught in a sludge of mown grass that had never been raked away. Poppy whipped out her phone and leaned on the fence. Opening her browser, she tapped into the search bar: *Brooke Warden, author, Into Thin Air, book*.

Nothing. She frowned and scrolled through the search results, but none of them seemed to be relevant. The same thing happened when she tried rearranging the words and adding things like *children's books* and *new release*.

Erasmus arrived a few minutes later, red in the face and out of breath. Poppy was stretching her thin arms. The first thing he said was, "I don't like running."

"Running is good for the soul," Poppy told him. "Do you have the clipping?"

"Yes," panted Erasmus. Standing on one leg, he pulled a folded piece of paper out of his left sock.

"Couldn't you have just put it in your pocket?"

"I didn't want to risk it."

"Risk what?"

"Our investigation."

Poppy snorted mockingly, and unfolded the piece of paper with her fingertips, wrinkling her nose a little. True to Erasmus's word, it was indeed an article about a piano recital, although not the kind she expected.

16th March

The North Riddling Musical Society wishes to pay tribute to one of its key stars. Andrew Booker was a major player in our Concert Crew, and his mastery of so many instruments will be truly missed. Watching his skills develop in a crescendo of musical ability has been a treat for us all, his forte on the piano being of particular note. "The North Riddling Piano Recital will not be the same without him," says Mrs Hetty Gwynne, chairwoman of the North Riddling Musical Society.

"Mrs Hetty Gwynne also runs the bookshop. She's profoundly deaf in one ear. I've put that in my notes."

Poppy remembered Mrs Gwynne – she was the lady with the hearing trumpet who'd stopped to pat Churchill.

"Underneath that," Erasmus said, pointing, and Poppy read:

MOTHER'S DESPERATE PLEA FOR MISSING BOY TO RETURN HOME

Saturday 15th March

Mother of missing boy Andrew Booker has put out an appeal for anyone with information concerning the whereabouts of her son to come forward. "We just want our Andrew back," says Elaine Booker. "It's times like this you wish you'd let your child do what they loved. Our Andrew always dreamed of being a champion sprinter. It was always a battle to get him to practise his scales on the piano."

Andrew went missing from his home two miles west of Suds yesterday, between 11 p.m. and 11.45 p.m. "It was as if he'd been plucked from his bed," says Detective Inspector Graves. "There was no sign of a struggle, and no suggestion that Andrew has run away. The only evidence collected from the scene was a fine blue dust on Andrew's pillow.

Poppy glanced at Erasmus nervously. Perhaps it was the same dusty powder they'd found in the woods? Blue powder wasn't exactly a common occurrence.

> Our forensics people will be conducting tests on the powder in the coming days to ascertain whether or not Andrew was drugged."
>
> Anyone with information about Andrew Booker's disappearance is urged to call our missing persons line listed below. Andrew has black hair, blue eyes and stands at 1.55 metres (5ft 1in) tall.

"I think the disappearances of Andrew Booker and Wendy Pocks—"

"The bald girl?" Poppy interjected.

"Yes. Her. I think their disappearances are connected, despite being almost four years apart."

"How? Wendy Pocks didn't vanish into thin air like Andrew Booker," Poppy reminded him, trying to convince herself more than anything. "You said so yourself: she was found."

"Not my point. And yes that's true, *but* both their disappearances happened between 11 p.m. and midnight on a Friday."

"Do we know why Wendy Pocks was in the woods?

Was she already there? Or was she…you know, taken there?"

Erasmus shook his head, and made a note to find out.

Something had been niggling at Poppy. "Do you not think having both these articles about Andrew in the same newspaper is…well, you know…insensitive?"

"I think it's enormously odd."

"On the one hand his mother is begging for him to come home. And on the other hand, the musical society are waving him farewell."

Erasmus stood suddenly upright, peering over Poppy's shoulder.

"What is it?" Poppy asked.

Erasmus gripped Poppy's arm and swung her around beside him.

"Alright!" Poppy snapped, brushing him off.

"Quiet!" Erasmus hissed, and Poppy reluctantly obeyed.

There were voices. Low voices. And they were coming from around the corner of the church. Erasmus dropped behind a nearby hedge, and Poppy felt his insistent grip on the back of her shirt, encouraging her to follow suit. She kneeled down beside him.

"What are they—"

Erasmus's hand interrupted her.

"Thanks so much for doing this, Simon," came a woman's voice. Poppy peered between the shadowy leaves of the hedge. The woman was actually a vicar.

She was holding open a door to the church hall. Her white collar was coming slightly loose and a ribbon of hair had fallen across her face. She brushed it away as she opened the door.

"Alright, Sue," an irritated man with flaky skin mumbled as he approached the door. "The old place looks as if it needs some TLC." He nodded at the scruffily patched tiles on the steeple above them and the rusted gutter battered beyond recognition.

"Well," Sue breathed, "I'm trying to get it heritage-listed so we can get some extra funding for a makeover, but this town isn't old enough or interesting enough. And the last time anyone moved here was too long ago to remember. I'm in an unfashionable business in an unfashionable town."

Simon glanced behind him. "Come on then!"

A small girl with a hat pulled down over her ears followed him. She tugged at his sleeve.

"*That's her!*" Erasmus mouthed to Poppy.

"*Who?*"

"Wendy, if you do that *one* more time, I'm going to explode!" Simon said to the little girl, irritably scratching his dry elbow.

Poppy froze. That was Wendy Pocks.

"Bring her in," the vicar said eagerly, "I've made tea if you're thirsty."

"Go on then." Simon sighed as he closed the door to the church hall behind him.

Poppy looked over to Erasmus. Erasmus wasn't there. He was standing on a broken piece of stonework and shamelessly gazing in the window between the curtains of the church hall. Poppy crawled over to him, her heart beating to the rhythm of her scurrying hands and knees.

Erasmus held his finger to his lips, pre-empting Poppy's disapproval as she sidled up beside him.

"Yes," sighed the vicar, as they listened, "that's the same colour as my William alright."

Poppy slid up the wall of the church, steadying her breath and swivelling her head so she could just see between the curtains.

The little girl with the hat was sitting in a chair beside her father. Her legs didn't touch the floor, but they weren't swinging. The vicar was looking anxiously into the girl's eyes.

"When did it start?" Simon asked, slurping his tea. His lips were dry too.

"A fortnight ago." The vicar fell into a stackable chair and pulled off her collar. "First it was his eyes. He kept telling me they were really itchy. Then they went all red, and he started having trouble finding his words. I didn't notice their colour fading at first. I just thought his eyes weren't as sparkly as normal. Then about three days ago, I could see it – they were going grey, grey like his dad's hair."

Her eyes, Poppy thought to herself, *something is wrong with her eyes.*

And Poppy was right. The small girl's eyes were grey as stone.

Poppy's blood ran cold. Why wasn't the girl talking?

"William!" the vicar called sweetly. "Could you come in here, pet?"

There was a moment of silence. The corner door shuffled open with a scrape and William stepped into the room.

Poppy's heart twisted in her chest. William's hair was patchy. William's eyes were like two small eggs.

Simon was obviously unnerved. "Why isn't it affecting *other* children then?" he asked, scratching his neck.

Sue the vicar leaned in conspiratorially. "You know Beverly Dart? Bev Dart?"

Simon shook his head.

"She's the short lady with the curly hair who sits at the back of the church with her two sons, Tim and Archie."

"You know I don't go to church, Sue," Simon muttered.

"Right," the vicar apologized. "Of course. Well anyway, she popped by last week after church to ask me how William was doing. I haven't told anyone else about him, but she and I talk a lot. Anyway, she said she started taking Archie to speech therapy a few weeks ago because he'd been having trouble with some words at school. But even with the therapy sessions, he's been getting worse."

"Do you think it's something in the drinking water?" Simon asked the vicar.

"Well, it can't be some strain of bug in the house," she replied. "I keep a spotless home. Anti-bac on every surface, every day, and not a cobweb in sight. All the window sills and ledges in our house see the fluffy end of my duster each morning."

Gran wouldn't stand for that, Poppy thought. *One of Gran's rules is to never dust the window sills.*

Simon itched his elbow again. And the little girl turned towards the window.

Her skin was the colour of a white room on a cold day, as if something had been drained out of her. Wilma Norbles – the girl Gran had told her about – she had faded away. But did it happen like this?

Poppy turned to Erasmus, who signalled with his head that they should make a dash for it.

A troubling sensation settled over Poppy as they made their way out of the churchyard. Perhaps there *was* a reason why Mum never really wanted to return to Suds. Something unnatural seemed to drift over the trees and through its drowsy streets. Her heart ticked with a strange curiosity. Despite it terrifying her, she wanted to know what was going on. She wanted to know what peculiar thing was out there.

Seven

MARLEY

"Do you think weird things like what happened to Wendy Pocks and that piano boy have been happening for long?" asked Poppy the next afternoon as they took a left turn down Old Suds Road. She'd spent the morning trying to search the internet for the names of the children Gran and Erasmus had mentioned. But Gran's computer was returning results so slowly that she'd been forced to continue looking on her phone. There was only the odd local newspaper article about them, but she did stumble upon a page in a missing persons archive for a girl called Minty Togs who disappeared from Suds in 1960. It seemed odd to her. Why hadn't anyone else tried to investigate the unusual number of disappearances from the area? Surely *someone* had noticed the incongruences? "Well, that's exactly what we need to find out," he replied matter-of-factly, taking his video camera out of his satchel and wiping the lens. Erasmus had arrived unannounced at Gran's front door with a tripod slung over his shoulder at two o'clock. He showed Poppy a map of Suds that he was compiling with any odd incidents marked on it, and after Gran had given him lunch, he had insisted that Poppy come back with him to the library.

Poppy bit her tongue, then said, "What do you think happened afterwards then?"

"If the incidents in Suds and Riddling that I've read about are connected," Erasmus said, "then it varies. Some of them aged quicker than their own grandparents and passed away pretty young. Others seem to have vanished almost instantly."

"Vanished?"

"I read this one article from the library archives about a parent who only left their kid for a few moments playing in the park and when they went to look for them, all they could find was a flock of grey leaves dancing in the wind."

"You're pulling my leg."

"I wouldn't pull your leg even if I wanted to," said Erasmus simply. "I've read other stories of parents coming into their kids' rooms at night to find nothing but a grey smudge on the pillow. Or the really weird story of Minty Togs, who got it into her head that she was a piece of laundry."

Poppy stopped walking and folded her arms across her chest to cover her heart, which was leaping up and down like a fish out of water. "I found a page about Minty Togs in a missing persons archive last night," she told him.

Erasmus raised his eyebrows and told her what he'd found out. "The day Minty Togs's eyes started turning grey, she went out to the washing line and pegged herself up to dry. No one knew why. She did this every day for months and her colour slowly faded, until one day Minty's mum came out to find nothing but a piece of grey cloth flapping about in the breeze. Minty was never seen again." He paused as Poppy visibly shuddered in horror. "There are some other cases. I made notes on a few of the unusual ones I've identified and made a copy for you."

Erasmus reached into his sock and produced a square of neatly folded pages. Poppy glanced at the immaculate handwriting in black ink before making a show of pocketing them.

"Have a read of them and see if you can spot any similarities aside from the obvious." Erasmus paused. "I'm not one for signs in the stars, prophecies in dreams and all that rubbish," he said as if addressing an assembly, "I'm a man of science." Poppy stifled a snort of laughter, but Erasmus continued. "I don't believe in feelings or premonitions or things that go bump in the night. But somehow – I don't know how – I just *know* that all this has something to do with the Peggs, whatever or whoever they are."

Poppy was equally fascinated and horrified.

"If we can just work out our focus point, then we can deduce why and how these things are happening," she said, trying to sound just as intelligent-yet-mysterious. "Do we concentrate on this blue powdery stuff, the kids fading away and disappearing, or the town itself?"

"Well, I've been making steady progress at the library," Erasmus said. "I've scoured the archives and set up a little interview for us."

"What interview? Who's it with? You said we were going to the library!" Poppy looked back down Old Suds Road. Come to think of it, she'd had a feeling they were heading off course.

"I just said that so your gran would let you come," Erasmus said smugly. "Don't worry. Everything will be illuminated shortly."

Erasmus led Poppy across town to a path through Riddling Woods. Presently, the knotted trees opened up into a clearing where the murky river stitched its way through the gloom. They followed the river for some time, until they came to a sign nailed to a stump. The sign read *Marley*, and had a little pail with a lid underneath, which Poppy guessed was a kind of letter box. But someone had spray-painted an addition so that the sign now read: *Lookout 4 Mumbling Marley*. Poppy had seen those same words carved into the carriage of the train she came to Suds on.

"Are we allowed to walk through here?" Poppy asked, her chest starting to feel the familiar heaviness of concern. "Isn't it illegal to trespass?"

As she stopped to make sure her shoelaces were tight, Poppy noticed three more handmade signs surrounding the path they were taking:

GO AWAY
NO TRESPASSING
MARLEY WILL GET YOU

What would Marley do if he gets us? Poppy regretted thinking it.

"It isn't his land," Erasmus said. "He can't tell us to get off his land if it isn't his."

"Well maybe he claims squatters' rights," Poppy offered quietly, but Erasmus ignored her. Poppy knew all about squatters' rights because Dad once did some legal work for his friend Hugo who had squatters living in his second home. Poppy didn't like Hugo, or his sour-faced wife, Leda.

"Don't you need to be home for dinner or something?" Poppy asked, trying to steer Erasmus back to town. Gran ate whenever she wanted to, which was usually eight thirty or nine o'clock.

"I make my own dinner," Erasmus told her. "And my own lunch, even for school."

Poppy pulled her cardigan around her. This evening was cooler than those before. Mum had been right about the weather in Suds. The seasons played out differently here, and even now the first winks of autumn were flecking the woods.

Gradually, bushes covered in yellow berries began to appear between the trees. The jostling clusters of yellow quivered in the breeze as if huddling together.

"They're poisonous," Erasmus said as Poppy eyed a particularly juicy-looking bunch. "Marley grows them to keep people away."

"Exactly who is Marley?" Poppy asked anxiously, forcing herself to keep walking forwards. Since her heart had started galloping, she'd found it more and more difficult to break the rules. The letters on the sign seemed louder and angrier: **GO AWAY**.

Mum broke the rules, she thought to herself reluctantly. *Mum didn't have the indicators on her car fixed, and look what happened to her on that corner.*

She brushed her fingers on the rough bark of the nearest tree to bring herself back to reality. She hated herself for even thinking that. It wasn't Mum's fault, was it?

"Poppy?"

"Yes?"

"You asked me who Marley was?"

"Yes, sorry."

"Marley, or Mumbling Marley to the Suds community, is homeless…except he has a house. Most people – in fact, I think *all* people – in town avoid him. He's considered a local pest because people think he is a bit light-fingered and has a problem with alcohol. It's generally thought that all the isolation has sent him a bit cuckoo. People who have been near his house often say they hear him shouting at himself. He's lived in Suds for at least fifty years."

"And *why* are we trying to find him?"

"There we are!" Erasmus suddenly shouted, pulling his video camera from his satchel. He flipped open the viewfinder and began to document, taking close-ups of the berries and the trees. "Marley's house," he said clearly as he recorded, "twenty-seventh of August at 16.08."

Through the bushes, Poppy could now see a set of rickety stairs leading to the riverside below. Moored against the bank was a tumbledown barge. Rotting planks and strips of tin were nailed to its hull, as if to plug a worrying number of leaks.

Erasmus finished filming and, overtaking Poppy, began to descend the stairs to the barge Marley presumably called home.

"I think this is dangerous!" Poppy whispered to him, noticing the rusty piles of junk that had collected along the water's edge. Erasmus stepped onto the tiny deck and rapped sharply on the low door. Poppy waited in terror, but quickly decided she'd feel less nervous with Erasmus beside her than with the woods behind her, and followed him onto the barge.

"I don't think anyone's home," Poppy whispered, tugging at Erasmus's sleeve.

"Then why is the chimney smoking?" Erasmus asked, and, sidestepping away from her, he knocked again.

"Whogoes?" came a murmur from inside. Poppy watched as what looked like a telescope protruded from the door and extended towards them. Through the glass of the telescope she could see a blinking, yellow, bloodshot eye.

"Erasmus Tall and Poppy Slub," Erasmus announced clearly, opening up his video camera again.

"Ain'tnever 'eard've no Erasmus Stall and Poppys Lub. Off withyer!"

Poppy tugged desperately on Erasmus's sleeve, shaking her head fearfully.

"We need to talk to you," Erasmus said even louder, yanking himself free.

"Haven'tyer 'eard stories 'bout Mumblin' Marley?" bellowed the voice. "Haven'tyer 'eard 'bout the monstrous beast I keep for a pet? Down, boy, down!"

There came a terrific scratching of claws on the other side of the barge door and Poppy took a step back, clutching the railing.

"Yer'dbest be off!" the voice warned. "I can't hold

him down for much longer, he'll rip yer apart like a Christmas cracker if he gets to yer!"

"We need to talk to you about the Peggs."

The scratching stopped. The voice went quiet. After a moment, the door unlocked and the yellow eye peered through the crack at them.

"Who toldyer 'bout the Peggs?"

Erasmus fished around in his satchel and pulled out a photocopied newspaper clipping. He held it out proudly as if it was the final piece of evidence in a case.

An enormous hand with grubby fingernails and sprinkled with silvery hairs reached out and snatched the clipping from him.

They heard mumbling from within as the great shape inside read the clipping with apparent difficulty.

"*Mumbling Marley*," Erasmus mouthed helpfully to Poppy, pointing at the place where the mumbles were coming from.

"*I got that, thanks*," Poppy mouthed back.

"Isitjus' the two of yer?" Marley asked.

"And a digital video camera," Erasmus said cheerfully, waving it about for Marley to see. Poppy rolled her eyes – as if marching up to a madman's front door and knocking wasn't reckless enough? Another great hand came swinging out, this time wearing a woollen glove, and whisked Erasmus inside. The door swung open fully and the towering shape gestured for Poppy to enter.

The first thing Poppy noticed as she forced her feet across the threshold and into the cabin of the barge was the smell; a deep, earthy smell. Like a compost heap and the bottom of an old clothes drawer rolled into one. She felt her heart see-sawing up and down. She closed her eyes for a moment and the **GO AWAY** sign seemed to be emblazoned on the inside of her eyelids. She shouldn't be here. This wasn't somewhere the Poppy Slub she knew would find herself.

When she stepped into the main living area she set eyes firstly on Erasmus: his neck craned; one eye squinting, the other glued to the viewfinder of his video camera as he filmed. Then her gaze fell to what must have been the monstrous creature trying to viciously claw through the door.

"That's a basset hound!" Poppy cried out before she could stop herself.

Marley turned on her and Poppy saw his face for the first time. He was old – *very* old – and treelike. Not like a thin wintry tree; he was burly and mighty. The ceiling was far too low for the likes of him, and he had to stoop as he made his way around the cabin, his scraggly beard hanging like a tangle of weeds from his chin.

"Is that what he is?" Marley shouted brightly, sweeping the drooping creature into his arms. He fumbled in his pocket before producing a boiled sweet, which the dog chewed gratefully but carefully.

"He's very fonda sweets!" Marley told them.

"He couldn't rip a biscuit in half, let alone a kid!" Poppy went on, feeling cheated. The basset hound watched Poppy mournfully, still trying to break the boiled sweet with his brittle fangs.

"Nor would he wan'to!" mumbled Marley, scratching the basset hound's head. "He is the kindest soul ever to have four legs. But I didn'steal 'im!" Marley told them, his voice becoming  deeper. "Wha'everanyone says – I *didn'steal* 'im!"

Poppy hadn't had time to take in the room around her. There were lanterns and compasses, boxes of nails and junk, trays of trinkets that looked like they'd been dug from the banks of the brook, watches and coloured stones, sacks of rich-smelling onions, jars of pilchards, strings of little dried fish, a scattering of empty cat-food tins and a large stack of unopened ones. Poppy tried to screw up her nose without drawing attention to herself.

Marley stoked the coals in a little stove with his boot and pulled up an armchair by the fire. Erasmus had already made himself at home and set up his video camera on a tripod, pointing directly at Marley.

"And we're rolling," said Erasmus "It's still the twenty-seventh of August, now 16.32."

"Whassat for?" Marley coughed, nodding at the camera warily.

"For recording sequences of images which constitute video for investigative purposes," said Erasmus calmly. "Mine has a special 'flash' for when I'm taking still photos."

Marley narrowed his eyes.

"Start by telling us your name," Erasmus said, focusing his camera.

"Why? Yer know me name already," grunted Marley suspiciously.

"That's not the point," said Erasmus. "We're compiling evidence and evidence must be comprehensive."

"Evidence?" Marley snapped. "What for? I haven't done anything wrong!"

"Ignore him," Poppy told Marley. "He's just taking himself too seriously." She threw Erasmus a warning glare. "Now, how about we start with your name, and I'll make us a cup of tea?"

Marley gave the flicker of a smile, and sighed. "Well, alright. Me name is Mr Marley Gust, known fondly as

Mumblin' Marley, and I usedt'work the engine room at the Helligan Mills," he said. Poppy's heart gave a familiar twitch. He went on – the more he spoke, the faster the words came gushing out.

"It was a weird place, e'en back then. That'd be going on forty-four years ago now. The gates opened e'ry mornin' at nine, and closed e'ry night at six. Two guards wi' torches would count e'ry night as we left. Forty-five people in all. On Fridays yer'd be 'anded a brown envelope with yer pay for the week. Until strange things began to 'appen."

The kettle boiled and Poppy brewed them a pot of tea, serving it in the cleanest vessels she could find: a chipped mug, a bowl and a ¾ measuring cup.

Marley lifted various cartons of milk up and gave them a shake until he found one that wasn't empty. Poppy put her hand up to indicate she would prefer black tea, but Marley had already tipped a generous dollop of the curdled milk into her measuring cup. He continued.

"One night, some kids broke into the Mills on a dare. One boy wen' in and he ne'er came out. Kids'd been disappearing in Suds for hundreds o' years, but no one e'er thought it was anything more'an the town being next to the Riddling Woods. The woods have gobbled people up more times'an yer can count. People stopped moving 'ere 'cause they were afraid of 'em. People stopped talking about it 'cause they were worried summin' might 'appen to 'em. They still don't talk about it. But it isn't the woods they oughta be scared of. Would either of yer like some Kendal Mint Cake?"

"Could we not get off topic, please?" Erasmus interrupted. "Go back to the disappearances of those kids."

"Er, right, sorry," Marley mumbled. "There were whisperin's in the town. Whisperin's that summin' was 'appening out there at the factory, summin' sinister. Then, with our Friday envelopes one day, we got a note. I still got it somewhere."

Marley got up from his armchair and put the kettle back on the stove. He fished around in his coat pocket. Poppy hadn't noticed the coat yet. It was broad and rugged, yet embroidered with a curious pattern she was sure she'd seen before. In fact she was almost certain she'd seen a scrap of the exact same fabric in Gran's odds-and-ends box.

Eventually Marley found a wad of paper held together with an elastic band. Separating a small note from the wad, he grinned and handed it to Poppy:

```
This is the last time you will leave
the Helligan Mills. From the time you
receive this note, your services will
no longer be required.
L.W.H.
```

"Who's L.W.H.?" Poppy asked.

"Nobody knew," Marley said, pouring hot water into the rusty-looking teapot. "Turns out, I wasn' a very good employee. When I got me envelope, I lingered back in the shadows, keepin' quiet. The hallways were empty, so it was easy t'make me way through the mill." Marley took a nervous gulp of his lumpy tea before continuing. "I didn' really think I'd find anythin', I just thought I'd 'ave a poke around. Then I saw the open door and the stairs leadin' down, down, down. And I 'eard voices."

Poppy saw Erasmus zoom into Marley's face with his camera.

"I 'eard whispers, strange whispers, saying words I didn' understand. I peered roun' the corner and I saw a trunk, like a luggage trunk, with long pipes comin' out from either side. The trunk was shakin' up an' down, as if summin' was trapped inside. Then I saw *them*." Marley's jaw shuddered.

"Who?" asked Poppy.

"Listen t'me without inneruptin'!" Marley bellowed back. "It's the least y'can do in return for what I'm telling yer! *Those three*. Three...creatures. Tall as trees, standin' over the trunk. I couldn'a watch any more, but before I could scarper, one of 'em saw me. I've ne'er been so fearful as when I saw those eyes: two drillin' 'oles in the creature's head. It stalked over t'me, pointed its finger at me and took a deep breath in – and I felt a 'ollow emptiness like I'd ne'er felt before. It was almos' as if it scooped summin' out of me very soul. Now this is where me silky book comes in."

Poppy couldn't help but put her hand to her pocket. Her book was there. She'd been carrying it with her everywhere.

"In my coat pocket, I used t'always keep a book of drawin's an' ideas – things I'd dreamedup in m'spare time."

"What kind of ideas?"

"Clev'r ideas," said Marley. "Like cleaning chalk off of blackboards wi'vinegar. Nuthin' works better."

Marley paused and chuckled to himself. "Vinegar is a wondrous substance. I used t'write everythin' in vinegar, so no one else'd be able t'read what I'd writt'n. That book was in me pocket when the creature came up t'me. Remember that. When the creature breathed in, I could feel summin' slippin' away from me. I thought I was goin' t'die. But somehow I managed t'pick meself up off the floor and climbed up the steps."

Poppy slipped her hand into her pocket and gripped her book tight. *It's there*, she thought, calming herself. *It's fine.*

There was a moment – only a moment – where she looked across at Marley's enormous frame, slumped in his chair, and saw a craze grip his eyes.

"I don' know how I got outta there. I really don'. And," said Marley, "I didn' come away empty-'anded."

There was a loop of string anchored to a paperweight at the foot of Marley's armchair. He gestured for Poppy to get up off her seat, then he pulled the string tight and the tatty rug over the floorboards slid away, revealing a trapdoor. Marley lowered himself to his knees and peered through cracks. He grinned.

"Who'd've thought that th'best watchdogs in th'world would be cats."

Poppy could hear a bubbling sound like boiling water from beneath the floorboards.

Marley told her to shut the curtains and stand well away from the edge of the trapdoor. He placed a lantern on the floor and, pulling on a pair of leather gloves, he heaved open the trapdoor.

Erasmus panned his camera around and focused on the teeming mass of bubbles they could now see through the hole in the floor.

Marley looped a length of rope over a hook hanging above them to create a sort of pulley.

"Fetchme one of 'em tins," he told Poppy, who did so as Marley stuffed two wads of tissue up his nostrils.

"Bitstrong f'me, the smell," Marley apologized, and ripped off the lid of the cat-food tin with one swipe.

Poppy gagged and Erasmus peered inside with intrigue. Using his gloved finger, Marley scooped a congealed glob of cat food out of the tin and flicked it into the water.

"C'mon," Marley cooed. "Here, puss, puss, puss!"

There was a surge of ripples, and the glob vanished.

Poppy edged away. Erasmus zoomed in.

Marley dropped in more globs and soon disintegrated flecks of fat and grease spiralled among the froth. Something was eating the stinking cat food. Poppy threw Erasmus a glance, but before she had time to wonder what it was that lurked beneath the boat, there was a grinding of gears as Marley began to pull on the rope to hoist something up.

From between the bubbles emerged a porcelain urn, chipped and coated in algae, and stoppered with a blackened cork. Marley unhooked the urn and placed it beside the fire.

"E'ryone in town thought I was a fool t'choose this place t'live. Lil' d'they know: Old Marley isn' as fool as he sounds. This river is deeper than any in the country."

"How deep?" Poppy asked.

"Well," said Marley, nodding to a huge coil of rope in the corner, "when I dropped that in the water, it didn' reach the bottom."

Poppy turned to Erasmus. He had repositioned himself beside the urn and had pointed his tripod and camera directly at it. His fingers were wrapped around the cork stuffed into the urn.

"Stoppit, don' open that!" yelled Marley, but Erasmus had already twisted the cork.

Marley grabbed Poppy's arm and yanked her towards him, covering her face with his gloved hand. Through his cupped fingers, Poppy watched as Erasmus gazed into the urn.

"Blue powder," Erasmus said slowly. "The same as the stuff we found in the woods."

"I can't look!" Marley moaned. "It makes me eyes itch!"

Poppy extricated herself and Marley pulled a moth-eaten scarf from his pocket to wrap around his eyes.

Erasmus had retrieved the matchbox with the powder they had taken from the woods and, opening it, he compared the two samples. Poppy kept her distance and tried to warn Erasmus to do the same. This could be the stuff making those kids' eyes go funny.

"It appears to be the same," Erasmus murmured without concern. "Same colour, same consistency, similar grain count."

Erasmus whipped out a tape measure and kneeled beside the colossal coil of rope. He quickly measured the height and width of the coil and then the width of the rope.

Poppy saw Marley raise an eyebrow beneath the scarf. He was feeling around the room, looking for something. Poppy quickly spotted what he was after and handed him a pair of purple swimming goggles. When he finally managed to squeeze them on, his yellow eyes bulged beneath the scratched plastic.

"And what do these supposed *creatures* use this powder for?" Erasmus asked.

"I dunno," said Marley, leaning over the two of them like the bough of a tree.

Erasmus replaced the matchbox in his satchel, Marley

watching him closely. He fitted the cork back into the urn, and filmed 360 degrees around it. When he was done, he panned his camera towards Marley again.

"You didn't tell us what happened to your silky book," Erasmus said bluntly.

"Lemme go back a li'l," he said, eyeing Erasmus as if he was a snarling police dog.

The basset hound had trotted across the cabin and was watching the bubbling water with great interest.

"Ge' away from there, Marley! Dogs'n'cats don' get on!"

The dog galumphed into a corner shamefully. A gritty slurp of water lapped over the edge of the trapdoor. Poppy peered into the murk. There couldn't be cats down there: cats hated water. She shuddered as images of something silver and tentacled lashed through her head. Before she had time to build up the courage to ask Marley what these underwater cats really were, Erasmus broke the silence:

"Why does your dog have the same name as you?"

The human Marley grunted and turned his back on the two of them to lower the trapdoor.

Erasmus motioned to Poppy and, shaping one hand like a mouth and the other like a dog, he pretended they were talking to each other.

Poppy had to think before she got the gist of what he was saying: *That's why people hear him talking to himself. He's talking to his dog.*

Marley threw down his leather gloves and collapsed back into his armchair. Marley the dog joined him.

"I tried tellin' people in the town 'bout what I'd seen – that there were creatures out there, and they'd trapped summin' and were doin' summin' 'orrible to it. But the townsfolk got all nervous when I told 'em, and 'stead of b'lievin' me, they thought I'd taken to the drink, on account of me mumblin'. I've tried loadsa times to warn 'em over the years 'bout what's out there, but nobody ever listens. Not even t' this day."

"And the book?" Poppy asked. She almost flinched as soon as she said the words, ready for Marley to snap at her, but instead he sighed heavily.

"I was shaken after what I saw. And that night, when I got 'ome, me silky book, which'd been in me pocket the 'ole time, was empty."

"Empty?" Poppy asked.

"Blank," said Marley. "All me pictures 'n' drawin's gone. Not a trace. As if they w're sucked out. That was the night that me mumblin' started. I talked normal 'fore then. But what turn' e'en stranger, I got 'ome a few weeks later to find my place'd been ransacked and the book was gone."

"You mean it was stolen?" Erasmus asked.

Marley shrugged. "All I know is when I got 'ome, it weren't there. I've ne'er seen it since."

Before Poppy could gesture for Erasmus to keep his mouth shut, he asked, "What did this book look like?"

"Er, greenish, kind of, I think." Marley scratched his head.

"Any other details? Was there something written in the book perhaps?" asked Erasmus, pushing his tripod closer with his feet.

Marley shook his head.

Poppy breathed deeply, slowing her heart.

"Wait a minute," Marley muttered, taking off his swimming goggles. The watertight cups had left two red rings around his eyes. "There *was* summin'. My initials. On the back. M.G. Stitched 'em meself. I'd covered the book with a piece o' silk I took from the Mills when I worked there, yer see. Found it scrunched up in the corner of a locked cupboard in the engine room."

Poppy's heart gave a *whack* like a timpani. She couldn't catch Erasmus's eye. Marley Gust. *That's* what the *M.G.* stood for on the back of her book.

Doing her best impression of a pickpocket, she slid her hand back into her pocket to touch the book again. Why was it so comforting to know it was there, with her? The book gave her comfort, but wondering who or what had written that poem in there made her feel physically sick.

"Could you tell us," Erasmus began to ask, "what you think happened to these creatures—"

He was interrupted by a piercing shriek from outside that made Marley spill his tea in fright.

"What the hell is that?" he shouted. "Who'd yer bring

with yer?" He shot up, knocking over Erasmus's tripod, and towered above them.

"We didn't bring anyone!" Erasmus shouted. "Watch out, you'll smash my camera!"

"I don' care what anyone says!" Marley bellowed. "All I know is, I've never stole nuthin'. They're liars! They're LIARS!"

Poppy bolted for the door. But it wasn't Marley that had frightened her. It was the shriek.

At the top of the riverbank between the berry bushes was Churchill. He was hysterical, squeaking madly and flapping his ears. Poppy bolted up the stairs two at a time and took him in her arms.

"What is it, Church? How'd you find me?"

"He doesn't speak English!" Erasmus shouted up, struggling with a tripod leg that was stuck in the door.

But Churchill wouldn't be calmed. Like a spaniel, he leaped from Poppy's arms and bolted in the direction of the woods. Poppy followed him without thinking. She clutched her pocket as her feet pounded the uneven floor of the woods.

It's still there. It's still there.

Eight

GRAN

An ambulance was parked in the drive outside Gran's house. The first thing Poppy thought was, *Its lights aren't flashing. That's good, isn't it?* Churchill dived through his pig flap as Poppy fumbled with her keys in the door. Before she managed to unlock it, the door swung open and a man dressed in a green paramedic's uniform greeted her.

"You must be Poppy?" The paramedic smiled calmly.

"Yeah, where's my gran?" She craned her neck to peer past him.

Why would he ask stupid questions in a crisis? Perhaps it isn't a crisis.

"Now don't worry, your nan—"

"Gran."

"—is fine," said the paramedic, raising his hands in

the air as if Poppy was an angry hen on the loose. "No need for panic! She just took a little turn."

What type of "little turn"? A little turn off a cliff?

Poppy pushed past him and headed straight for Gran's armchair. She was lying on the floor next to it with a cushion behind her neck. Beside her was a second paramedic, who was checking her pulse. Gran lifted her head as Poppy rushed to her side.

"Poppy, darling, you came."

Gran's eyes looked tired. For a moment Poppy thought that the ringing sound which hung in her ears was something to do with the blood pumping furiously around her body, but then she spotted the phone lying off the hook next to Gran.

"Churchill came and found me," she whispered.

"He's a good pig. He's a clever pig. Not to worry, dearest. I'm sure it's nothing. Just a turn – old people have them all the time."

Churchill had curled up next to Gran on the floor and rested his snout on her tummy as she patted him softly. Gran shifted as if she was uncomfortable.

"Take off my bangles, will you, Poppy? They're hurting my wrist," she said in a weak voice that didn't sound like hers at all.

Poppy took Gran's arm and rolled up her sleeve. It was covered in lots of little soft brown spots. "Because I had my time in the sun," Gran liked to say.

Poppy slipped the bangles off one by one. Gran's wrist

was a little swollen. When they were all off, she rolled down the sleeve of her blouse.

"Thank you, darling," said Gran. "Just make sure no one else sees my knobbly wrist bone. I have to cover it up with bangles, or else people will get a shock when they discover I'm not quite the gorgeous oil painting they thought I was."

Poppy reached over to pick up the phone lying beside Gran and popped it back on the receiver on the side table. As she did so, the second paramedic beside her turned to her and spoke in a measured but somehow foreboding voice.

"It's Poppy, isn't it? Poppy, we're going to need to take your nan—"

"Gran."

"—sorry, *Gran*, into hospital for observation overnight."

"Not on my watch!" said Gran, finding a sliver of strength again. "If you think I'm going to let you strap me to a bed and test me like a guinea pig in a chemical plant, then you don't know how wrong you are."

"What happened to you was a bit unusual, but *hopefully* nothing too out of the ordinary for someone of your age, Mrs Herisson," said the female paramedic, standing up and folding her arms.

"*Of my age?*" Gran cried out. "What do you mean, 'my age'? The cheek."

"How old are you, Mrs Herisson?"

"Twenty-one…and a bit."

"Mrs Herisson?"

"She's sixty-eight…and a bit," said Poppy, rubbing Gran's wrist.

Gran scowled at Poppy.

"How long will she be away for?" Poppy asked the paramedic.

"Hopefully just for the one night."

Poppy decided she didn't like the word *hopefully*. *Hopefully* wasn't a hopeful word at all. Whenever people used it, they meant there was something that could go wrong.

At first the paramedics said there was no way that Churchill would be allowed to ride in the ambulance. But then Gran folded her arms and said that, "If that pig doesn't ride in the vehicle, then I'll drive myself to the hospital. And if I cause a road accident on the way, I'll be sure to tell the police *exactly* why I wasn't in an ambulance."

Gran was in Ward C, but Poppy stayed outside with Churchill. A couple of hours passed and, just as she was getting a can of drink from the vending machine, a nurse came out to say Gran was going to sleep for the night. The woman reluctantly agreed to wait with Churchill for a few minutes while Poppy said goodnight.

Gran was in better spirits when Poppy eventually

found her, despite being tucked away in the geriatric ward.

"The food tastes like something I scraped off my boot," she whispered to Poppy. "And that old biddy in the bed opposite me keeps waking up and shouting blue murder. I'll be lucky to get twenty minutes' sleep altogether. Oh! Poppy, dear, would you mind?"

Gran reached for a paper cup on her bedside table and handed it to Poppy. She nodded in the direction of the tea trolley parked beside the bed opposite her. Poppy knew what Gran was getting at straight away and, slipping over, she popped the upside down paper cup over the bowl of sugar cubes beside a tower of disposable paper cups.

"I'm definitely no stick-in-the-mud," Gran sighed, "but no one keeps the old rules any more. Whatever happened to stop people caring about little details like that?"

Poppy kissed Gran's head. Gran cared about little details. Little details like initials stitched onto hemlines and acorns embroidered onto lapels.

"I'm really sorry to tell you this, Poppy," Gran began, and Poppy's heart fluttered, "but I've texted my friend Dalia Terce to come and stay with you just while I'm in here. In the morning, she'll drive you to the uniform shop at your new school for your fitting and then get you all enrolled."

Gran doesn't text. Something really must be wrong.

Gran told Poppy that Dalia had her own key and would be there when Poppy got home.

"Dalia is easy enough, but whatever you do, *don't* go all polite on me and call her Mrs Terce. She'll skin you like a carrot. Bad blood between her and her husband. She's about ten years younger than me, but she cares a lot more about getting older than I do."

A plump nurse with one streak of purple hair moved through the ward, announcing that visiting hours were over. Gran was looking sleepy anyway, so Poppy kissed her goodnight and went to find Churchill.

"You've got a vicious little pig there!" said the nurse who had waited outside. "When Mrs Gwynne from the bookshop wandered past, he started snapping at her heels and made a complete din!"

She tossed Churchill's leash to Poppy and power-walked through the automatic doors, glancing back as she did so, as if to say, *Crazy pig!*

Dalia wasn't there when Poppy arrived home, but there was a message waiting on the telephone that explained she was in the middle of her massage therapy and had "Already paid the man sixty pounds, so I'll be there just as soon as I've got my blouse back on, girlie. Two shakes of a lamb's tail."

"Eewww." Poppy shuddered, hanging up the phone.

Usually Gran's house was glowing with the soft

twinkle of lamps and candles. But tonight the house was dark and quiet. There was a pinkish stain and a smashed teacup on the floor beside Gran's Seat of Wisdom (her armchair) that Poppy hadn't noticed before. The stain smelled a bit like sherry, but Poppy tried not to think about it and gave it a scrub with some soapy water. She wrapped the broken porcelain in newspaper and put it in the bin. She had a moment of panic when she realized that it was after six and there might still be washing hanging on the line. But when she peered through the window she saw that Gran had already brought it in. Gran always stuck to her rules, because Gran never forgot. Poppy noticed the neighbours' washing was still hanging on their line, flapping like a row of ghosts in the breeze. She lit some candles and boiled some pasta for dinner.

While she waited for the pasta to cook, Poppy hung her cardigan on a chair at the dining room table and laid out the notes Erasmus had copied for her. The paper wasn't lined, but Erasmus's handwriting still moved like ruler markings across the page.

Poppy snorted to herself. She didn't need his Grandness the Duke of Know-it-all there to make his smart comments every twenty seconds. She took a separate piece of paper and tried to write down everything she could see that connected the seemingly inexplicable occurrences. *What was the psychology behind it all?* That was the question that all the detectives in the shelf-loads of Agatha Christie she'd read asked when they had a case to solve. *Modus operandi* was the phrase they used. *Why and how was the committer of the crime doing it?* She read:

1952

Albert "Berty" WINTHROP: Male, 13 years old, 5'1", blue eyes, brown hair.

Mother claimed that after Berty came home from school following a rugby game one evening, she made him wash the mud out of his jumper and leave it hanging on the washing line all night. The next day Berty put the jumper in question on before going to school. When he returned home he discovered he couldn't take the jumper off. It was as if it had become part of his skin. Mrs Winthrop reported that Berty's hair slowly turned grey, his eyes faded, he stopped talking and when Berty eventually died many years later, he was buried in the Suds cemetery still wearing that same jumper.

Note: There is an old wives' tale in Suds which is largely ignored these days that says it's bad luck to leave your laundry out after six o'clock.

Poppy leaned forward in her chair so her cardigan wasn't touching her. Gran didn't ignore that "old wives' tale". It was one of Gran's unbreakable rules.

Below that Erasmus had written something similar for Andrew Booker, the pianist, Minty Togs, the washing-line girl, and beneath that another report on bald Wendy Pocks, the site of whose reappearance they'd visited just a few days ago.

Poppy scanned all four accounts and noted down what commonalities they shared. Aside from the obvious similarities like the colour draining away and all of them losing their ability to speak, the only thing she could come up with was that three of them disappeared on a Friday, but Erasmus had already told her that and it just seemed like coincidence to her. Finding a black ballpoint pen, she added her own report for Wilma Norbles, the girl Gran had told her about who had vanished while swimming:

1973/4

Wilma Norbles: Female, 10 years old, appearance unknown. Swimming champion, attended North Riddling School. During summer, Wilma practised swimming up and down the Suds River. Timescale is unclear, but over time Wilma's eyes began to fade in colour. She soon stopped speaking, her hair faded to grey and one day Wilma went swimming never to resurface.

Poppy glanced out the window at the darkened front garden, and the paint flaking off the street light across the road. She became suddenly conscious of the fact that she was by herself in the house, and after checking the lock on the back door, she made Churchill come and sit next to her in the lounge room.

When Dalia arrived, Poppy discovered that she was much less interesting than she had hoped. Dalia had a big mouth with too much lipstick, and spent most of the evening on her diamanté-covered phone, convincing her sister to pay a visit to her "world-class" continental masseuse.

"Therapeutic, you understand, Mogs. You know how much I hate extravagance," she said every thirty seconds, adjusting her bob of aubergine-coloured hair and sipping her Chardonnay.

She only stopped to complain about how expensive her contact lenses were, and to suggest that Poppy could play Monopoly if she was bored. For a moment she thought it might be nice to buy out every hotel, train station and utility in London, just for a change. But Poppy was happy sorting buttons. She wanted to have something useful completed for Gran when she got back from hospital.

Every ten minutes she found herself checking her phone to see if Dad had called. She'd sent him a message from the hospital to tell him about Gran and that she was okay.

At a quarter past midnight, just as she was dozing off in bed, her phone lit up with a message from Dad that read:

Hope she's okay. x

Poppy had to stop herself from messaging back:

What's up? Too busy circumnavigating Canada on your bike to give a rat's? xxxxxxxxxxxxxxxxxxxx
(<---- look how many kisses I put)

She'd only just lapsed back into a light sleep when her phone went off again, but this time it was a call from a number she didn't recognize.

"Hello?"

"It's Erasmus. Erasmus Tall."

"Hi, Erasmus Tall, it's one. One in the *morning*."

"It's 12.57. You shouldn't exaggerate – it's widely considered an unattractive quality."

"Whatever," said Poppy.

"I'm telephoning you because I wanted to say that I'm really disappointed you left halfway through our interview."

"Really? I kind of thought things were wrapping up nicely. We had him in the bag, Ras."

"Well, they weren't and we didn't," said Erasmus sharply. "There was so much more he could have told us if your stupid pig hadn't interrupted and if you hadn't gone running off with it."

Poppy's heart somersaulted. "Firstly, Churchill is a *he*-pig and secondly, you've got to be joking!"

"I most certainly am not. When there's an investigation under way, we don't rest – night or day, for better or worse."

"This isn't a marriage ceremony, lay off the analogies."

"That's *not* an analogy, it's a figure of speech."

"An analogy *is* a figure of speech," began Poppy hotly. "And my gran is in hospital. So thanks for checking everything was okay."

"Is she alive?"

"Yes," Poppy choked out.

"Is she speaking coherently?"

"Yes."

"Then I really don't see why you had to rush off on me like that. What you did wasn't logical. Do you see?"

Poppy felt an angry thumping in her chest, and, tapping the "end call" button, she flung her phone on the bedside table.

She dreamed that night, but her last thought before she drifted off to sleep was, *He won't make me cry. If death can't, then Erasmus Tall can't either.*

Nine
BOYFRIEND

"Who were you on the phone to in the wee hours last night, girlie?" asked Dalia as they drove in her dented, pale-gold estate car to the uniform shop at school. It was a nothingy sort of day and the sky was flat and grey. Dalia turned the radio up as she asked the question, almost as if she didn't care whether Poppy answered or not.

"Just someone I know," Poppy murmured, pressing her nose to the glass and watching the fields flashing by.

"Ah!" said Dalia knowingly, undoing her bottle of green health smoothie with her long teeth. "Boys, eh? You can't fool me, girlie."

Poppy ignored her, thinking: *You'd be easier to fool than a deaf pigeon in a blindfold.*

Dalia began singing to the radio in a voice Poppy

could only describe as unearthly. The car sped through a tunnel and Poppy held her breath and counted.

1, 2, 3, 4, 5, 6...

The school grounds looked nothing like the ones Poppy was used to. For starters, there was a paddock of deer to one side of the playing fields and the Riddling Woods hovered behind them.

In the uniform shop, it wasn't so much a "fitting" as an opportunity for the lady who ran it, Mrs Felt, to pull plasticky-smelling jumpers over Poppy's head. Mrs Felt's daughter, Mitsy, listened from between a row of hanging blazers, reading a well-thumbed copy of *Fairytales of the English South*. Mitsy was small and thin, with a rustle of wiry dark hair and enormous violet eyes that watched Poppy with great curiosity.

"I think it's too big, Mrs Felt," Poppy coughed in a muffle as the sports jumper smothered her limber frame in a cavernous labyrinth of nylon.

"Nonsense!" sang Mrs Felt, now wrapping the school kilt around Poppy's waist. "If I know anything about children, it's that they grow. Everything grows: their legs, their arms, their heads and – well – *hopefully* their brains."

The sleeves of the jumper felt like Poppy was wearing a sleeping bag on each arm and when she finally managed to free her hands she had a peek in the mirror.

I look like I've robbed a giant's clothing store.

"Has *my* brain grown, Mum?" Mitsy asked Mrs Felt thoughtfully.

"Well, how old are you now, nine and a half? Ten? Then it would be about the size of a large grapefruit, I'd say," Mrs Felt said, examining Poppy with new enthusiasm. "Provided you stop reading those stupid fairytales." She leaned in closer to Poppy. "Mitsy found that tatty old fairy-tale book at a second-hand shop. Never lets go of it. And if her sitter hadn't cancelled on me last minute, maybe I could think for a second!"

Mitsy closed her book and clutched it tight.

Poppy had Mrs Felt worked out very quickly. Mrs Felt ran the parents' association at school. Mrs Felt baked cakes for the bake sale and coached the netball team. Mrs Felt ran the uniform shop, the tuck shop, the stationery shop and couldn't remember her own daughter's age.

"Do you have any friends you'll know at school when you start, Poppy?" asked Mrs Felt.

Poppy didn't quite know how to answer. She wasn't going to pretend Erasmus was really her friend. He was too interested in himself and his precious investigation. Erasmus didn't give a rat's about anyone, probably not even his own mother.

"Yes, she does!" Dalia chimed in, looking up from her copy of *What Makes a Good Crack: A Chiropractor's Guide*.

"Who?" asked Poppy, swivelling round and nearly

tripping over her school kilt.

Dalia turned to Mrs Felt, looking very pleased with herself. "She has a boyfriend. I heard her on the phone to him last night!"

This seemed to interest Mitsy greatly, and she crept out of her hiding place to listen in more closely. Poppy's heart leaped into action and she *willed* her cheeks not to flush an alarming shade of scarlet.

"He's *not* my boyfriend," she insisted, trying desperately not to scowl at Dalia.

"What's his name?" Mrs Felt asked Dalia, resting her chin on her fist.

"Lazarus!" Dalia declared loudly, blinking her contact lenses into position.

"Erasmus!" Poppy corrected her without thinking, instantly regretting it.

Mitsy's eyes widened.

"Were you listening in?" Poppy demanded of Dalia.

"Oh, stop being such a prude," Dalia moaned. "It was just for a moment!"

Poppy didn't want to make any more fuss about it, even if Dalia had been nosey – she was in danger of losing her battle with the blush rising up her cheeks and would have given her left leg just to change the subject.

"Do you know who he is?" Dalia asked, directing her question at Mrs Felt.

"Asparagus Boy!" Mitsy piped up.

"Mitsy!"

"But, Mum, that's what everyone calls him!" Mitsy insisted. "Asparagus Boy! He's in the year above me."

"Yes, we heard it the first time, Mitsy. Bite – your – tongue," said Mrs Felt, looking embarrassed.

"Great name!" Dalia grinned. "Why do they call him that?"

Mitsy thought. "Be-because he once brought a tin of asparagus to school for lunch."

Mrs Felt laughed nervously. "He's a...a...nice boy, isn't he, Mitsy?"

Mitsy remained silent.

"His mother..." whispered Mrs Felt to Dalia, and gestured as if she were glugging from a bottle.

Both grown-ups thought Poppy didn't see this, or perhaps they thought she didn't know what they meant. But she did. She wasn't going to let herself feel sorry for Erasmus though. After all, he didn't give a flying fig about her. Why should she suddenly gush out with an apology just because his mum was a drinker? Worse things had happened.

"He's a nice boy," Mrs Felt assured Poppy. "He's just a bit...troubled."

"Ahh, we like lone wolves, don't we, Pops?" Dalia nodded wisely.

She's just old and lonely, Poppy told herself as she felt another wave of scarlet bloom across her cheeks.

As they headed off for enrolment with her new uniform, Poppy heard Mrs Felt and Mitsy talking.

"Goodness, it's almost time for pilates with Harriet!" Mrs Felt said as she began furiously steaming a blazer. "Why don't you read me that story you like while I pack up here, Mitsy? Nice clear voice and *enunciate*. The lips, the tongue, the tip of the teeth – is that how it goes?"

Mitsy cleared her throat and began slowly.

"In...th-at town, where the river cut deep and the trees gr-e-ew black, there had al-ways been four ugly sis-ters...sisters."

Almost every day that weekend and the following week, Gran would call Poppy to say that her doctor had insisted on keeping her in "just one more night", because, according to her, the nurses wanted to "conduct a few more experiments on me before they let me out – it's not often they get a beauty like me on the ward". Poppy spent most of those days swotting up on her German in Gran's workshop. She wanted to have at least one subject completely under control before starting at the new school. When she'd had enough of declining nouns and conjugating verbs, she set about reorganizing the workshop. She loved rolling up, pinning and sorting the miles of shimmering ribbons, the twists of wire and the bolts of fabric in every colour from a musky purple to golden greengage.

Poppy had to swallow her disappointment when Gran called again that evening with her usual excuses.

Sure it was "just one more night", but Gran had already been there a week and a bit.

"Be careful, precious," Gran had said before Poppy hung up. "Always be careful and kind. Have you been sticking to my rules? Do you remember all of them?"

And she'd repeated them back to Gran: "Don't do the washing or leave it out after six o'clock, hide all the sugar in the house, close the windows and most importantly of all…"

They said the last bit together.

"Never, don't you ever, dust the window sills."

When that Monday came suddenly swinging around, Poppy realized just how apprehensive she really was about starting at a new school.

A new school, she thought. *New smells, new teachers, new people, new shoes, new uniform, new cliques, new books.*

Dalia dropped Poppy right at the school gates that misty morning. Not around the corner, or demurely in the street. *Right* at the school gates. Her parting advice as she gulped her green smoothie and roared off was, "I think the school office is that way."

Poppy's fists were clenched tightly around the straps of her backpack as she made her way through the chaotic school grounds towards the office.

Kids can be so violent, she thought as a tennis ball ricocheted off the basketball hoop and grazed the back of her shoe. A bunch of sweaty boys scrambled for the ball behind her, colliding in a shouting heap. Her old school wasn't all *that* different. The boys still threw punches and the girls still queued outside the loos chewing gum, but she was used to them. Right now, she didn't know if someone was about to punch her in the face or offer her a crisp.

One of the least enthusiastic people Poppy had ever met showed her to her first classroom. Dennis was a short, sweaty, bowling pin of a man with flared nostrils, who worked in the school office alongside Beth, who seemed to enjoy peppering the office with sticky notes.

"Mr Hern," Dennis called out to the man Poppy thought must be her teacher. "New."

Poppy got the feeling Dennis was pointing down at her from behind her back.

Mr Hern was bright and young, wearing tortoiseshell glasses and a flags-of-the-world novelty tie.

"Nice tie, Herny!" shouted someone from the back of the class.

"New day, new tie!" Mr Hern sang back.

Dennis slumped off towards the office, fishing a chocolate wafer out of his pocket for the journey as he left.

"You are Poppy," said Mr Hern, taking her bag for her and showing her to a desk.

"Yes," she croaked. She was glad he had told her what her name was. She didn't think she could have mustered the courage to tell him herself.

"Poppy, welcome to North Riddling School. I'm sure you'll find us a little less..." He looked around the disorderly classroom and was distracted by a ponytailed girl who was trying to fit a copy of *The Pickwick Papers* into her mouth. Poppy recognized her mustard-coloured hair immediately. She'd seen her in Bonhilda Bonhoeffer's sweet shop, stealing sweets.

"Regina Pocks, get that book out of your mouth right now!"

"But, sir, she dared me to!"

"Who dared you to?" Mr Hern demanded.

"She did, sir," Regina whined, pointing to Poppy. "That new girl."

Poppy opened her mouth, knowing full well that she didn't have the strength to actually say anything in her defence.

"The new girl's name is Poppy, and I find that *incredibly* hard to believe, Regina," said Mr Hern, and a warm glow ran through Poppy's cheeks.

Regina obviously wasn't too bright and, blinking desperately, she ignored what Mr Hern had said. "But, sir, if someone dares you to do something, you *have* to do it."

"That's codswallop. I've never heard such a spineless, nonsensical statement."

"You can't call her that, sir!" another girl cried out.

"Call her what?"

"Cod-wallop, you called her a cod-wallop, sir," the girl replied. "And what would you do, sir, if someone dared *you* to do something? Would you be gutsy? Or would you just chicken out?"

"Alright," said Mr Hern, gesturing for Poppy to take a seat and stepping onto the raised part of the floor where his desk sat. "Let's get this whole 'daring' business cleared up. For starters you are, all of you, misusing this word. Can anyone tell me where the word 'dare' comes from?"

Germanic origin, Poppy said in her head. Poppy *especially* loved the way old German words slipped so quietly into English etymology. Her lips must have moved, because Mr Hern said, "Poppy?"

Her heart began doing its usual routine of making her feel as if she were hanging upside down off a cliff. She could *feel* Regina Pocks and the other girl folding their arms behind her.

"Ger-*ahem*-manic," she croaked, pausing to clear her throat.

"What was that?"

"Germanic," she whispered, as quietly as a spider.

"Yes! Germanic. It's from the Old English word *durran* which has Germanic origin, but also some Indo-European roots, as the word is similar in both Greek and Sanskrit."

Poppy liked Mr Hern. He was bubbling with energy, as if longing to share what he knew about language with the dull-eyed children of North Riddling School.

"The original meaning of the word 'dare' was to have courage, bravery. To venture out and do new things. To *know* your fears and confront them. So, Regina, when you tell me that someone 'dared' you to swallow the abridged edition of *The Pickwick Papers*, I don't call that brave. I call that senseless."

"You didn't tell me it was *abridged*!" shouted the second girl with the ponytail, snatching the book from Regina.

Mr Hern sighed. "And I give you *another* successful lesson in etymology at the glorious Riddling Woods School."

Poppy knew she wasn't supposed to have her phone out at school, but at lunch she desperately wanted to call Gran. So she thought she'd try asking Dennis to let her use one of the phones in the office.

As she crossed the school grounds she spotted Mitsy, the uniform lady's daughter, leaning on the supporting beams of the swings.

Poppy attempted a "cool" wave and Mitsy smiled back, before burying her huge eyes back in her book of fairytales.

"She's not answering," Poppy heard Dennis saying lazily as she heaved open the front door to the office.

From around the corner in the waiting area, Poppy

could hear the sounds of someone quite obviously in distress.

"Are you here to see the headmaster?" Dennis asked Poppy when he finally noticed her.

"No!" Poppy shouted, by accident. "I was wondering if I could call my gran on your phone?"

"Do you have a temperature?" Dennis asked, not looking away from his computer.

"No."

"Have you barfed in the loos? Cos if you have, you need to tell me, so I can get Ned to clean it up before someone slips over and lands face-first in it. It's happened before."

"No," Poppy said again. "My gran's in hospital. I just want to see how she is."

Dennis reluctantly pushed the phone across the bench towards Poppy with one miserable finger.

"Has she called back yet?" came a familiar voice from around the corner. The voice sounded worried and made little anxious wheezing sounds as it spoke.

"I'll tell you when she does," Dennis told the voice.

Poppy dialled the hospital, but the receptionist told her Gran had been discharged earlier that morning.

"Where did she go?"

"'Fraid I dunno, love," the receptionist said. "I just started me shift!"

Poppy dialled Gran's house when Dennis wasn't looking, but no one answered. What if Gran had been taken to another hospital? She didn't have time to mull for too long before the phone rang, and Dennis leaned over to snatch it from Poppy as if she'd been hogging it for hours.

"It's for you," Dennis sighed, holding the phone out to whoever was hiding round the corner. Poppy heard a scrambling, and out of the waiting area shot Erasmus, who grabbed the phone off Dennis.

"Steady on!" said Dennis, who wiped his hand on his shirt as if he'd touched something disgusting.

"I need you to come to school, Mum," Erasmus said loudly. He was crossing his legs and had one hand covering the zip on his trousers. Poppy began to tiptoe out slowly.

"I need you to come to school, Mum," Erasmus said again as he fidgeted and made odd little panicking sounds. He held the phone out to Dennis, who recoiled as if someone was brandishing a snake in his face. "She needs to talk to you."

Dennis looked incredibly displeased and held the receiver away from his ear.

"Erasmus!" Poppy hissed. But he didn't turn. "Erasmus!"

The boy suddenly turned. There was a pained expression on his face, and then Poppy saw the problem. The top part of his trousers was soaked.

"Are you okay?" Poppy mouthed.

Erasmus said nothing. He just stared at her vacantly. It was as if he didn't know who she was.

130

"Your mum can't come," said Dennis, slamming the phone back into its cradle with unnecessary force. "She's working. You'll have to go to the sick bay or something to get cleaned up. I'll call the nurse."

Dennis dialled an extension with surprising dexterity and within a few moments the school nurse came swooping in with a towel.

Erasmus lifted his hands in the air, his fingers clenched like claws, as she wrapped the towel around him. Poppy didn't see an articulate, brilliant young man. She saw a boy. A little, frightened boy.

"What happened here?" the nurse asked Dennis.

"He was doing 'research' on some little project of his in the library." Dennis smiled insincerely. "Apparently he got so into his book that he missed his mouth and spilled apple juice all down his front. Students aren't allowed drinks or food in the library," Dennis reminded them, and lifted a juice-stained book up for the nurse to see. "There will be consequences for damaging school property, and I'll have to send a bill to his mum for the book."

The book was called *The Martha Godwit Diaries: A History of the Town of Suds*. Erasmus had been working on the investigation. If Poppy had been helping him this might not have happened, and better still, they might have been a few steps closer to working out what was going on.

The nurse put her arm around Erasmus and pulled him close to her. She wasn't afraid of children like Dennis was.

"Where's my portfolio?" Erasmus said to himself, his eyes searching around the room. "I've left my portfolio, Edgar, in the library. I have to get Edgar."

"What portfolio is that, love?" the nurse asked sweetly, ushering him out the door.

"What are you waiting for? An autograph?" Dennis snapped at Poppy.

"He's my friend," Poppy said without thinking.

Dennis snorted as he poured himself a milky tea. "Pretty weird choice of friend on your first day. He's got a problem, hasn't he? Has trouble speaking or something? Never says anything to anyone."

"He's not weird," Poppy said, closing her fist.

Dennis reached with great effort for an exposed bowl of sugar. "And my name's not Dennis."

Unfortunately for Erasmus the sickbay was on the other side of the school, which meant a humiliating trip across the playground.

Poppy heard the first of the taunts as she followed him from the office. The freezing wind whipped at the towel around him, threatening to take it off.

"Oi, Asparagus Boy!" shouted a thin, blond boy, pretending to pee. "Whoops, I did it again!"

"Hey, ET!" jeered a toothy girl in a headband. "Need to phone home?"

"Was Mum too busy at the pub to make lunch for

you again, runt?" called out another. "What was it this time? A tin of garden peas?"

The nurse gave them disapproving looks, and shielded Erasmus with her arm. Poppy saw Mitsy observing from her spot by the swing. Mitsy wasn't saying anything, and neither was Erasmus. His head hung; he stared silently at the ground.

"Hey, Asparagus!" shouted Regina Pocks from beside the girls' loos. "Who are The Peggs?"

This got Erasmus's attention and he looked up to see Regina dangling his dossier, Edgar, from between her finger and thumb. Poppy froze. She knew she ought to go and thump Regina in the mouth, but she didn't. Regina handed the dossier to a beefy boy standing beside her and, with athletic vigour, he flung the dossier high in the air. Sheets of loose paper streamed out like white birds shooting across the sky. The dossier somersaulted and, with a soft *plonk*, landed right in the middle of the grassy playing field.

Erasmus wriggled free from the nurse's grip, and as he did so the towel fell to the ground, exposing the apple juice stain covering his trousers. A joint guffaw went up from everyone watching. Everyone except the nurse, Mitsy and Poppy. Poppy could see Dennis poking his sweaty face through the blinds of the office, trying to get in on the action.

Erasmus darted about the playing fields, gathering the loose pages to his chest and clutching Edgar under his arm. He was a picture of panic, as hours and hours of his work danced across the grass in front of him.

"You couldn't make this stuff up!" hooted the beefy boy, doubling over. "Whatta scream!"

Poppy saw Mitsy catch one of the pages that blew up against her leg and place it carefully between the pages of her fairy-tale book.

But Poppy was still frozen. She knew she had to do something. Most of the pages had drifted beyond human reach and were now floating like runaway kites above the woods.

Be careful, she remembered Gran saying. *Be careful and kind*.

Her little heart was contracting and expanding so quickly, Poppy felt certain it was going to burst through her ribcage and take off down the road at any moment.

They'll laugh, she thought. But it wasn't enough to stop her. Like an ice sculpture coming to life, she raced across the playing fields and, dropping to her knees in the mud, began to snatch the pages together as fast as she could. Erasmus didn't look up.

The bell rang and with moans of dismay the other kids headed back to class, leaving Poppy, the nurse, Erasmus and Mitsy. When all of the pages were gathered, Erasmus clambered to his knees and, without looking at or saying anything to Poppy, he snatched the wad of pages from her and stuffed them into Edgar.

Mitsy kept her book closed. The nurse wrapped the towel around Erasmus again and steered him off towards the sickbay.

There was no *Thanks a million, Poppy*, no *Cheers for your help, mate*. Poppy liked to think she didn't mind, but she did. And she minded more when Mitsy said, "You shouldn't have done that."

"I had to," she said, wiping her muddy hands on the underside of her kilt.

"Regina will be mean to you now though," warned Mitsy.

If Mitsy hadn't been in year seven and Poppy in year eight, she might not have said what she did: "Well, Regina Pocks can just buzz off."

"Can I, newbie?" came a voice from behind them.

Poppy knew it was Regina before she mustered the courage to spin around. The beefy boy was with her and so was the other girl with the ponytail.

"Buzz off, can I?" Regina asked, sizing Poppy up. "You think I'm a fly or something? I'm not gonna buzz anywhere."

Poppy opened her mouth to say something, but instead of an articulate comeback, a long strand of dribble came oozing out. She flushed scarlet and hurriedly wiped her lips on her sleeve. That hadn't happened before. Poppy felt her eyelid twitch, and for a moment Wendy, the little girl from the church hall, danced through her head: those eyes. Those stony eyes.

"Ha!" screeched Regina, slapping beefy boy on the shoulder. "Did you see that? Like watching the Niagara Falls!"

Poppy admitted to herself that this was one of the cleverer things that Regina Pocks had ever said.

"I think Asparagus Boy's got a girlfriend: Asparagus Girl!" howled Regina.

She stepped towards Poppy. Poppy hadn't noticed how tall or thickset Regina was until then.

"If I hear you talking behind my back, *ever*, I'll knock you out so fast you won't have time to yell 'Help, Mum!'"

Poppy wondered if maybe Regina knew about her mum. She hated thinking it, but somehow she was happy Regina had said it. It proved she was cruel. But best of all, it had evaporated Poppy's fear.

For a moment, she didn't even feel scared, because her fingers and chest brimmed with a strange, air-punching power.

Poppy Slub felt angry.

Ten
ASPARAGUS BOY

On the way home Poppy found her phone in the bottom of her bag and switched it on. Dalia was supposed to pick her up from school, but after forty minutes of waiting, Poppy had decided to walk. She found a picture message waiting on her phone from Dalia. It was a photo of her posing with a bandana around her head and a pair of Marigolds on as she scrubbed the bath. Poppy grimaced.

Heeeeeey girlie, had big spring cln for ur Gran
2day and got carried away, won't b able to pick
u up from school. Soz! Sum1 waitin 4 u @ home.
Big kisses. Dals. XXXX

Poppy wondered why Dalia had jammed six "e"s into

the word "Hey" and yet somehow hadn't managed to put one in "be".

When Poppy got home Dalia's car wasn't in the drive and, to her surprise, waiting in her Seat of Wisdom armchair was Gran. Poppy threw her arms around the old woman's neck and kissed her. A man in a blue shirt popped his head out of the kitchen and Gran introduced him as Richard, her new home help.

"Richard will be coming in twice a week to lend me a hand while I'm on the mend," Gran told her.

When Richard was gone, Poppy made them tea and set about cooking dinner. She made a cheesy cauliflower and bacon gratin, and Gran clapped when she laid it, piping hot, on the dining room table. Gran lit the candles and they talked for hours, about school and the nurse who accidentally farted while taking Gran's blood pressure.

Poppy noticed Gran only ate half of her gratin, but she didn't mind. Gran was home. She hadn't felt somewhere was really home since Mum died, and even though she didn't like to think it, let alone say it, she could feel the edges of that warm, wrapped-up love beginning to creep back once again. The kind of love you feel when you've been for a cold swim and a great, big, cosy towel envelops you in a sheltering hug, away from the wind and sand.

"I have some other news," Gran said mysteriously, pouring herself a sherry. "Your dad sent me an email. He's coming to visit for a little bit."

Poppy's mouth opened.

"But he's not back for good just yet," Gran added hastily, a weak smile flickering across her face.

Poppy tucked Gran into bed, did the dishes, had a quick bath, filled Churchill's water bowl and tiptoed up the stairs to her room. Reaching underneath her pillow, she made sure the tailor's chalk Mum had given her was still there. The box was intact, save for one of the red triangles of chalk, which had snapped right in two. Something made Poppy want to fix the chalk, to glue it back together and make it right again. But chalk and glue wouldn't gel any more than Gran and Dad did.

"You attach way too much significance to things," Poppy's dad had once said, when they were clearing out their house. He emptied a crate of Mum's *National Geographic* magazines into a rubbish skip. "They're just things," he said. "They don't mean anything. Besides, they'll just get dusty. Mum would have wanted us to get rid of them."

Mum would not, Poppy muttered in her head. On Sunday afternoons, Poppy and Dad would each choose a random issue of the magazine and read them in the lounge together. Just twelve months ago, Dad would never have dreamed of throwing them away. Dad used to lick his fingertip and turn each page with a reverence that Poppy had never seen in anyone else. And then Mum slipped away.

Poppy threw an extra blanket across her bed. She fell asleep with the chalk in her hands and faded into a peculiar dream.

She was in the waiting room at the hospital. Although it wasn't really a waiting room at all. It was a train carriage, and where the doors of the carriage were supposed to be, that was the entrance to the ward. The lady who had disappeared from the train was standing at the door, with her arms covering the entrance. Poppy couldn't see in. She couldn't speak. She tried to shout at the lady, but her jaw felt dull and heavy. Dad was in the room. Poppy could hear his voice.

"Take her heart," he said to the nurse with the purple streak of hair she'd seen with Gran at the hospital. "Take her heart."

The lady at the door turned to Poppy and grinned, showing her white teeth. One by one the objects in the room began to fade to grey.

"Her heart," said the lady at the door, looking straight at Poppy. "Take her heart."

Poppy woke up in a cold sweat. She'd left the heating on before she went upstairs, but her room was freezing. There was a sudden weight in her chest. The window was open, swinging gently in the breeze.

Something was standing on her window sill. Something tall. Something billowing. Something breathing heavily.

Her arms wouldn't move. Her jaw felt as if it had been clamped shut.

"Her heart," the tall shadow whispered. *"Take her heart."*

Something began to rattle in Poppy's dresser. The rattling grew louder until, with a final twang, a drawer shot open and the box with the bone comb inside came whizzing out and landed in the outstretched palm of the tall shadow. Poppy saw its fingers for the first time. Great wooden things, with mechanical-looking joints.

"Take her heart! Take it!" hissed another voice, that seemed to be coming from behind the shadow.

Poppy couldn't feel herself; it was as if someone had cut the wires that connected her body to her head. The tall shadow stepped off the window sill with a click of its wooden foot and stalked towards her. She didn't know how, but Poppy got a sense that something ancient had stepped into her room.

She managed to free her hand and threw the only thing she could at the black shape: the tailor's chalk. There was a sound like a loud spark as the box of chalk hit the creature smack in the head. With a screech, the shadow sprang back onto the window sill as little triangles of chalk skidded across the floor.

There was a pounding downstairs on the front door.

Poppy watched in horror as something like a wide basket sailed down from the sky to float in mid-air outside her window. The tall shadow leaped like a cat into the basket and off it soared. Poppy rushed to the window, the breeze chilling the sweat on her forehead. She couldn't see anything for a moment, then the basket-shape glided across a white patch of clouds and vanished in the direction of the towering Riddling Woods.

Poppy heard Gran's voice downstairs. A door opened and closed and Gran told someone to sit beside the fire. Poppy drew the window shut and pushed the bolts in at the top and bottom. She snatched up her dressing gown and, wrapping it around herself, hurried down.

Standing beside the fire, his hands and face blue with cold, was Erasmus, wearing oversized men's pyjamas. Wrapped around his neck, like some kind of ridiculous scarf, was a thin sleeping bag.

He didn't move, but his eyes darted towards Poppy. In a crisis, Poppy knew she had to do something sensible.

"I'll make you a hot-water bottle and tea," she said firmly.

"D-d-do you have hot chocolate?" Erasmus stammered.

Even the steam gabbling out of the kettle couldn't warm the chill that gripped Poppy's spine. She was glad Erasmus showed up when he did. Maybe that was what had frightened that thing away.

Pushing the door open with her shoulder, Poppy

carried in a tray with the works: a hot-water bottle, hot chocolate with a melting dollop of Martian-Mallow, and toast with generous pats of butter and jam. When she put the tray down, Gran beckoned to her from the hall.

"His mother was working a late shift," Gran told her in a low whisper. "She works down at the pub, but she never came home. Between you and me, I've heard she does that a lot. Their electricity and gas is on a pay-as-you-go system, and apparently she forgot to top it up. So the poor boy was home alone and near frozen. You can't be too careful in Suds. The winter comes early, the summer comes late, and as for autumn and spring, they sometimes arrive at the same ruddy time!" Gran sighed and then chuckled. "Blossoms bloom as leaves fall."

Poppy felt a pang of guilt.

"I think he'll have to stay here the night," Gran said. "At least it's toasty warm."

"Is that alright?" Poppy asked. She couldn't think of anything more articulate to say, so she said, "He needs people to be kind to him."

"Of course it is, darling." Gran smiled, her crinkly eyes glittering in the dim light. She put her hand out and touched Poppy's cheek. "You're *so* like your mother it frightens me."

Gran helped Poppy set up an inflatable mattress in the living room beside the fire and went back up to bed, leaving Poppy and Erasmus with Churchill, who by now was wide awake.

144

Poppy didn't want to talk about the events at school; nor, she imagined, did Erasmus. As soon as she heard Gran's bedroom door close, she launched into her account of what had just happened in a low voice. Erasmus fell into a stunned silence, punctuated only by the crunches of toast. Poppy didn't feel like eating. She told him about the figure entering her room, about the comb, the chalk and the strange basket-like shape that had carried the figure away.

"Just like the poem said!" Erasmus gawped and the corner of his fourth piece of toast fell out of his mouth. Churchill snuffled about for the crumbs on the floorboards. "Across the sky they fly by night in airborne wicker hamper. Once they've got you in their sight, there's nowhere else to scamper."

His green eye twitched anxiously.

"I managed to scamper," said Poppy quietly, and a shudder coursed up her neck as the image of the tall shadow loomed in her mind's eye.

"But why did they come for you now? And how did they get in, because you've always been safe before? You must have done something differently, Poppy."

"I locked my window, I—" Poppy stammered. "I did. I can remember doing it."

"I don't think they'd have a problem unlocking windows." Erasmus grimaced. "If these creatures can turn kids' eyes grey and zoom around in a flying basket, I doubt a window would stop them. There must have been something else you did that was different. Try and think."

Poppy couldn't think of anything. Why had she been targeted? Why had she been singled out by those things? Her head swirled like a windstorm.

"At least tell me what it looked like," Erasmus said. "Did it look…human?"

Poppy shuddered. "Well, yes," she said softly, "and no."

Erasmus frowned.

"It was tall, like the things that Marley described, and sort of hunched over. And it had these eyes. These eyes that looked like…no, no it's too weird."

Erasmus raised his eyebrows.

"Like they knew it was me, specifically me, who was going to be in that bedroom. Like they were expecting me."

Erasmus insisted she show him the scene of the crime. The sleeping bag came off, and Erasmus went down on hands and knees as he sniffed about the room. Poppy held Churchill in her arms so that he didn't disturb the evidence. He wanted to get involved and sniff too.

"This is the dresser the comb flew out of?" Erasmus asked, pointing at the drawer lying lopsided on the floor. Poppy nodded. Erasmus methodically collected the pieces of tailor's chalk and placed them back inside their box. Poppy liked the way he did it, full of care and consideration. She found the wooden peg under the window sill and clipped Mum's note back to the front of the box, then examined the package closely. What was so special about Mum's old chalk?

Erasmus opened the window.

"What are you doing?" Poppy hissed. "Those things could still be out there!"

A breeze wafted through and Erasmus inhaled deeply through his nose.

"Bleach," he said finally.

"What?"

"Bleach. Sodium hypochlorite dissolved in water? There are traces of bleach on this window sill. Has it been cleaned in the last forty-eight hours?"

"Absolutely not," said Poppy. "We never clean the wind—"

She stopped. The window sill was clean. The tangles of cobwebs were gone.

Dalia, she thought, *Dalia was spring-cleaning*. She'd sent Poppy that awkwardly posed picture of her doing it.

"She's wiped all the cobwebs away," Poppy whispered.

Dalia had probably smeared them onto a piece of kitchen roll and plonked it proudly in the bin.

Erasmus was far less concerned and muttered, "Something to do with cobwebs then, eh?" as he examined the gleaming window sill. He looked up at

Poppy suddenly. "You don't happen to still have a loose page from Edgar, do you?"

Poppy shook her head.

"One of the missing pages was an odd if not important piece of research, but it must have been blown away with the others."

Poppy shifted.

"You've got something in your hair," Erasmus said, squinting.

"Oh, it's just that white spot," Poppy said self-consciously, wondering how he'd forgotten about it so quickly.

"No, not that."

He lifted his hand to brush Poppy's shoulder, which made Poppy twist away automatically.

"Don't move!" he whispered, combing something from her hair.

On his outstretched finger, glistening like tiny crystals in the moonlight, were a few grains of *fine blue powder*.

Poppy wanted to be sick. Her head swayed. This was it. This was how she was going to die, all laid out in front of her. Her eyes would slowly turn grey. Her head would shrivel and wizen like a wilting toadstool. She'd lose her voice. And then…she'd vanish.

The wicker hamper bumped and twisted its way over the tops of the vast forest. From the hamper swung a rope dotted with pegs, which dangled behind like a kite tail.

It was a westerly wind tonight.

As the highest twigs began to scrape the bottom of the hamper, a pair of creaking, splintery hands unfurled a tatty grey bed sheet, which billowed open like a sail, carrying them higher.

There was a sudden fluttering above them. The three ancient creatures looked up.

"What white leaf blows our way?" asked the first.

"Pages! Paper pages with words," said the second, standing up to snatch at them with its long clicking fingers.

The pages dipped and circled the wicker hamper, like a flock of birds scaling the currents.

"These are written by the boy one," hissed the second creature, ripping Erasmus's notes to shreds. "Them two clever ones know too much – too much by half, I tell you! You should have taken her while she slept!"

"But the chalk!" cowered the first. "She knows the power of the chalk!"

"Chalk or no chalk," whispered the third, "I shall have her heart and you, my sisters, will have her eyes, her hair and her dearest dreams."

The creatures threw their heads back and shrieked to the new moon, as their sail filled with a whisper of the westerly wind and carried them over the misty rise.

Eleven
TALL STORIES

Early the next morning Poppy heard Gran making a phone call. She heard Gran offering to "walk them to school" and then saying, "Well, if that's how you feel, Ms Tall, you'd best come and get him right away."

To her surprise, Poppy had slept surprisingly well. There was still some blue powder on her pillow, which she brushed under the bed with a shoe, and remembering the events of the night before, she dashed to the mirror and examined her eyes in the light. To her relief they were still blue, but she double-checked for any grey spots or signs of her impending doom. She recited tongue-twisters to herself, enunciating each word.

"Blue...bug's...blood," she said slowly. "Blue, bug's, blood. Blue bug's blood. Boo, blug's, bud." She started again, wondering each time she stumbled if this was an early sign of the mysterious vanishing voice.

Before long there was a knock on the door, and when Poppy went down, Gran was readying Erasmus to leave. She'd folded his sleeping bag into a shopping bag and even managed to pack him a ham and cheese baguette for school that day.

Erasmus was hungrily eating a croissant, stuffed to bursting point with anchovies. When Gran opened the door, Ms Tall was outside, speaking loudly into her phone and jangling her car keys.

"You said I could drop a few of my shifts this week, and pick up a few next week, Tom," Poppy heard Ms Tall say in her gravelly smoker's voice. "I have rent to pay, Tom. We aren't millionaires, you know. Dammit."

Ms Tall wore dark sunglasses and you could only tell what she was thinking from the occasional movement of her thick, dark eyebrows. She ended the call.

"I told you to stop wearing those. They're not yours," Ms Tall whispered to Erasmus, flicking his pyjamas. Then she saw the sandwich tucked beneath his arm.

"What's that?" Ms Tall asked him, prodding the baguette with one of her glossy black fingernails.

"I made him a baguette." Gran smiled warmly. "For school!"

Ms Tall prised the parcel from Erasmus and handed it back to Gran.

"That's nice of you," she said coldly. "But we don't need charitable donations."

"It isn't caviar," said Gran, taken aback. "It's just a ham and cheese sandwich. Nothing more to it."

"We're alright, you know," said Ms Tall with no hint of a smile. "My boy and I, we're alright. We might not have the fancy house or the huge TV, but we're okay. We get along just fine, don't we, RazzleDazzle?"

She nudged Erasmus, but he didn't say anything. Ms Tall turned to Gran. "If he comes here again, send him straight home. I don't want him wandering off with strangers. We might not live in the big city, but it only takes one odd person to be out on the streets at night, if you know what I mean."

Poppy caught Gran's gaze, but only for a second.

"Sometimes I worry," said Ms Tall softly. "I worry that he's got this bug that I've heard a couple of kids at his school have. The one where their eyes go that funny colour and they stop talking. But Erasmus never spoke much even when he was tiny, did you, baby?"

Other boys would have fidgeted and groaned when their mum called them baby, but Erasmus stood silently.

"Well, I know you're a busy working mum," said Gran. "And I certainly remember what that was like. So if you ever need him to stay somewhere after school or for the night, we'd be more than happy to have him."

"What makes you think I can't take care of my son, Mrs Herisson?" Ms Tall said, turning on Gran. She shook her head. "Everyone in this town is so bleeding nosey. They all think it's their personal business to make comments behind my back about how I should raise my child. Well believe you me, none of *their* husbands left them on welfare with three months of rent arrears."

Poppy glanced at Erasmus, then looked away so as not to embarrass him. Erasmus had told her his dad was dead. Either he was lying or in denial. Poppy couldn't decide between the two and guessed both.

Gran straightened her back. She was tall and noble.

"I don't think it's any of my business to tell you how to raise your son," she said with a pleasantly firm tone. "But being kind to a fellow human being is not the same as poking my nose into other people's affairs. And, seeing as your son is a friend of my granddaughter's, I'm afraid that makes him a friend of mine. Making lunch is what friends do for each other."

"We don't need lunch. Or friends," Ms Tall said, ushering Erasmus away. "I see what you're doing as charity. I've seen this all before. Next you'll be asking us to come to your church, where we all sit in a circle and hold hands and talk about how rubbish our lives are. We don't need any of that either. We're alright."

Ms Tall steered Erasmus down the drive towards their dumpy cream-coloured car.

"Erasmus," Gran called out, and he turned. "You are always welcome."

Ms Tall pushed Erasmus into the front seat and did up his seat belt before slamming the door and shooting Gran a filthy look. Erasmus's arms lay motionless at his sides and his eyes were fixed on the dashboard. Poppy didn't recognize him. She slipped her arms around Gran's waist.

Gran wanted to walk Poppy to school, but her leg looked swollen that morning so Poppy insisted she go alone. There was a moment as Gran tried to zip up Poppy's backpack – which was near bursting point on account of all the lunch Gran had packed – where Poppy thought she'd tell Gran about the thing that had come into her room last night. But as she looked from Gran's swollen leg to her weary eyes, she decided not to.

Before she left for school, she nipped back up to her room and put Mum's box of chalk in her pocket. She felt safer with it.

"You've still got the hospital band around your wrist, Gran!" Poppy said, noticing the white plastic ring hidden amongst her bangles as she said goodbye.

Poppy took the scissors from the kitchen drawer and Gran laid her forearm on the table. A dark purple bruise had bloomed all the way up Gran's arm. Poppy flinched.

"It's just from where I fell, pet," Gran said, touching Poppy's hair with her other hand. "Nothing serious."

Poppy wanted to believe her, but Gran was also the same woman who told anyone who'd listen that she'd once met a maharajah in the grocer's. Poppy cut the bracelet and binned it.

As soon as she got to school, she washed her hands. There was something she hated about touching things from hospitals.

Mr Hern's class was first that morning. He had given Poppy's English classwork (a paragraph on an aspect of a burgeoning industry during the Industrial Revolution) such a glowing review that Poppy had nearly floated out of her chair in delight. Poppy had picked Gran's brains about how weaving with a loom worked and Gran had explained in extraordinary detail how the loom lifted and dropped the criss-crossing threads of varying colours.

Miss Nnamani took their next class after lunch, which was biology. Poppy soon learned, by way of Regina Pocks, that Erasmus mostly took special classes "because he's actually a dumb alien".

Poppy wanted to whip around in her chair and say something to the effect of *He doesn't take them because he's thick, it's because you are.*

"Now," Miss Nnamani began, "today's lesson is going to get a bit icky. If you don't have a strong stomach, come no further."

Of course, when a teacher says something like that, no one in their right mind is going to put their hand up and say, "Sorry, miss – I'm a chicken, can I sit this one out?"

They all followed Miss Nnamani down to the school lab, which looked like a converted locker room with

Bunsen burners screwed to the yellow bench tops.

When they were all properly kitted out with white lab coats, gloves and paired off into duos, Miss Nnamani opened one of two large plastic bags and, reaching inside, hoisted out a large white rat. It was quite dead. Its long front teeth hung miserably from its pink mouth.

There was a joint groan of horror from everyone there. Regina Pocks made a show of jumping up onto a stool and falling off into the beefy boy's arms. The boy's name was Sid, or Mean Sid, as Poppy's lab partner Eleanor told her.

Miss Nnamani walked round the classroom, pulling white rats from her bag and plonking them onto cork boards in front of each pair. Reaching the front again, she drew a sketchy diagram on the whiteboard. Miss Nnamani was an excellent teacher, but a rubbish drawer. "Today, you're going to dissect one of these poor blighters. Take it in turns – one of you can take notes while the other cuts, then I want you to swap. I want you to locate the rat's stomach, its lungs, its heart and – if you're feeling particularly adventurous – see if you can spot its kidneys."

Eleanor opened a cereal bar and consumed it noisily as powdery crumbs showered the poor white rat.

"How do we know if they're boy rats or girl rats, miss?" a boy called John Wharf pondered from the back.

"I'm sure you'll find out without too much trouble," said Miss Nnamani. "Why do you want to know?"

"Well," said John, "when I'm taking notes I need to know whether or not to refer to the rat's kidneys as *his kidneys* or *her kidneys*."

"You start with the cutting," Eleanor told Poppy, still spraying crumbs everywhere. "I'm eating."

Sid had already tucked into his rat, and was expertly using the pins Miss Nnamani had provided to hold back the skin from the rat's belly.

Poppy looked down at their rat and picked up the scalpel. Its legs were splayed apart. It wasn't the kind of creature you would generally describe as *cute* or *appealing*, but Poppy took pity on it.

"I'm so sorry about this," Poppy whispered to the rat.

"Should I write that down?" asked Eleanor, licking sticky crumbs off her fingers.

Poppy wasn't aware that Eleanor had been listening.

"I'll make the first incision," she said practically.

In it goes, she thought.

Poppy's scalpel slipped into the rat's ribcage with a crunch.

Carefully, she thought.

Once she'd made one long slit down the body, she peeled back the fur, leaving the muscular rat shape exposed. She pretended she was cutting material for Gran. It was a blessing there was no blood.

"Do you want to cut for a bit?" she suggested to Eleanor, but Eleanor had started on another cereal bar and just shrugged her shoulders.

"Probably not a good idea if I'm eating and dissecting at the same time, is it?"

Thanks, Eleanor. Thanks a bunch.

"Well done, Poppy," Miss Nnamani said, looking over her shoulder. "Very neat! Now use your surgical scissors to remove the tissue surrounding the organs. That's it!"

Poppy did as she was instructed almost cheerfully. The moment came when the long incision up the rat's sternum had been made and Poppy peeled away the flaps of glistening tissue.

And there it was. A village of entrails, sleekly fitted together in twists of gizzard and gut. Her eyes flickered, and a sickening dizziness swarmed over her, like a goldfish swimming circles inside her head. She gripped the edge of the bench top and the scalpel clanged to the floor.

"Ouch!" shouted Eleanor, rubbing her foot. "That hit my shoe!"

Poppy's throat tightened and her heart began to pound, racing, galloping, twitching and recoiling inside her chest.

A clammy sweat surged across her body. She didn't have time to think what was happening, all she could do was dig her nails into the bench top to stop herself from toppling sideways.

She couldn't breathe. Her lungs felt like two punctured balloons that refused to inflate.

"Oi! Oi, new girl!" Eleanor whistled. "Snap out of it!"

But Poppy couldn't hear her. All she could hear was the sound of her heart beating its way to exhaustion, and a voice:

Its heart, it said. *Take its heart.*

Poppy's fingers dropped to her pockets and she fumbled manically for the box of chalk. The box came loose and, clenching her fist, she came away with some crumbling chalk and the wooden peg from Mum's note.

Take it! Take the heart! sneered the voice.

Poppy's knuckles turned white and her body trembled in a seizure-like terror.

It wasn't an out-of-body, eyes-rolling-white experience though. This was real. This was a bottomless pit of fear that was swallowing her up. The dead rat seemed to grin at her, its innards laid bare for all to see, the flaps of skin and fur hanging like gargoyle-ish wings from its ribcage.

She could hear a pulse in her ears that seemed to be coming from the rat. At any moment she expected its claws to twitch or its tongue to quiver thirstily.

"We got a problem here, miss!" shouted Eleanor, backing away from Poppy.

"What's Asparagus Girl up to now?" Regina Pocks sniggered, nudging Mean Sid.

Poppy couldn't hear any of them. All she knew was that, more than anything else, in that ever-narrowing tunnel of terror, she wanted to get herself away from the rat.

Miss Nnamani fluttered over and gripped Poppy's shoulder.

"Poppy, love," she said softly. "It's alright, it's just a rat."

No sooner had she said those words than there was an explosive bang right in front of Poppy.

Miss Nnamani screamed and covered her mouth. A few bits of powdered chalk fell through Poppy's fingers and scattered across the bench top. Thin ribbons of smoke issued from the blackened ribcage as the rat's organs popped and sizzled within.

"John Wharf," Miss Nnamani said firmly. "Fire extinguisher. Now!"

John nearly fell off his stool, but before he could unhook the fire extinguisher there was another loud pop and the rat burst into yellow, smoking flames. Poppy slipped off her stool, but her legs had become like two slumping pillows and the last thing she heard before she was knocked out cold on the laboratory floor was Miss Nnamani yelling, "Everyone out!"

Poppy woke up to the sound of Dennis's reassuring drone, and rolled her eyes beneath her eyelids. She was lying down, on something that felt white and clean.

"You can go now. There's nothing to see here. She's not going to spontaneously combust again," Dennis told someone. "I've got a bucket of water waiting beside the door just in case."

Poppy opened her eyes. She must have been in the sickbay, because there was a poster staring back at her which showed a frightening mascot tooth with arms and legs, warning kids to floss.

Dennis loomed into view, peering at Poppy with equal fascination and disgust as if she was some medical curiosity. Then she remembered. The rat. The explosion. The rat explosion. She *was* a medical curiosity. When she lifted her head, she felt a throb of pain across her temple. That must have been from where she hit the floor.

What had happened? She couldn't help feeling that it was something to do with the creature and the blue powder in her room the night before. What if *her* eyes were about to turn grey?

"Alright!" Dennis shouted at someone. "Enough gawking – back to class."

Poppy lay still, ignoring him. Her thoughts went something like: *Gran, rat, fire, sore head and knees ouch*. She couldn't seem to get a clear grip on what she was actually thinking about. Her throat felt dry and she could feel the scummy remains of dried saliva around her mouth.

"Are you ignoring me?" Dennis continued testily. "I will *not* be ignored – I'm an administrative pedagogical assistant, Mr Tall!"

"Dennis!" came a voice that Poppy recognized as the

school nurse's. "Keep your voice down! This young woman is in need of rest. She's had a very nasty knock to the head and more besides."

More besides? What else happened?

"And they need you back in the office. I'll watch Miss Slub for a bit."

Poppy craned her neck just in time to see the nurse wink at her as Dennis reluctantly waddled out of the room. The nurse threw a smile to someone sitting at the foot of the bed before slipping out of the room too. Poppy lifted her head despite the pain.

Erasmus was sitting with his arms to either side of him, watching her cautiously.

"You came!" Poppy smiled weakly.

"I heard what happened," said Erasmus matter-of-factly. Then he told her exactly what had happened, "You were cutting open a rat. You panicked. The rat caught fire. You fainted."

Poppy frowned. "I didn't panic! And *I* didn't set the rat on fire."

"According to an unreliable witness, fire-beams shot out of your eyes, igniting the rat in question," Erasmus said, squinting at the pages of Edgar like a policeman.

"Balderdash. Who told you that?" asked Poppy, but she didn't wait for an answer. "I had some of Mum's chalk in my pocket. I started feeling unwell—"

"You panicked," interrupted Erasmus.

"—and when I took the piece of chalk out of my

pocket I felt something different. Something more than just being unwell. And then the rat just blew up."

"Just like that?"

"Like a kernel of popcorn."

"Popcorn doesn't blow up," said Erasmus quietly, although he seemed to be thinking about something else. "It expands rapidly under heat." He took a pencil from his satchel and made a note in Edgar.

"Adding popcorn to your shopping list?" Poppy asked, although she wished she hadn't. The attempt at humour made her head swing and her stomach contract.

"No," said Erasmus. "Cobwebs... Chalk... Explosion."

Erasmus looked up at her.

"I think you've just done, for want of a better word, magic."

Something about what he said made sense to Poppy, but that was impossible.

Of course she'd seen something horrible on her window sill, and something strange was definitely happening in Suds. But she knew that if she opened a copy of the *Reader's Digest Greatest Mysteries of the World* there would be cases similar to this in towns all over England that claimed to have their own connections with witches and goblins. The idea that she was rumoured to have performed magic tickled her, despite her achy head.

"Do you really think so?"

"I've taken a look at the school lab. Those Bunsen burners don't run any gas through their pipes. They were switched off a few months ago because they didn't meet health and safety standards. The cork board was coated with anti-inflammatory paint. And finally: rats don't just combust on their own."

"Could it be something to do with gas building up in its stomach?" Poppy asked. *Probably concussion speaking*, she thought.

At first Erasmus looked at her inquisitively, as if she'd said something surprisingly clever. Then Poppy said, "You know, like those whales you can see exploding online?"

Erasmus's face dropped and he looked away as if bored.

"You don't have internet," Poppy said quickly.

"Firstly, no, I do not have an internet connection," Erasmus said coldly. "And secondly those whales do not 'explode' in the detonative sense that you so kindly mentioned, they simply burst because of the gaseous pressure which builds up inside of them."

Erasmus went on unsympathetically, "It happens to human bodies too. It might even happen to you one day if you're lucky."

Poppy wasn't in the mood. "Yeah, I get it."

"Now," Erasmus said, readying his pencil above Edgar once more, "we need to go over the case notes that you lost. What can you remember that we've discussed?"

"Hang on – the case notes that *I* lost?"

"Yes, that's what I said."

"I'm sorry, just remind me – *how* did *I* lose *your* case notes again?" Poppy asked, flushing with anger.

Erasmus put down his pencil and used his forearm as a bookmark.

"I'm not saying it's your fault. People can be skittish, especially around bullies. I understand that. But if you *had* rushed over sooner to assist me in gathering up the case notes, we wouldn't have lost so many, which is why I'm asking you to try and remember what it was we've discussed over the past weeks."

"I thought you were the one with the thousand-terabyte memory?"

"It's called a petabyte, and I'm not a computer," Erasmus said, but he wasn't joking.

Poppy had had enough. "Well that's funny," she snapped, sitting up and sliding off the bed. "Because sometimes you act just like one."

As she stormed towards the door, Miss Nnamani popped her head into the room and gave such a cheery "Hello!" that Poppy jumped with fright.

"Sorry, Poppy!" she laughed. "I was just coming to see how the patient was doing. But she's obviously doing just fine."

"The patient?" Poppy said.

"She means you," said Erasmus.

"O-oh, right." Poppy coughed. "I'm fine."

"I see you have your trusty nurse with you." Miss Nnamani smiled.

"She's great, isn't she?" Poppy said.

"She means me," said Erasmus.

"Oh…oh right, of course," Poppy said. "Nurse Tall employs the 'tough love' approach. Nurse Tall is all about how many milligrams or how many megabytes of medicine you're allowed."

That came out wrong, Poppy thought. *Maybe I do have percussion to the head?*

"What Nurse Tall doesn't realize is that's not what being a nurse is about at all. Being someone's nurse is about being kind and looking out for one another."

Poppy had almost forgotten that Miss Nnamani was there, and with a vapid "Well I'll see you in class! Good day, Erasmus!" she was gone.

Poppy limped down the hallway towards the office, feeling vaguely like an escaped asylum patient minus the white hospital gown.

Dennis begrudgingly telephoned Gran, watching Poppy cautiously as if at any moment she was about to erupt like a volcano.

"Thank you, sir. All the best," Dennis simpered as he hung up.

"My gran isn't a man," Poppy told him.

"Well she sounded an awful lot like a man to me." Dennis snorted, flaring his nostrils. "Your 'gran' will pick you up in the next ten minutes. Would you wait outside?"

"Gladly," Poppy said, smiling sarcastically, thinking that she'd much rather do that. Being around Dennis was like being powerless to swat a mosquito enjoying a good long drink on your arm.

A snot-coloured car with a large sticker saying *Rental* on the side pulled up in the school car park. Poppy didn't really notice until the driver, invisible behind the reflection on the windscreen, beeped at her and waved an arm out the window. She pointed to herself, and the driver gave a thumbs up.

She could see Dennis was watching her with his beady little eyes through the office blinds, so she approached the car. The window rolled down.

"Dad?"

"Hiya, Pops!"

"Dad?"

"Poppy?"

"What are you doing here?"

"I've come to pick you up," said Dad, moving his eyes from side to side.

"No. What are you doing in England?"

"I'm surprising you! I got my five days off two weeks earlier than I told you and I thought, hey! Poppy likes surprises, so why the heck don't I just head on over?"

Poppy got into the car and grabbed his arm. She'd missed him. A flood of happiness washed over her. Dad kissed her on the head.

"Did ya miss me?" he asked.

"Yep," Poppy managed, swallowing a dry sob.

Poppy couldn't stop watching Dad as he drove them back to Gran's. His tousled mousey hair, his crooked nose and his soft eyes. He still drove the same way, carefully apexing each curve. But his cheeks were gaunt and there was something quiet about his mouth.

It had been weeks since she'd seen him. All her irritation seemed to fade away into a mellow warmth that only a homecoming could bring. She told him about school, about sorting Gran's buttons, about Suds and its sweet shop, but she didn't mention the silk book, Erasmus or Mum's chalk. Every now and then, Poppy checked her eyes in the rear-view mirror to make sure there weren't any grey spots developing, and Dad watched her.

"So, the school nurse called and told me what happened," he said, after a while.

"What did she tell you?" she asked casually.

"That you had a panic attack," Dad said.

"Is that what they're calling it?" Poppy snorted.

"Pops, if you're worried…" Dad began, then sighed and bit his fingernail. "You can always talk to your gran."

"Why would I be worried? Stop biting your fingernails," she told him, tapping his wrist.

Dad sighed again. "Poppy, you don't have to pretend that what happened wasn't a big thing. It was huge. It *is* huge."

Poppy turned away in her seat and folded her arms awkwardly. How could a moment of such elation turn into a "life talk" so quickly?

"You've been so tense ever since Mum left us, and…" Dad paused and lifted his fingers to his mouth to nibble at his nail, but then let his hand drop back to the steering wheel. "And God knows it hasn't been easy for me. I've been tense too. But you can't worry your little life away. It won't do any good to fret and lose sleep over things that might not happen."

"I'm not worried," Poppy lied, gazing out the window.

"Have you been reading too much?" Dad asked thoughtfully, as though this was a thing parents often asked their children. "I think you should take up cycling. It will get you outside. Cycling has helped me no end. I've met loads of new people and you get to—"

Poppy felt a hot surge flush across her cheeks. Her fingernails dug into the silk book in her pocket as she cut him off.

"You can't just swoop in every now and then to parent me, you know," she snapped, grinding her teeth. "And stop saying that Mum 'left us'. She didn't leave us. She died. She's dead. End of story. I'm not a little girl, Dad – I do a lot of growing up when you're not around."

They pulled into Gran's drive and Poppy slammed her way out of the snotty, clean-smelling car. Gran was waiting for her at the front door.

It hurt Poppy that she was so angry with Dad. He hadn't done anything really. But that was just it. He *hadn't* done anything. As soon as the going got tough, Dad nipped off on a group cycling retreat to the Alps where he could meet "other like-minded people".

When Poppy went down to dinner she had made up her mind not to be civil.

Gran tried to fill the silences by plying Dad with questions about what it was like acting as legal counsel for new companies in Canada. He wasn't touching his spinach and walnut pasta bake (with extra, extra cheese), he was just moving it around in little circles with his spoon.

Churchill sat on the floor beside Dad, gazing up at him as if to say, *Are you going to eat that?* Dad didn't seem to like Churchill and without thinking asked, "Can pigs carry diseases?"

Gran finished her mouthful and said, "Yes, they're

just like people that way."

Dad threw Churchill an awkward glance and shifted in his chair.

"You're not going to catch swine flu," Poppy muttered bitterly.

"I've had some exciting news," Gran interjected, looking pleased with herself. "I've been commissioned to design and build a costume for three of the leads in a new West End musical called *Oh, Cairo!*"

"That's excellent news!" Dad chimed. "What's it about?"

"It's a comedy about six female archaeologists working in the Valley of the Kings."

Poppy didn't say anything, and Gran threw her a sideways glance.

"I've decided I'm going to cook for you both tomorrow," Dad announced, putting down his spoon and folding his hands as if he were a news anchor. "Something healthy and nourishing," he went on.

Gran and Poppy watched him.

"Since when have you *ever* cooked?" Gran asked, half joke, half jab.

"I can cook, ask Poppy!" Dad insisted.

"I once saw you microwave some leftover pad thai?" Poppy offered.

Dad frowned. "Well, I'm glad you've brought this up actually," he said, dodging the insult and putting his napkin on the table. "Because—"

But Gran cut him short. She seemed to know exactly what he was going to say.

"Because you've met someone," she interrupted.

"Sorry?"

"Because you've met someone who showed you how to cook. And this is your way of telling us."

Dad was stunned. "A-as a matter of fact, yes. I have met someone," he said pleasantly. "She's a lawyer actually, *very* smart."

Gran was amazing. She was civil. She was calm, as if she'd known this day would come. But her smile still looked hurt.

Poppy, on the other hand, was spitting angry black curses through her head. Along with thoughts like: *Will I have to call her "Mum"?*

"A lawyer?" Gran asked. "What did she teach you to cook?"

"Fibre-free juices," Dad said proudly.

"Oh," said Gran.

"Fibre-free juices?" Poppy repeated. "So this woman teaches you how to squeeze an orange and all of a sudden you're marrying her?"

"I'm not marrying her, I haven't even…kissed her yet!"

"Bleurgh! I don't want to know!" Poppy covered her ears.

Dad smiled weakly.

"Poppy!" Gran snapped, staring at her across the

table with firm, disappointed eyes. Poppy was shocked. Gran never snapped at her. Wasn't Gran on her side? She'd never usually give up the opportunity to pick a bone with Dad.

"What's her name?" Gran asked politely.

"Josie," Dad said softly.

Poppy reared up like a phantom horse. "THAT IS NOT HER NAME. THAT IS MUM'S NAME!"

"She can't help her name, Poppy," Dad pleaded. "She's a really lovely woman. And she has two cats. You're bound to like her."

"Oh yes, I'm sure," Poppy drawled. "She's a lawyer with cats who cycles and makes fibre-free juice – what's not to like?"

"Poppy, you've said quite enough," Gran cut in, staring at her again with those powerful eyes.

Poppy snatched up her cutlery and plate. Moving around the table, she aggressively cleared Gran's and Dad's dishes as well. But she wasn't quite finished.

"And like it or not, this –" she pointed to his untouched pasta bake – "is what we eat here."

Poppy did the dishes and had them washed, dried and put away within ten minutes. She slunk up to bed and waited until she'd heard Gran and Dad bidding each other goodnight.

When they were definitely asleep, she tiptoed downstairs to Gran's computer and started googling. On Dad's Facebook page she quickly found Josephine

Parsons, who worked at Bristol & Davenport Solicitors. Poppy snorted in disgust. There were one or two pictures of Dad and this Josie cycling in Canada. The truth was, Josie did look like a perfectly decent person, despite the cats, but Poppy wasn't going to have any of that. Josie Parsons was a conniving, manipulative creature with kind blue eyes, a crooked smile and frizzy brown hair. Poppy angrily clicked too fast and accidentally closed the web page.

When she opened it up again and typed in *Josie*, the first name to come up was Josie Slub. Poppy clicked.

There was Mum. As alive as anyone could be, wearing a green dress, her eyes closed, her arms around Dad's neck as he pecked her on the cheek. Poppy scrolled through. One of their weekends in Cornwall as a family – several pictures of them at the beach with Mum kicking the waves and Dad crouching beside a jellyfish. Why had no one deleted Mum's account? Her page was just left here, floating somewhere in cyberspace like a lost child.

Some of Mum's more distant friends had written goodbye messages on Mum's wall, which Poppy stopped herself from reading because she knew they'd make her angry, sad and disgusted all at once.

As she flicked through the pictures, she wished desperately that Mum had said something significant the last time she saw her; some parting advice that would stay with Poppy for the rest of her life. In truth Mum had just said, "Pops – don't forget your lunch."

That was it. The last thing. The last time Poppy heard her mum's voice, she was telling her not to forget her salmon and cucumber sandwich. She watched her fingers trembling ever so slightly above the mouse for a moment before closing the browser window.

She typed *panic attack symptoms* in the search bar and waited for Gran's ancient computer to sputter something onto the screen. Then she clicked on the most promising-looking website.

As she read, she got the distinct impression that what she was doing was not a good idea. The website listed all of what Poppy had experienced in the school laboratory and more. Everything except for rats spontaneously combusting.

Anxiety, the website said every ten words. *Apprehension. Panic disorder. Post-traumatic stress. Sweating. Twitching. Itching. Imagining.*

Poppy closed the window again. She was right. This wasn't a good idea. Her fingers reopened Mum's Facebook page without her asking them to. There Mum was in the green dress again.

Poppy's neck stiffened. The dress was one that Gran had made for Mum.

Poppy felt for the silk book in her pocket. She slowed her breathing and held the book up against the dress on the screen. The black spot in Poppy's mind from when her mum had died had clouded her memory: the silk on the book in her hand and Mum's dress were definitely cut from the same cloth. The white patch on the back of her head began to itch. This new knowledge made her feel more connected to the book somehow. Why were they both the same silk?

She dreamed about her mother that night, the horrible dream where the woman from the train stood in her way, and she couldn't see Mum's face, just her green dress. Before she knew it, it was morning and the night had passed as if Poppy had only blinked her eyes.

Twelve
On Deaf Ears

Dad dropped Poppy off at school the next morning. On the way there he told her that he only had five more days left in England and wanted to make the most of his time with her.

"We'll hang out tonight?" Dad asked as Poppy picked up her bag.

"Yep," Poppy muttered, slamming the door.

The snot-coloured car glided off down the school driveway and a horrible thought punched Poppy in the gut. What if Dad crashed? What if the last thing Dad ever said to her was *We'll hang out tonight?* Her heart did a backflip. She turned to wave him down, but the car was now an indicating speck of greeny-yellow at the far end of the drive and, turning smartly into the road, it vanished between the trees.

Poppy got out her phone to text him.

"Slub! Is that a mobile phone?" came Dennis's yap from the entrance to the school office.

"Nope," Poppy lied, sliding the phone into her backpack and feeling for her calculator key ring.

She held out the key ring for Dennis to inspect. He wasn't satisfied but told her to "push off to class" anyway.

Poppy spent the day tapping her knees on the bottom of her desk. She thought about faking another panic attack just so she could see Dad again, if only for thirty seconds. He was flying out on Monday evening. Monday was headed for her at breakneck speed.

The next afternoon, Poppy had to attend choir trials. At enrolment, Dalia had claimed she'd heard Poppy singing in the bath and that her voice was "bewitching". Mrs Picardy, who oversaw enrolments and ran the choir in her spare time, had been so overcome with enthusiasm that Poppy was forced to sign up for try-outs on the spot. Poppy had never sung a note in the shower, let alone the bath.

Erasmus was already there when she opened the door to the school hall, reading a sheet of music in the corner. There were some other kids sitting on the stage, their legs dangling over the edge.

"Can you read music?" she asked casually, sitting down beside him.

"I haven't learned properly," Erasmus said. "But Mum once showed me that that note" – he pointed to a note on the manuscript – "is an E. Like E for Erasmus. So I worked out the rest on my own."

"Impressive," said Poppy. Then before she knew it, she'd grabbed Erasmus's forearm.

"I'm sorry," she whispered, "I'm really, really sorry for yelling at you like I did."

Erasmus didn't look at her. He looked at her hand, wrapped around his arm.

"You didn't mean it," Erasmus said softly. "You were upset."

She smiled briefly. "Anyway, we've got way too far with this investigation to give up now. I intend to give it my undivided attention. And I mean that."

"Gather round, gather round," came Mrs Picardy's deep voice. She was short and round, with tangled hair and glasses. "Gerty, you're on piano."

Gerty Raisin, an eleven-year-old piano maestro with buck teeth, leaped onto the piano stool and arranged her sheet music. Mitsy, with her fairy-tale book tucked under her arm, had been cajoled into turning the pages for Gerty.

"First, introductions – I'm Mrs Picardy," the woman shouted, hoisting up her skirt around her stout body a little. "And we're going to begin by sorting you into voices. Line up for me."

The door creaked open and the lady from the

bookshop poked her head in.

"I'm not late, am I, Mrs Picardy?" cooed the old woman, blowing her nose forcefully on a rotten-looking handkerchief.

"Ah!" Mrs Picardy cried out. "Mrs Gwynne, *au contraire*, just in time. Boys and girls, this is Mrs Gwynne, who you may know from the bookshop. Mrs Gwynne is the chairwoman of the North Riddling Musical Society, and she's joining us today to listen out for new talent to enlist. So don't be silent: sing like nightingales!"

Erasmus laughed and Poppy questioned him with a frown.

"*Enlist*, *listen* and *silent* are all anagrams of each other," he told her.

Poppy rolled her eyes. More importantly, she thought, Mrs Gwynne was the chairwoman of the North Riddling Musical Society, the society that Andrew Booker, the pianist boy who vanished, had been a part of. They'd quoted her in the newspaper article. Poppy made a mental note to mention this to Erasmus.

Mrs Gwynne positioned herself at the back of the room, polished her hearing trumpet and pointed it towards the front of the hall. She was wearing a dull beige suit with brass buttons. Gran would have hated it.

It turned out Poppy and Erasmus were both altos. The older boys seemed to enjoy this.

"Asparagus!" one of the basses shouted. "Do computers' voices ever break?"

Poppy felt a pang of guilt. Only yesterday she herself had accused Erasmus of being computer-like. She saw now that he wasn't like a computer at all, even though he could do maths really, really quickly.

Gerty rolled off with a mournful introduction to "Greensleeves" and they began.

Poppy almost jumped out of her skin when Erasmus started singing. There was a titter of laughter as he bellowed the words to "Greensleeves" in what Poppy could not deny was an exceptionally high voice. Erasmus continued unfazed.

Poppy couldn't hear herself singing. Mitsy was missing Gerty's cues to turn the music, and instead was gazing fondly at Erasmus and swaying on the spot.

"Exceptional projection, Mr Tall!" chimed Mrs Picardy. "I'll wager they could hear you two towns over at that rate!"

Mrs Gwynne beckoned to Mrs Picardy and they spoke and pointed at Erasmus for a bit, but he didn't seem to notice.

Mrs Gwynne grinned toothily at Erasmus and watched him with great interest throughout the rest of the trial songs. She bobbed her head jollily to the music and tapped her boot on the floor.

Halfway through one song, something smacked into the hall door. Poppy had just sidestepped away from Erasmus for fear of losing her sense of hearing. Mrs Picardy encouraged them to continue singing despite the noise. There was a clatter, the door swung open and Ms Tall stumbled in. She had a can of energy drink in her hand. Her hair was teased into a frazzled mania, as if she'd tried desperately to comb it, without success.

Erasmus ignored her and kept singing as he watched Mrs Picardy's hands.

"Sorry!" Ms Tall slurred, tiptoeing across the floor and wobbling in her high-heeled boots. She still had her sunglasses on.

"Shh!" Mrs Picardy hissed, signalling to Ms Tall.

Poppy tried to ignore them. Ms Tall made her way clumsily over to Mrs Picardy and waited beside her, mouthing the song and swishing her fingers in the air, as if mimicking the choir mistress. The song they were all singing seemed to be a weird local ditty Poppy hadn't heard before about a girl who bought a magic ribbon. Everyone else seemed to know it already.

Poppy could see that Ms Tall must have put on her make-up in a hurry. There were quick stripes across her cheeks that were too orange.

They finished the song and Ms Tall began to clap loudly. Mrs Picardy looked quite put out.

"We used to sing that one at school too. My baby's got such a beautiful voice, doesn' he, Mrs Piccadilly?" Ms Tall garbled.

Mrs Picardy smiled awkwardly and there was a rustle of giggling from the choir.

"When he was a baby he would be silent as a mouse."

Ms Tall laughed loudly, taking off her boots and using Mrs Picardy's shoulder for balance. "Then, when I'd walked out of the room, he'd start singin' in his cot, lulling himself to sleep like a li'l dove! I used to listen at his door."

The boy singing the bass part who had shouted out before now doubled over in hysterics.

Poppy shifted on the spot, turning to Erasmus. He was staring at Mrs Gwynne, ignoring his mother. Mrs Gwynne hadn't stopped listening with her trumpet. Her foot was still tapping to the music which had stopped playing, her trumpet pointed directly at Erasmus. It was as if she was listening to a song nobody else could hear.

"Baby?" Ms Tall called out.

Erasmus didn't look at her. Everyone had fallen silent.

Ms Tall pushed past Mrs Picardy and made her way through the choir to Erasmus, dropping her empty can of energy drink on the floor.

"Baby?" Ms Tall sobbed, wrapping her arms around Erasmus's head and caressing him. As she jostled past, her handbag swung into Poppy and Poppy got a whiff of cleaning fluids. Erasmus stayed mannequin-like.

"Can you hear me, baby?" Ms Tall whispered, great big tears streaming down her cheeks from beneath her sunglasses. Her black hair fell across Erasmus's pale skin like a dark curtain.

"I'm sorry about what I said, baby," she wept, "I was—"

"You were upset," Erasmus said quietly. "You didn't mean it." He was rigid in her grasp.

She let go of him and wiped the running mascara from around her eyes. Then she saw Poppy.

"What are you doing here?" Ms Tall sniffed, wiping her nose on her hand.

Poppy's throat was as dry as sand. She clenched her fingers around the silk book in her pocket.

"Is it you filling my boy's head with worry?" Ms Tall snapped, fumbling through her handbag and producing Edgar. Erasmus snatched it off her and cuddled Edgar like a favourite blanket.

Ms Tall pointed her finger and glared at Poppy, her mouth sour. "Is it you tellin' him there's such a thing as magic and flying washing tubs and blue powder, eh?" She snorted. "I've read about it all in those notes he makes. Just you stay away from my son. You don't understand what's good for him. I do."

Poppy hadn't noticed, but Mrs Picardy must have sent Gerty to fetch someone, because she slipped in the door with Dennis, who took a nervous breath and approached Ms Tall.

Poppy's chest was heaving up and down. Ms Tall was terrifying in all her drunken glory. She homed in on Poppy, the lenses of her sunglasses like two black glassy eyes.

"Alright, Ms Tall." Dennis trembled, beckoning her

from a distance. "Why don't you come with me and we'll rustle you up some nice tea and a biscuit, eh?"

Ms Tall sniffed her acknowledgement, as if deciding she wasn't going to make any more of a scene. She straightened her hair, turning back to Erasmus and pulling him into a tight squeeze again.

Dennis had picked up her boots and, taking her arm, he escorted Ms Tall from the school hall.

There were a few taunts as they gathered their things, but by now Poppy was learning to ignore them just as well as Erasmus did. Before they left the hall, Erasmus picked up the can his mum had dropped and stowed it away in his satchel.

"Vodka," he muttered, sniffing the can as they walked home from school. The enormous trees which lined the road shuddered their leaves away, as if tickled by the autumn wind. Ms Tall hadn't been anywhere to be seen when choir finished.

Now that everything was out on the table, Poppy felt she could ask a few more questions.

"Does she drink often?"

"She's drunk often," Erasmus said. "Whisky when she's happy. Vodka when she's not."

Poppy heard a shoe scuff behind them and turned to see Mitsy, still caressing her fairy-tale book, following them cautiously at a distance.

"She follows me home every night," Erasmus said without turning. "She keeps trying to show me her book."

"Erasmus?"

"That is my name."

"Why are you so different from everyone else?" Poppy asked. She tensed, waiting for him to snap at her. "It's just that, I don't understand," Poppy ventured on when he didn't reply. "I don't understand how you can—" She stopped herself, then launched in. "– how it's so hard for you to speak to people or say what you really think to them and yet...and yet you find it so easy to tell what people are thinking. You can read people as if they were newspapers. But then other times, I try to tell you something and you just don't get what I'm saying at all."

Erasmus thought for a second. He obviously hadn't been asked this before and oddly it struck Poppy as the most ordinary thing she'd seen him do.

"I don't use my instinct like other people do," Erasmus told her, opening Edgar to rearrange the notes his mum had sifted through. The pages weren't numbered, but Erasmus had a method. A very particular method. "People let how they feel get in the way of decisions or assumptions they make regarding people and they call that 'instinct'. I don't do that. I look at people. I can watch them, without their being nice or their not being nice affecting what I think of them."

"What about Regina Pocks? You must see she's a complete beast?"

"She's incredibly sad."

"She's a bully!" Poppy exclaimed.

"She *is* that. But she's mostly sad. You can't see that, can you?"

Poppy bit her bottom lip. "As soon as she says nasty things about people – about you – I can't, I *don't* feel anything else but angry," she said.

"Watch her," Erasmus told Poppy. "Watch the way she checks her hair in the window reflection every two minutes. Watch her at break time and see how she pretends she isn't hungry, but in reality she doesn't want to show everyone that her dad packed her a piece of two-day-old fried chicken for lunch. She eats by herself in the toilets."

Poppy looked at him. She couldn't read resentment in his eyes. This was real. Erasmus Tall truly thought Regina Pocks was sad.

"Only it's different with you," Erasmus said finally, looking away across the hedged fields.

"What about me?" asked Poppy.

"I can't read you like other people," Erasmus said quietly. "You're a riddle to me."

Poppy fell silent.

"That's why I talk to you," Erasmus said, staring at her with uncommon nerve. "There is a problem in you that I can't solve."

Poppy let the sun catch her eyes, so she didn't have to look at him. What was it about this boy? He could be as cold as glass, as unfeeling as stone, and yet seem to know her. To know that Poppy harboured a terrible fear – of what, she didn't know herself. It just gripped her sometimes, like a cold hand in the dark.

There was a low snarl from somewhere in the nearby hedge. Poppy ducked behind Erasmus, making more fuss than was necessary.

The thing snarled again. Erasmus swung off his satchel and crept towards the undergrowth.

"Erasmus, watch yourself!" Poppy hissed, backing away.

The thing rustled and Poppy spotted a pair of doleful eyes peering back at her.

Erasmus dipped his hand into his satchel and pulled out a Lemon Romp (from Bonhilda Bonhoeffer's shop, no doubt). He quickly unravelled the wrapper and held the sweet in his outstretched palm.

Mitsy caught up with them and kneeled down beside Erasmus without saying anything.

"Why are you following us?" Erasmus sighed at Mitsy. "Shouldn't you be at home with your babysitter?"

"She's my sitter, not my *baby*sitter, and she's always asleep," said Mitsy. "She only wakes up when Mum comes home from bingo."

There was a wolflike growl and out of the hedge trotted Marley the dog. He sniffed the Lemon Romp and promptly devoured it.

When he was finished, Marley trotted up the road, turning back to look at them. He gave a sharp bark, which now seemed almost pathetic compared to when he'd been brooding in the hedge.

"He definitely wants us to follow him," Poppy said.

Erasmus sighed. "I don't know why you always think you can understand animals. For once and for all, they *don't speak English.*"

Marley gave one last bark before he veered left and bounded along the high street towards the supermarket.

"All we want to know is how you came by fifty pounds," said a bored-looking constable standing at the supermarket checkout. The girl behind the checkout chewed her gum furiously.

A bell clanged as Poppy, Erasmus and Mitsy bundled through the door.

"I...er...sold me old washing machine," mumbled Marley.

The constable, whose name tag said *Bunty*, narrowed his eyes.

Marley's enormous head hung on his chest. On the conveyor belt was an enormous pile of cat-food tins. Whatever it was in the water beneath the barge must be hungry.

The basset hound had curled himself up on Marley's foot.

"What's happened?" Poppy asked, sidling up to a toothy woman who was watching from aisle six.

"He was trying to buy all that cat food with a fifty-pound note," the woman told her. "And the girl on the checkout smelled something fishy about him. It turns out that last night Bonhilda Bonhoeffer's shop was robbed. She's a smart woman – first thing she does is check the CCTV footage from the night before and sure enough, large as life – there he is! Pokin' around behind the till like it's going out of fashion. It's a wonder he didn't take more!"

The woman paused, leaning in closer, and Poppy could smell horseradish on her breath.

"He stole *five hundred pounds* from her!" the woman said grimly. "It isn't the first time he's done something like this. He's bad news. Do you know last year he stormed into the bingo night at the church hall and was trying to convince people that some…*things* were out there in the woods, trying to steal our kids! Mad as a monkfish."

Poppy watched Erasmus flip open his video camera. She blinked hard for a moment, trying to commit what the woman was saying to memory.

"Well, we've had reports that the money came from somewhere…elsewhere, Marley," sighed PC Bunty. "I'm going to have to ask you to come with me to the station."

Marley turned his shaggy head frightenedly around

the shop as Bunty took his arm and steered him towards the door. He caught Poppy's eye.

"Poppyslub! Whatever they say, I didn't steal, Poppyslub," Marley said to her desperately. Then his face changed and he spoke clearly and specifically to her across the shop.

"The cats need cat food!" Marley said, nodding as if she were meant to know what he was saying. "The cats need cat food."

Poppy nodded, remembering the bubbles under the trapdoor on the barge.

"Look after my little Marley!" the great man called out to the three children.

Mitsy kneeled down beside the whimpering basset hound and held him by the collar.

Erasmus elbowed her suddenly and pointed to the back of Marley's head as he was bundled out of the shop. It was unmistakable. Between the masses of scraggly hair was a large white spot. A spot just like Poppy's.

Poppy felt responsible for Mitsy and made sure to walk her home. The little girl insisted on taking the dog with her, and said she'd be lucky if her mum, Mrs Felt, even noticed.

Erasmus lived on the road behind Mitsy's, and his house was the only one on the crescent that wasn't lit up merrily. The windows were dark, except for a lonely security light, which flickered on when he walked up the mossy driveway.

"What time do you call this?" Dad asked when Poppy pushed through the front door.

Poppy checked the clock in the hall. "Ten minutes past six."

"I thought we were going to hang out again?" Dad said. "I'm flying out in a few days."

Poppy felt a pang of guilt. She hadn't meant to forget.

"Marley's been arrested," she told them by way of apology.

"Oh, not poor Marley." Gran winced. "What for?"

"Pinching cash from that sweet shop you like," Poppy told her.

Dad was looking between them in confusion. "Who's Marley?" he asked.

Gran was about to give a more delicate answer when Poppy said, "He's a local drunk who lives in a house on the river. Well, sort of a drunk. The thing is he's not *actually* drunk. And his house isn't actually a house. It's a barge."

"And what were you doing with a local drunk?"

"Well, he's sort of an…acquaintance," Poppy offered, checking what was on the stove for dinner.

"Uh-uh, no. No." Dad wagged his finger parentally.

"My daughter is not spending time after school with a local drunk."

"He doesn't really *drink*, Dad. He has a speech impediment." Poppy sighed, leaving out the bit that it was inflicted by some terrifying magical creatures of unknown origin.

"Is that what he calls it, eh?" said Dad cleverly. "A *speech* impediment?"

He turned on Gran, obviously wanting to have a go at her for letting Poppy spend time with "barge people". But he looked from her swollen leg to her bruised arm and seemed to have second thoughts. He swivelled back to Poppy.

"I want you to *promise* me, Poppy," he said, holding up his finger again, "that you'll come straight home from school from now on, no dilly-dallying. People like that man can be seriously dangerous."

"Whatever," Poppy said, unpacking her backpack. Any feelings of remorse were gone now. Dad could be so narrow-minded about people.

Dad was shocked. "Where did you pick up this attitude? Is it from that weird boy Gran was telling me about?"

Poppy saw that Gran obviously wanted to protest the use of the word *weird*, but Dad was straight back in there.

"Because if it is, I don't want you seeing him either."

Gran opened her mouth to speak, but Dad silenced

her rudely by raising his hand and his voice. "I know things aren't easy for his family, but we have enough rubbish in our own lives without taking on everyone else's problems."

"Oh, stop being so 'normal'," Poppy told him. "You don't understand people who don't spend their lives trying to fit in, do you? That's why you don't like Gran."

Poppy felt like a cat who had helpfully dropped a dead rabbit on the dinner table. Gran stepped in.

"Your dad and I haven't always seen eye to eye, Poppy. But that doesn't mean we don't have a great deal of respect for what the other thinks," she said, raising her eyebrows at Dad to help her out.

Dad opened his mouth, but all he said was, "Exactly."

Poppy was confused about their sudden insistence on backing each other up. And she knew what she was about to say was manipulative and hurtful, but she said it anyway.

"Mum would've let me hang out with Erasmus."

"Well, Mum can't make that decision any more can she, Poppy?" said Dad, perhaps more aggressively than he meant to.

Poppy put her hand into her pocket, and her knuckles brushed the silk book. The hairs on the back of her hand pulsed, and she felt the book ignite her anger. It spurred her on. "Mum never made any decisions anyway," she struck out fiercely. "You made them for her. That's why Gran never liked you. That's why her indicators weren't fixed on her car. You wouldn't let her get them fixed by our usual mechanic because you said he was becoming too expensive. That's why she's dead."

She was suddenly aware that her fingers were clenching the binding of the silk book, the fire of her anger was snuffed and Gran was in tears. Dad was staring at something on the floor. Churchill was asleep. Poppy felt the white spot in her hair itch furiously, and the boeuf bourguignon spluttered and popped as it seared on the stove top.

Poppy woke up three times during the night. She knocked on Dad's bedroom door at 1 a.m. but didn't get a response, even though she could see his lamp was on.

"Let him sleep, pet," came Gran's voice from along the corridor. She stood in the dark like a stooped, pale ghost. Her hair was plaited and a thin, blackberry shawl was draped around her nightgown.

"I think he's awake still," whispered Poppy. "I can see his lamp."

Gran shook her head and her brow furrowed with hurt. "He can't sleep without a light beside him any more," she told Poppy and sighed. "When one light goes out, people like to burn a candle in its place."

She steered Poppy back to her room.

Poppy climbed into bed, and Gran tucked her in. She perched herself on the edge of Poppy's bed, her bruise falling like a shadow across her arm in the dim light.

"He hurts too, Poppy," Gran said.

Poppy felt a sob rise in her throat. If anyone could make her weep with guilt, it was Gran. She ran her fingers through Poppy's hair. Her voice was like honey.

"Do you think your dad wouldn't give away every penny he has to get back the girl he loves?"

Poppy shook her head.

"He's hurting, Poppy. He's hurting like nothing else, and you remind him so much of her. You're so like her it frightens him."

Poppy felt the beginnings of a tear in her eye.

"Don't be hard on him, Poppy. There's nothing like guilt to destroy hope, and there's no greater guilt than the guilt of something that happened for an inexplicably silly reason."

Poppy wiped her eye with her blanket.

"But why don't you hate him, Gran? Mum asked him to get her indicators fixed because she was super busy at work. I heard her ask him twice, and he kept putting it off."

Gran kissed Poppy on the forehead and went over to the window.

"Because," said Gran, "I look into your dad's eyes and I see that, with all his heart, he wishes it had been him and not her."

Poppy ached, hating herself for what she'd said.

"Death can bring people together, or tear them

apart," Gran said wisely, gazing up at the starry sky. "And I for one choose to let it bring us together. I might not have been crazy for your dad when I first met him. I can't abide the way he dresses, particularly when he's cycling. I can't bear his taste in food or music, or his stuffy friends. But he loved my daughter. And on that point, we've never had reason to bicker."

The room was still as Gran pulled the curtains across and her eyes rested on the window sill.

"Poppy," she said sharply, "Poppy, did you clean this window sill?"

Gran ran her finger across the pane, and then down onto the window frame as if hoping to find dust.

"Dalia did," said Poppy, sitting up in bed. "She went nuts and cleaned everything when you were in hospital."

Gran hurried out of the room with a concerned mutter.

She reappeared a few minutes later with her finger outstretched and bustled over to the window sill.

"I've been watching him set up house in the laundry," she told Poppy.

Poppy watched as Gran rested her finger on the pane, and a large, almost translucent spider tinkered off her hand and ventured across the sill.

"Spin away, little friend," Gran whispered to the spider, and almost as if it were caught in the wind of her breath, the spider skipped to the nearest corner and began to weave itself a lair.

"When your mother was a girl," Gran told Poppy, "she was very gentle, like you. When the boys at school would pull the wings off flies for a laugh, she'd come home in tears! If anyone was ever downtrodden or victimized or ignored, then they were a friend of Josie's. She had this uncanny knack of seeing something in people that no one else could. You have that in common, you and your mum."

Poppy knew Gran was referring to Erasmus.

Gran smiled a crinkly smile as two fat tears made their way across her paper cheeks.

"She'd never let me wipe the sills. Never. It was the one thing she absolutely insisted on. And I never have. As long as I'm alive, spiders will always be welcome to linger in the corners of these windows."

That didn't sound at all like the Mum Poppy remembered. Not that Mum wasn't kind. Mum volunteered at homeless shelters. But Mum would never leave a window sill coated in cobwebs. Hers were always wiped to the point that they were reflective.

Gran pulled a hanky from her sleeve and blew her nose loudly.

"Enough," she said to Poppy. "I'll bring you up hot cocoa, and then it's time to sleep."

When Poppy finished her hot cocoa, she pulled the covers up to her nose. Her heart gave a little flutter as if sighing before it fell back to sleep. How she ached to think of Dad sleeping with the lamp lit beside his bed every night.

It was a good thing Gran hadn't told Poppy any more than that or her heart may have broken. For the truth was that Mr Slub, the serious, ever-thrifty man who cut his own hair, tucked in his shirt and wore sandals over his socks, fell asleep every night with his wife's favourite dress tucked into the bed beside him. A green dress her own mother had stitched for her in finest Helligan silk.

Thirteen
EVIDENCE

After a weekend spent nose deep at the library, on Monday morning Poppy packed herself anything she thought looked remotely useful for the day's main task. She'd promised Erasmus to spend all of lunchtime recalling their lost notes. Apparently there was somewhere he knew where they wouldn't be disturbed.

She made a list of everything she'd packed.

3 x pencils
1 x reporter's notepad
3 x box of paper clips
1 x map of Suds (courtesy of the tourist information centre)
1 x map of England (courtesy of Google Images)
1 x box of drawing pins (brass)
1 x ball of red yarn (courtesy of Gran's supplies)
2 x chocolate-peanut bars

2 x apples
1 x box of Strawberry Wheels
The silk book
The tailor's chalk

Dad emerged from his room as Poppy swiped her lunch from the fridge. His hair was tousled and his eyes were red. He looked as if he hadn't slept a wink. He'd been that way ever since Poppy's outburst in the kitchen.

"I'll do the school run," Dad said to Gran as he tucked in his shirt and did up his belt. Without looking at Poppy, he unhooked his keys from beside the door and went outside to wait in the snot car.

The ride to school was silent. No small talk. No humming to the radio.

It wasn't until the car turned left into the school driveway and they were gliding up the avenue of great trees that Poppy realized this was the moment to say goodbye.

Erasmus was waiting for her at the top of the driveway, gripping the straps of his backpack as if he were five and this was his first day of school. Dad pulled up beside one of the school buses and Erasmus began to wave frantically, as if it wasn't a wave of welcome, but a wave of farewell.

Poppy struggled not to read into this as an omen of things to come.

"I'll see you in a few months then," said Dad, staring out at the strange waving boy. "I know it wasn't meant to be quite so long originally. But…"

Poppy opened her mouth ever so slightly to ask if there was any chance he might be back earlier, but she thought better of it.

"That's Erasmus," Poppy told him, hoping that might diffuse the tension.

"You'll be late," said Dad, gripping the steering wheel as if he were about to drive off.

"What I said the other night," Poppy began, but Dad cut her off without looking at her.

"You'll be late," he said again. "And look after Gran. She needs you right now."

Poppy got out of the car, feeling sore and hurt. She wanted Dad to wrap her up in a tight squeeze. She wanted to ask him why he kept away, and why he needed someone else in his life when he already had her. She wanted to explain everything to him. Surely he would understand. But before she knew it, the door was closed and once again Dad had become a snot-coloured blob indicating at the end of the drive on his way back to a world of lawyers and meetings and weary nights poring over contracts. A world she and Dad didn't inhabit together.

"Was that your dad?" Erasmus asked.

"In the flesh," Poppy told him as they crossed the playground.

"I want you to meet me at twelve-thirty exactly beside the deer pen," Erasmus said, looking up at the sky. The deer pen was on the outskirts of the school, which themselves bordered the Riddling Woods.

"I'll be there," Poppy said beneath her breath. Regina Pocks was approaching. And worse still, she was handing out flyers.

"Oh, and by the way," Erasmus said, quickly turning to Poppy, "Regina is having a Halloween-themed birthday party at her dad's house, and I want you to come with me."

"Ha!" Poppy snorted. "If she invites either of us then you can call me Mr Buttocks for the next month."

"Deal," Erasmus said cheerfully. "Oi, Regina!"

"What the hell are you doing?" Poppy hissed out of the corner of her mouth.

Regina finished handing out flyers to a huddle of excited, doting girls and marched over. She licked her teeth with excitement.

"Can you invite us to your party?" Erasmus asked earnestly.

Regina jerked her head, gesturing for Sid and another girl to join her. This was apparently too good to enjoy by herself.

Poppy felt her neck lowering into her shoulders,

imagining that this was how it felt to be a tortoise.

"And why would I do that?" Regina scoffed.

"Because we really, really, *really* want to come," said Erasmus.

Poppy almost muttered, *Speak for yourself*, but Regina was looking particularly bloodthirsty this morning so she didn't. She'd hiked up her school kilt, and somehow managed to make the ladders in her tights look incredibly threatening.

Regina flashed a grin to Sid and the other girl. Any thought of Regina being sad or somehow lacking in self-esteem had vanished from Poppy's mind. Regina Pocks was a tower of terror.

"It's Halloween themed." Regina pushed two photocopied invites into Erasmus's hand. "I'm an autumn baby. Oh, and no costume means *no entry*. Asparagus Boy and Asparagus Girl better start planning their couple's outfits."

"But it's not Halloween, yet?" Sid wondered looking like a confused jellyfish. "Isn't Halloween in December or something? Yeah, isn't it near Christmas?"

"It's in October, you idiot. And that's what I mean," Regina snapped. "It's Halloween *themed*. The real Halloween is still, like, a month away. Try to keep up, Sid."

The three bullies turned and swaggered towards the classroom. Sid turned back towards them, grinning wickedly.

"Your invitation, Mr Buttocks," said Erasmus, bowing and handing the photocopied sheet of paper to Poppy.

"Oh, shut your mouth," Poppy muttered, hitting him with her invite. "It's obvious she only gave us these because she thinks we won't come."

She found herself biting her lip and hoping that to be true. The tricky, calculating side of Regina was a point of interest that Poppy could live without.

"Blast!" said Erasmus, thumping his thigh.

"What?"

"Mum threw out my Sherlock Holmes costume last year."

"Oh." Poppy laughed. "Don't worry about that, my gran has more costumes than you could shake a stick at."

"Would she have any in my size?"

"Loads," said Poppy. "In fact, I think we have a whole cupboard devoted to people with big heads."

"Would she let me borrow one?"

"That's why I suggested it," sighed Poppy.

"In that case – good thinking, Mr Buttocks."

Erasmus was checking his watch when Poppy jogged over to the deer pen at exactly twelve-thirty.

"I'm not late," she panted, "I can't be!"

Erasmus looked at her quizzically. "I never said you were. Come on – I'll lead the way."

Erasmus was acting strangely, almost as if he thought someone was watching them as they darted along the fence to the deer pen. He kept glancing up at the sky and checking the direction of the wind by wetting his finger and holding it up in the air.

Soon Poppy realized they were at the back of the lovely old main school building, which rose up above them. From this side she could see that a section of tiles had slipped off the roof. Presumably no one had bothered to replace them because no one usually saw this side of the school.

On the narrow steps was a tray of jars filled with paintbrushes left over from Ms Ghanoush's art class, baking in the midday sun. Erasmus climbed the slippery steps and headed inside. Taking Poppy's hand, he wheeled her around the corner as a teacher wandered out of the staff room. Poppy felt like a Cold War spy. Erasmus led her up to the third floor, which had been left derelict, in a paused state of constant renovation. He opened a rickety door and Poppy entered.

There was a flutter as a sparrow escaped through a hole in the attic roof. In the distance she could hear the cries of boys playing handball and someone screaming as they hung from the middle of the monkey bars.

The attic was so filled with dust it had become like a small desert. Poppy got the impression that the staff must have kept dumping things up here over the years until it got so full they just wedged the door shut and forgot all about it. There were cricket stumps and punctured world globes, boxes of protractors and compasses, the backdrop of a school play from 1987, shoes, pins, pencils, rolled-up maps, disintegrating textbooks, hymn books and, in one corner, five or six boxes of sugar cubes.

"Gran has sugar hidden in her house too," Poppy said quietly, admiring the room. "Do you think that the sugar has something to do with the Peggs?"

"I'd say it's highly probable," Erasmus said. He moved over to a bulletin board, which he'd already begun to pin things to. "Let's get down to brass tacks." At which point Poppy fished some out of her bag, and Erasmus used one to attach the clippings about the disappearance and reappearance of Wendy Pocks to the board.

"Pocks!" Poppy said loudly.

"Cow or Small?"

"Pocks," Poppy repeated, "as in, Regina Pocks?"

Erasmus looked as if he was trying not to draw attention to this fact. "Ah, yes," he said, "Wendy is her sister."

"You never told me that!" Poppy cried in outrage.

"I thought you'd deduced it yourself," said Erasmus defensively.

Then Poppy realized.

"Oh no," she began, "I see your little plan."

"We don't have any other option," Erasmus insisted.

"It's unethical!" said Poppy. "To get an invitation to someone's Halloween Party just so you can interrogate their sick sister."

"We won't be interrogating her so much as just talking *to* her," said Erasmus. "She hasn't spoken a word since the incident."

Poppy sighed.

"You're a cunning little fox, you know that?" she told him.

"I'm more of a hedgehog," he said thoughtfully.

"Explain."

"Well the fox has *many* tricks, my dear Mr Buttocks," said Erasmus, "while the hedgehog has but one, and that is the best of all. Now, facts about Wendy Pocks. Go!"

Poppy remembered that Wendy had been found bald and confused, with discoloured eyes and insect bites all over her arms. At the woodland site where Wendy had reappeared, the police and Poppy and Erasmus had all found traces of the blue powder.

"Blue powder," Erasmus murmured. "It's the one thing that connects them all. Are there any more cases we can recall?"

"Well," said Poppy, shifting some dust with her foot. "There's me."

"What about you?"

"The blue powder we found in my room, on my pillow."

"Oh, that's different," said Erasmus. "That's nothing."

"What do you mean 'nothing'?" Poppy said indignantly. "I've been checking my eyes in the mirror every ten minutes in case I start to see grey spots appearing."

"Why would you be worried? Those creatures on the window sill didn't come near you."

Poppy shook her head in confusion. "How could you know that? You saw the blue powder on my pillow. That thing was in my room!"

"Yes," said Erasmus impatiently, "but it's very basic ballistics. The powder wasn't clumped like the other samples we found."

"I'm beyond confused," said Poppy.

"I'm sorry, this one's on me," Erasmus laughed. "I sometimes just think we're the same person and I forget that you haven't read *Blaise Sparks's Science of Ballistics*. It's a propelling read."

"No," said Poppy half-bitterly. "As it happens, I forgot to pick that one up last time I was at the bookstore."

"Well, if you *had* read it," Erasmus began, "you'd realize that the powder on your pillow wasn't sprinkled like the other samples. It was blown through something."

"Go on," said Poppy, beginning to get the gist of what he was saying.

"It's my personal belief that those creatures either climbed or flew onto your window sill and blew that powder through an implement like a pea-shooter or a trumpet, so that it landed on your bed without waking you."

"But I woke up anyway before they could get to me?" Poppy said, the sickening fear of turning grey slowly ebbing away.

"Exactly," said Erasmus. "And *I think* that has

something to do with your chalk. Perhaps the blue powder has something to do with subduing the victim?"

"So all things considered, I shouldn't worry about the powder?" Poppy asked, as if waiting to hear her chances of contracting a rare illness.

"I know it's hard to believe, but there is nothing amongst your affairs that is worthy of great anxiety."

That made Poppy want to snap. The white spot in her hair had appeared well before the incident in her bedroom. Of course she had reason to be anxious. But she didn't. No good had come of snapping recently.

"What do you think the relevance of the silk book is then?" she asked, changing the subject.

"You mean Marley's book?"

"Yes."

"I don't know. Perhaps the same thing happened to the book as happened to the kids. After the Peggs had been near Marley's book, it was left empty and vacuous. It seemed like all his dreams and ideas were sucked off the pages."

"Leaving it with the ability to recite poetry?"

"Perhaps," Erasmus said slowly, "some of the Peggs magic was sort of...left inside the book?"

"And then there's the chalk," Poppy reminded him.

"And then there's the Helligan Mills."

"Gran said that fabric still comes down the river whenever anyone orders it."

"I wonder how they order it?" asked Erasmus. "I read

in the library that the only way of accessing the Mills was by the river."

Poppy unpacked her lunch and handed Erasmus a chocolate-peanut bar.

"By the way, I've been thinking: you really should probably stop carrying that silk book around with you."

"Why?" Poppy asked, trying not to sound as though she cared. She'd carried the book everywhere she went ever since she found it.

"Because they're after it," said Erasmus. "You took it from them."

"Some old lady dropped it on the train!" scoffed Poppy. "It's not my fault she's careless."

"But don't you see?" said Erasmus. "That wasn't just any old lady. And she definitely wasn't careless."

Poppy felt her lip twitch. She didn't want to ask the question.

"You mean it was one of the Peggs?"

"In the flesh," said Erasmus grimly. "Marley said he wrapped the book using a scrap of green silk he found at the Mills. What if the Peggs stole the book back off him because they wanted the silk back. And what if the silk had some quality which allowed them to follow it maybe, or track it. It's ingenious really. That lady that you saw on the train must have left it there deliberately. For you. Who knows? They could have done this to kids in the past too."

Poppy fished the book out of her pocket and laid it

on a desk with three legs. She felt a twist deep in her stomach as her fingers left its cover. Was this book the thing that had led the Peggs to her window sill?

"So could it be like a homing beacon?"

"That's one way of putting it," said Erasmus darkly. "And I've seen you with that book. You hate not having it with you. There's something magnetic about it."

"What about the poem then?" Poppy asked, trying to swallow. "Surely they wouldn't give that away deliberately?"

"Maybe the silk has an effect on the book that they don't know about. Something to do with their magic." He thought for a moment. "Do you remember that song we sang at choir practice about the girl who bought the green ribbon?"

How could she forget? Poppy had been lucky not to lose her sense of hearing after listening to Erasmus belting it out.

"Do you remember any of the words?" Erasmus asked her, sifting through a box of dusty books.

"Vaguely," said Poppy. "Something about a peddler?"

Erasmus found a songbook and flicked through it until he found the page he wanted. He showed it to Poppy.

A poor girl from Dover went one day
To buy herself a ribbon.
Her hair was bland, her eyes like clay,
As ordinary as a pigeon.

"Here have I," said a peddler lass,
"A silk of riddling green.
You won't need scarves or cloaks or hats,
For this will make you queen."

The peddler pulled a strip of silk
From the bottom of her sack,
But the girl was wary of her ilk,
And tried to give it back.

But the peddler tied the ribbon through
The poor girl's simple hair.
And she danced across the woad fields to
The song of sea and air.

The girl, she kept a-dancing,
Until the day was night.
O'er mountains she went prancing,
Till she lost herself from sight.

The riddling green, it sent her crazed
With a maddening, deep desire.
The lust for silk made her eyes turn dazed,
And her feet climb ever higher.

They say some birds, perhaps it were,
Swooped in from the West.
And tried to pluck the silk from her

And take it to their nest.

But the peddler's knot was tied so tight
The girl was lifted too.
And carried shrieking to her plight,
Where the hills run mulberry blue.

Her vanity, it got her where
She had thought last to look.
But these stories foul, I do declare,
Should fill another book.

"It doesn't say it's about the Peggs though," noted Poppy.

Erasmus picked up the silk book and examined it. He tapped the spine. "What if this *was* magic silk?"

He put the book down again and, sitting back, looked at it from a distance, leaning on his fists.

"What if this silk," he said again, "is 'riddling green' silk."

"Like in the song?"

"The same as in the song," Erasmus murmured, still watching the book.

Poppy felt green.

"What if the silk has a quality that makes you want to touch it?" he went on. "Something that draws you to it, so that when the moment's right, they'll know where you are to come and…find you."

Erasmus had taken out his notepad and was doing a sum at the bottom of the page. He paused for the tiniest of moments, and then wrote the answer to the maths problem he was working out and said to Poppy, "You need to destroy it." His mind was made up.

"No," said Poppy. She slid the book towards her.

"I wouldn't touch that if I were you," he said warningly.

Poppy's hand recoiled but only for a moment.

"It's my book," she said definitively, but her stomach twisted and lurched.

"It's not your book, it's Marley's, and we can't leave it with him," insisted Erasmus. "They might be after him too. It might draw them to him."

Poppy bit her bottom lip to stop it from trembling. She couldn't chase away the feeling that while they were hunting for answers, their answers had crept up behind them.

"But why did the Peggs leave the book for *me* to find? Why would they be after me?"

Erasmus finished pinning up the last of the articles he'd collected on his most recent trip to the library.

"I don't know, Poppy," he murmured, shaking his head. He drew a line underneath the maths problem and held the notepad up for Poppy to see. "I don't know why they might be after you, and I don't know the first thing about them. But I will tell you this. There's something odd about this town and the woods. Not least of which is this: the bend in the river where Marley's boat is moored is deeper than I ever imagined, assuming my measurements were accurate." He tapped the notepad. "Actually, I've factored in a few variables, meaning the coil of rope could have been even longer. But at the very least, there is a trench beneath Marley's barge that is five-*hundred* feet deep." Poppy let out a slow breath.

"OI!" Erasmus barked suddenly. "Get lost!"

And Poppy was just in time to see Mitsy's bob of hair vanish like a squid beneath the trapdoor.

Fourteen

UNSELFISH

When Poppy got home that afternoon, she noticed Dad must have water-blasted the garden path before he'd left. He used to love doing that. Apparently, there was nothing more satisfying than blasting moss, dirt and the occasional ant to kingdom come.

Richard, Gran's home help, was there getting stuck into the laundry. He wasn't supposed to be there more than twice a week.

"Richard's going to be coming a few more days a week," Gran told Poppy. "Just until I'm really back on my feet. Oh, I've told him not to touch the window sills. So not to worry on that score!"

Gran had her specs on and was adding some intricate embroidery to the lapel of one of the archaeologists' costumes she was making for the West End musical.

She had her legs up on a stool. Her ankles were fat and red. Richard took off Gran's flat canvas shoes and eased on her slippers.

"I'm more than capable of doing that myself, Rich," Gran said.

Richard didn't ask questions. Richard didn't take notice of Gran's grumbling. Richard was nice.

"How are you feeling?" Poppy asked.

"Super," said Gran. You could tell when Gran was really concentrating, because her tongue poked out just a little bit, and she looked over her specs not through them.

"We're planning a visit to the police station on Thursday," Poppy told Gran. She looked over to Richard, waiting for him to raise an eyebrow or smirk, but he didn't.

"To see poor Marley?" she asked, picking out her last stitch. Gran was meticulous.

"No one else will," said Poppy.

"Quite right," said Gran. "He doesn't deserve to be abandoned. I've known Marley for years, and it's nothing but bad luck that gets him his time in the clink."

Gran put down her embroidery and, reaching on top of the cupboard, she peered around the corner to make sure Richard was busy in the kitchen before heaving down a trunk.

Laying it on the floor, she fished out a silver coat. It was a great, heavy thing with indigo lining.

"Mmm, yes," Gran said, holding it up and examining it. "Yes, as I thought. Just needs a few stitches to tighten up the seams." She fumbled through her tin of thread, searching for a spool of the right colour.

"I made this coat for a film of *The Selfish Giant*," Gran told Poppy, expertly threading her needle. "They used an enormous puppet to play the giant. But I think this will fit Marley nicely."

She looked at it again and scrunched up her lips. "It might be a little broad in the shoulders," she decided. "But it's warm and that's what counts. It's lined with mohair – the wool of the Angora goat. Terrifically warm. God knows why I bothered for a puppet!"

She finished closing a hole in the lining, and cut the thread with her teeth. Then she folded the coat and gave it to Poppy.

"Tell him it's from a friend," Gran told her.

After the delicious dinner Richard had cooked, Poppy asked Gran if she could help them with the costumes for Regina's Halloween-themed party. Gran of course said yes, but for the first time Poppy could see she was worried about her workload. Gran had toiled on the costumes for the musical late into the night and got up at the crack of dawn that morning to begin work again.

Back in her bedroom, Poppy got the faint smell of bleach again as she passed the window. Was Erasmus right? Was it Mum's chalk that had somehow protected her from the creature in her room? Poppy took one of the triangles of chalk and drew a white line along the window sill. She felt pathetic. But for a reason she couldn't explain, it made her feel safer.

Poppy and Erasmus had arranged to meet at the bottom of the school driveway on Thursday afternoon and walk to the police station together. Somehow Mitsy had managed to get it out of Poppy where they were going. She'd cornered her in the library that day at lunch as Poppy tried to research blue powders that had a soporific effect.

When Poppy finally got out of class, she spotted Mitsy with Marley the dog on a leash waiting for her at the end of the driveway. Erasmus was leaning against a nearby tree, unimpressed by Mitsy's presence.

"You need a lesson in discretion," whispered Erasmus to Poppy as they headed out of town. "Why'd you have to tell Mitsy? She'll spoil everything."

"Why does she follow you everywhere, anyway?" Poppy asked, struggling under the weight of the enormous coat Gran had given her.

Erasmus sighed. "It's like having a personal stalker. She started doing it a little while back..." He looked back to make sure Mitsy was far enough behind them so she couldn't hear. "I was walking to school and I heard someone crying. It was Mitsy. She must have been trying to crawl under a fence when her backpack got caught on some barbed wire. I helped her slip the backpack off and walked her to school. And ever since she's been following me around like a bad smell."

Poppy turned and grinned at Mitsy.

"Who shall I say is requesting a visit?" asked the policeman at the station reception, whose name tag suggested he was Constable Rogers. Erasmus flicked open his video camera and pressed the record button, but let it hang around his neck as if he wasn't filming. Poppy did the talking.

"Poppy Slub, Erasmus Tall, Mitsy Felt and Marley... Marley the dog," she said with a smile.

But Rogers wasn't in the mood for bonhomie. "I'll see if Mr Marley will accept your visit," he said flatly, plonking away at his computer keyboard.

The double doors swung open behind them, and Rogers looked up and positively beamed. "Miss Bonhoeffer!" He smiled boyishly.

"Good to see you, Rogers." She whistled amorously, flashing him a wicked grin. Miss Bonhoeffer was a stout woman with dark straps of liquorice-coloured hair, horn-rimmed glasses and an orange suit. In her arms was the most enormous box, bursting with sweets. Poppy instantly liked her, even though she didn't want to.

Although there's something too *sweet about her*, she thought, pardoning herself for the pun.

"I was just popping by and thought I'd drop off a little something for you all, as a symbol of my appreciation for your tireless efforts in returning my five hundred pounds. I am *so* obliged!"

She leaned over the reception desk and kissed Constable Rogers on both cheeks while balancing on one foot. Constable Rogers was left with a great big smack of orange lipstick across his jaw.

Bonhilda plonked the box of sweets in front of him.

"You shouldn't have, Ms B!" Rogers said.

"Call me Bonny!" she laughed. "Now just you make sure you share this with Sergeant Reg and that nice Constable Bunty, won't you?"

Constable Rogers nodded without listening.

"I've put in all your favourites," she said, pointing at the elegant gilded packets and jars of fantastic sweets. "We've got Martian-Mallow in every flavour, Lemon Romps, Custard Cusps, Strawberry Wheels – they're out of season at the moment, but, shh, I won't tell if you don't! – Gooseberry Gizzards, Wickers Gutsmack Ganache, Rumpletooth's Fudge, Whirling Whistlers and Dried Sourapple Skins."

Constable Rogers's mouth was watering, but whether it was for the sweets or Miss Bonhoeffer, Poppy couldn't tell.

The phone rang, and Miss Bonhoeffer blew kisses to Constable Rogers as she bustled out of the station.

The minute she was gone, Rogers's mood changed back.

"He'll see you," he told Poppy, slamming the phone down, "but Bunty needs to search whatever it is you're bringing for him."

Rogers pressed a buzzer and a set of automatic doors opened up. Poppy led them through to a room where there were plastic tubs into which they piled their belongings. Erasmus was reluctant to put his camera in there, but did so when Poppy flashed her eyes at him with gritted teeth.

Bunty fished through Poppy's backpack first, then moved on to Mitsy's.

"What're you doing here anyway?" he asked Erasmus, who remained characteristically silent.

"We've come to visit Mr Marley," Poppy told him and, feeling a little bolder, she said, "The man you wrongfully arrested."

"Sure, sure," Bunty laughed, prising open Erasmus's satchel with vigour.

Poppy felt a mean pinch when he said this and she

told herself firmly that she believed what Marley had said: he didn't steal.

When Bunty had finished scanning the great silver coat, and swab-testing it for the remains of explosive material, he led them down the corridor to the holding cells where Marley was being kept.

"This is all highly irregular," Bunty muttered as he locked them in and shuffled away.

Marley was sitting in the corner. He looked enormous on the steel chair, as if he were sitting on doll's-house furniture.

"Yer came!" He smiled weakly. Marley the dog suddenly leaped into animation and perched his two front paws on Marley's leg, licking his hand excitedly. Marley plucked the basset hound from off the floor and cradled him like a baby in his arms.

"Well th'food's not exactly howt quiseen, you know… gour-may!" said Marley when Poppy asked how he was.

She fished a chocolate-peanut bar, an apple and the box of Strawberry Wheels out of her bag for him to eat. Then she took the silk book wrapped in newspaper from the bottom of her satchel and placed it on the table. Both she and Erasmus had made a point of not touching it since they'd discussed that it could be covered in riddling silk. Although neither of them really knew what "riddling silk" meant.

"What's this?" asked Marley, downing two Strawberry Wheels at once.

"I think it's your ideas book," said Poppy quietly.

Marley went to grab it excitedly, but she stopped him.

"Be careful," she said. "We think the silk could be magic or cursed. It seems to draw the creatures you saw at the Mills to it."

Marley nodded gravely and, like a crab, used his forefingers and thumbs to peel away the newspaper.

His yellow eyes widened, and he nodded again.

"Tha'sit!" he told Poppy. "This is me book. How'd yer find it?"

Poppy looked to Erasmus.

"You need to bury it," said Mitsy quietly, brushing one of the now sleeping dog's paws.

"You don't know what we're talking about," said Erasmus pertly.

"Yes, I do," Mitsy told him. "You need to bury it in the white dirt."

"How would you know?"

"It said so in my book."

Erasmus groaned. "Not that stupid book of yours again. Fairytales are for nitwits."

"I'm not a nitwit," insisted Mitsy. "I'll show you."

"This is none of your business. I don't even know why you're here *anyway*," snorted Erasmus.

"My sitter is asleep, and Mum's at her pub quiz."

"What do you mean, 'white dirt', Mitsy?" Poppy asked her gently.

"The white dirt on the island in the river," Mitsy told her.

Poppy presumed Mitsy meant the chalk seams she had seen on the train, but she hadn't seen any more of the white pockets of earth in Suds, and the only island she could think of was just up the river across the paddock beyond Gran's house.

"By the way," Poppy said, heaving Gran's coat onto the table, "this is for you."

Marley stared at the coat in wonder and lifted it up by the shoulder pads. The tails fell to the floor in a swoop of rippling silver. Marley tried the coat on for size. Gran was right. It was a little too big in the shoulders, but it was generally a good fit.

"How'd I look?" Marley asked them, spinning on the spot.

"Divine," said Poppy.

"Silver," said Erasmus.

"Like an elf," said Mitsy after much thought.

Before long, Bunty poked his head into Marley's cell and told them they had five minutes left before visiting hours were over.

The hound whimpered and pulled on his leash as Bunty lead them back out to reception.

"What's going to happen to him?" Mitsy asked Bunty, pulling on his sleeve.

"Proper prison," said Bunty with an air of glee. "Five hundred quid isn't the only thing he's been caught nicking."

"Oh?" said Poppy.

"Someone accused him of stealing a puppy once. But they could never prove it, so he was never charged."

Bunty had a lanyard with a white plastic pass-card around his neck and was trying to swipe open the double doors to the reception area, but they weren't responding. As he stooped down to use his pass-card again, he tried hopelessly to wedge the doors apart with his fingers.

Erasmus had cocked his head to one side, as if seeing something that no one else could.

"Why won't this blasted door open?" Bunty cursed.

"May I use your toilet?" Erasmus asked.

Bunty turned to him, his sweaty face glistening, and pointed Erasmus down the corridor to a sign which read *Tea Room*.

While Erasmus was in the toilet, Bunty continued trying to force the door, even trying to call in backup on his radio at one point.

Within a few minutes, Erasmus returned and made a show of drying his hands on his trousers.

Bunty stood upright, and put his hands on his lower back.

"May I?" asked Erasmus, and Bunty snorted.

Erasmus took Bunty's white plastic card and, smartly flipping it over, used the alternative side to swipe against the door lock. There was a sickly *beep* and the doors chugged open.

"Oh," said Bunty as Constable Rogers shot him a bored look from behind his desk. "Must've been fixed."

"We've got to burn the silk book," said Erasmus as they walked along the high street. Most of the shops had closed for the evening.

"No," said Poppy suddenly, shifting the newspaper parcel which contained the book.

"Are you mad?" Erasmus snorted. "If you don't get rid of it, those things might come back for you."

"I don't have to touch it," she said, buttoning her pocket. "I can keep it in my sock drawer or something."

"You have to bury it on the white island!" Mitsy piped up.

"Why can't you leave me alone and just keep out of this?" Erasmus snapped at her. "You don't know what we're talking about. We're going to get rid of it."

Erasmus's hand made a move for the silk book in Poppy's pocket, and she jerked away.

"No!" she shouted. She had to keep it safe. It was her book. *Hers*. She found it.

But burying the book was better than burning it. At least then she'd know where it was when she wanted to look at it.

"We'll bury it," Poppy said softly. "On the island."

"What?" Erasmus moaned.

Mitsy grinned with satisfaction.

There was a little blue dinghy moored to the river's edge just opposite the island, which was completely barren save for a few weedy bushes. Erasmus protested that he couldn't swim, but when Poppy said that she couldn't either, he climbed warily into the dinghy.

True to Mitsy's word, on the island was a pocket of earth where the grass had slipped away, exposing white, chalky dust. They took turns burrowing, using a trowel they'd picked up from Gran's house. Mitsy managed a few scrapes before Erasmus impatiently took her shift for her, muttering that if she wasn't going to dig properly, he'd rather she didn't dig at all. Marley the dog tried to help for a moment, but then curled up beside a bush in a state of pure exhaustion.

Among the other things Poppy had taken from Gran's house was a hefty jar of buttons. Gran had said buttons were magic things. Gran had said that buttons kept things safe. When there was a hole large enough, Poppy squeezed the silk book inside the jar and covered it with buttons.

Once the jar was in place, they pushed the dirt back over it and patted it down. Erasmus took a deep breath and blew a cloud of white dust on top of it, so it would look less like something had just been buried, sending Poppy into a coughing fit.

"We should have burned it," he muttered as they steered the dinghy back to the shore.

Poppy and Erasmus walked Mitsy back to her front door and waited until she and Marley the dog were both inside. Instead of Erasmus peeling off and heading home, he followed Poppy back to Gran's house, so she invited him in for dinner if he promised not to tell his mother. Poppy scanned the street as they slipped indoors, making sure Ms Tall wasn't watching them from somewhere behind her dark sunglasses.

Gran's eyes looked glassy that evening, the same way they did when she had an extra sherry. She moved slowly around the kitchen, slicing onions and chopping the basil with extra care. On the bench was an empty box of sugary Lemon Romps.

"Are you alright, Gran?"

"Fine, popsicle," she murmured. "Had a busy day, and feeling shattered is all."

Poppy and Erasmus laid the table. Well, Poppy laid the table, and Erasmus followed closely behind her, straightening the cutlery.

When they sat down to eat, Gran poured Erasmus and Poppy a sherry each.

"Gran?"

"Yes, love?"

"We aren't supposed to drink alcohol."

"Oh!" Gran frowned. "Oh, sorry, I was in a daze. I was a million miles away."

She took their sherry and poured it back into the neck of the bottle, singing softly as she did so. *"And she danced across the woad fields to the song of sea and air..."*

Erasmus glanced at Poppy and she knew he was recognizing the song. Gran looked weary beyond belief, but Poppy wanted to tell her something.

"Gran," Poppy began.

"Yes, Poppy love?" Gran mumbled, droopily twirling some bolognese onto her fork.

"We've been conducting an investigation."

"Oh, yes?"

"An investigation into some of the strange events that have happened in Suds. Specifically, what's been happening to some of the kids."

Gran slurped up some spaghetti as if she was a chicken greedily wolfing down a can of worms.

"Do you remember what you told me about Wilma Norbles, that girl who went grey and vanished while she was swimming?"

Poppy waited. Gran kept slurping.

"Well," she continued, "we think the same thing, or something similar, happened to Wendy Pocks, that little girl who vanished and then reappeared in the woods about six and a bit months ago. We think it's even happening to the vicar's son too, right now."

Normally Gran wasn't exactly ladylike at the table – in fact Poppy had seen her licking her plate a couple of times out of the corner of her eye. But this was a new low. Tomato sauce was smooshed across her chin, and little red droplets were flecked over the tablecloth.

Poppy looked at Erasmus nervously, and continued. "We also think that whoever is responsible for this might be using some force other than science. Something like magic."

"I think they might have framed Marley too," Erasmus added. "To try and get him to stop warning people about them. I also think that might be our fault – maybe they've noticed that we've been sniffing around."

"Is that so?" slurred Gran, pouring herself another sherry. Poppy could see an empty box of Strawberry Wheels over Gran's shoulder. She must have had a go at those as well. "Do be careful though," Gran warned them, downing the sherry. "Marley has a habit of letting trouble find him. I...um...I don't want you getting mixed up in...er...that sort of thing."

Poppy felt a mean little twinge in her chest. She didn't like Gran saying that. It didn't sound like her at all.

Erasmus dipped his hand into his satchel, which he'd hung on the empty chair beside him, and pulled out his video camera. His other hand disappeared into his jacket pocket and reappeared with a plastic ziplock bag. Inside the bag was a tiny memory card.

"What's this?" Poppy asked, as Erasmus inserted the memory card into his camera.

"Evidence," said Erasmus, flicking through the clips on his camera screen. "Evidence from the laughably accessible evidence room at the Suds police station."

"You *stole* evidence?" Poppy coughed, widening her eyes. "That's, like, ten times worse than normal stealing."

Gran seemed amused by the whole thing.

"But this is what the police don't realize," Erasmus told her, scanning through the CCTV footage to the part he wanted to show them. "They think it's evidence of Marley stealing, when *really* it's evidence that he didn't."

He held out the camera and Gran and Poppy watched.

"I can't see properly, it's all blurry," said Gran, shaking her head. "Oh, wait, now I can. That's definitely Marley."

But Poppy had noticed something else. "There's no white spot at the back of his head," she said slowly.

"Just so, Mr Buttocks," said Erasmus to his apprentice, and Poppy narrowed her eyes. "But there's something else."

Erasmus paused the playback and toggled with the zoom buttons until Marley's hand filled the screen.

"He's missing a finger!" Poppy squawked.

"Ah yes, but which finger?"

"Poppy," Gran said suddenly, placing her hands flat on the table and looking over the tops of their heads, "this dun't've anythingta dowith the laundry…"

Gran stood up quickly, but no sooner had she done so

than she collapsed back into her chair and tumbled sideways. She must have grabbed at the tablecloth as she blacked out, because there was a grinding shudder as the sherry bottle, the jug of water and a bowl of peas hurtled towards the table edge and toppled with a deafening smash onto the floor. Churchill went into hysterics. Poppy dropped her fork and, forgetting herself, clambered across the table to where Gran had fallen.

Erasmus was already at the telephone by the time Poppy looked up. She noticed first that she wasn't crying, although there was a pain so sharp in her chest that she wondered if at any minute she would keel over too. She checked Gran's pulse. She could feel it. She checked Gran was breathing. She could feel warm, sweet-smelling breaths escaping Gran's mouth. Lifting Gran's head into her lap, Poppy ran her fingers through the thin, grey hair and whispered the only thing she could:

"Stay with me, Gran."

And Gran said, "Wait with me, Poppy."

Fifteen

TRICK

When the paramedics arrived, Poppy recognized them as the same pair as last time. No one asked any questions, although the female paramedic did pick up the empty box of Strawberry Wheels and give it a funny look before tossing it in the bin.

Churchill was allowed in the ambulance, and the nurse with the purple hair even let Poppy take him into the waiting room, provided he didn't attack anyone.

At quarter to eleven a doctor with a vanishing head of hair pulled up a chair beside Poppy, Erasmus and Churchill.

"Well hello, Poppy, Erasmus and this must be Churchill," he said, smiling and nodding to the pig. "Poppy," he said again, in a more serious tone, "your gran isn't very well at all, I'm afraid."

Poppy stayed calm and waited for the doctor to continue.

"I know your gran hasn't told you yet, but she has type 2 diabetes. Normally this is a very controllable condition, but in your gran's case, it's started to affect her heart."

"Is she going to die?" Poppy asked, picking at something underneath her seat with her fingernail, which she quickly realized was actually dried-out chewing gum.

The doctor scratched the back of his neck awkwardly.

"I mean," Poppy began again, "we're all going to die someday, but is she going to die any sooner than she would if she didn't have diabetes?"

Erasmus turned to the doctor and folded his arms.

"Why don't you pop into your gran's ward and have a chat with her?" said the doctor. "But I must ask you, Poppy, to hide anything sugary in the house. No sweets, no puddings, no chocolate and *no sherry*."

Gran was sweating when Poppy and Erasmus rounded the corner into her ward. The nurse with the purple streak of hair was on reception and told Poppy she could watch Churchill for a few minutes.

Poppy massaged Gran's knobbly wrist, and Erasmus straightened the drip beside her bed.

"Insulin," Erasmus said, and Gran smiled.

"Clever clogs," said Gran, and Erasmus smiled back.

"I'm sorry I gave you both such a fright," Gran said,

closing her crinkly eyes. "These things are never fun, are they?"

"That's alright," said Erasmus. "I've always wanted to dial 999."

Gran smiled again, but Poppy could see she was tired.

Before they left, Poppy got Gran a glass of water, and Gran told them that Dalia would be waiting outside to take them home. Poppy's heart groaned loudly.

To her relief, Dalia was subdued. She was wearing a crimson dressing gown, slippers and plastic rollers in her hair. On the seat beside her was a travel bag which she hadn't bothered to zip up. Hair straighteners, purple pants, contact lenses and make-up tubes came spilling out as she twisted and turned the car out of the hospital car park.

When the street lights began to vanish and they got back onto the road towards Suds, Poppy fell asleep. The last thing she remembered was the arm of a boy reaching around her, and gently resting her head on his soft shoulder.

Dalia must have dropped Erasmus at home, because when Poppy woke up to find her knocking gently on the car window, he was nowhere to be seen.

"Oh," said Dalia as she surveyed the sherry spilled across the dining room floor, the peas peppering the table and the shards of glass on the carpet. "Right," she said, snapping into action and rolling up her sleeves.

"You go straight to bed, girlfriend, I'll deal with this."

Poppy didn't argue. No sooner had her head hit the pillow than she fell into a deep, dreamless sleep.

"I can't see," Mitsy told Poppy as she fidgeted from beneath her costume. They were outside Regina Pocks's house. Plastic skeletons had been hung loosely from the trees, and fake cobwebs caked the fence and surrounding garden. Carved pumpkins with electric candles inside flickered with a mechanical rhythm, casting shadows across the grass. The first drops of rain began to darken the footpath as they approached.

Gran had made two costumes; one for Erasmus, one for Poppy. She'd cobbled them together in between finishing the costumes for the West End musical. They'd found Mitsy waiting for them at the Pocks's front gate, dressed in a white sheet.

"How did *you* get an invitation from Regina?" Erasmus demanded.

"I didn't! I'm friends with Wendy from school," Mitsy said proudly. "Oh, it won't be any fun if I can't see," she mumbled, tucking her fairy-tale book beneath her arm and adjusting her sheet.

For a reason unbeknownst to Poppy, Gran had made Erasmus a worm costume. A worm with an extensive tail and beady eyes, which now had Erasmus's leather satchel and camera slung around it. Poppy didn't get off any easier. She was fitted out as a great big furry rat with polystyrene claws. The only detail Gran hadn't quite got around to finishing before she went into hospital was the whiskers. There were three on one side and none on the other.

"We're not *going* to have fun," Erasmus said firmly. "We're going to continue our investigation, of which you are not a part. We're going to find out what really happened to Wendy Pocks. The police don't know what made her the way she is, but we will."

"You're going to ask Wendy questions?" said Mitsy, touching one of Poppy's whiskers.

Poppy nodded.

"But she can't talk!" Mitsy squawked. "Urgh! My ghost clothes are getting wet!"

Erasmus ignored her and knocked on the front door.

"Walk around the back!" shouted someone from inside. "They're in the annex."

Erasmus led the way, and Poppy dragged Mitsy around the side of the house past the bins, peeking through a window as they did so.

There was a football game playing on a tiny TV in the living room. On a dusty-looking couch was a beleaguered man who Poppy recognized immediately, scratching his elbow. She had seen him at the church hall with his daughter when they'd visited the vicar. He was eating fried chicken, lumpy gravy and mash on a little dinner tray, like the ones Poppy and Gran used.

The garden out the back was an empty block of grassy land with a washing line strung across it and surrounded by a rickety wooden fence. They could hear music coming from the room attached to the corner of the house, which meant it must be the annex.

Poppy imagined Regina the Terrible must have enjoyed decorating the windows and doors with the plastic decapitated heads. Red paper chains were strung like guts drying along the washing line.

Erasmus knocked, and almost immediately the curtains parted and a sliding door swooshed open.

"Ha!" Regina greeted them as she slipped out from behind the curtain. She was dressed in a daring costume which involved a miniskirt and a T-shirt tucked up over itself. Her hair was teased up into a frightening arrangement which loomed over her head like a spot of bad weather.

"Oi, Sid!" Regina hollered back into the room. "Come and get a load of this! What the hell have these three come as?"

"A worm," said Erasmus.

"And a rat," said Poppy.

"Ghost," said Mitsy.

Sid appeared from behind the curtain, dressed, rather originally, as a football player.

"Ha!" he joined in. "A snake, a mouse and is that a bed sheet? Rubbish costume."

"Why didn't you come as a piece of asparagus?" Regina snorted at Erasmus.

"Or maybe you could have all come together as a can of asparagus?" Sid sniggered. He was proud of that one.

The annex was filled with kids from school dressed as everything from witches to vampires and penguins. Poppy was still quite sure she would recognize Regina's sister, Wendy, given she didn't have any hair.

Regina was showing off her new magnetic dartboard, which involved everyone else watching her lob the darts across the room with Olympian skill.

"My mum sent it to me," she boasted. "And *no one* is allowed to use it except me."

"Wendy's not here," Erasmus whispered after a few minutes, nodding towards the door. The rat, the worm and the bed sheet slipped out of the annex.

Mitsy knew where Wendy's bedroom was. Making sure Mr Pocks was still watching TV in the living room, they slipped in through the back door and slunk upstairs.

Wendy was sitting up in bed. She had a dinner tray beside her with some untouched soup. Next to the soup bowl was a medicine bottle, a tube of yellow skin cream and a glass of water. The rain pattered noisily on the roof as they entered.

Wendy's head was quite bald. Not the type of bald that older men went. Her scalp was waxy smooth. She seemed to recognize Mitsy, who'd taken off her sheet, but didn't make an effort to communicate with her. Poppy took off her rat head and placed it on the floor beside Wendy's bed.

"Don't be frightened, Wendy," said Poppy, but Wendy didn't seem frightened at all. Poppy hadn't seen Wendy's eyes properly until that moment. The black pupils had faded to a charcoal colour and the irises were grey and speckled. They shocked her.

Poppy felt ashamed of herself. Mum had always been very strict with Poppy on this subject. It didn't matter if someone was missing a foot, or had a wart the size of the London Eye on their upper lip. You always looked them straight in the eyes with the same warmth you did everyone else.

Mitsy found a pile of drab-looking soft toys on top of a trunk in the corner and, settling down, she began reading her fairy-tale book, which she'd managed to conceal beneath her cumulus of sheets.

Poppy sat herself on the bald girl's bed and folded her hands. Erasmus produced his camera and, pressing record, he placed it on Wendy's bedside table, pointing towards her.

"Wendy," Poppy began, "I know you can't speak, but I need you to try and tell me what happened to you. My name is Poppy and this is Erasmus."

Wendy looked at Mitsy, and Mitsy nodded encouragingly.

"We're trying to work out what's going on with some of the kids in town who seem to have the same, er... *thing* as you have and we...we want to help them."

Wendy lifted her frail hand and pointed to the roof.

Poppy thought for a moment.

Wendy pointed to the frame of her bed.

"Er, sleep? You were sleeping?"

Wendy shook her head and rubbed her finger along the bed frame.

"Wood," whispered Erasmus. "She was in the woods."

Wendy nodded and raised her hand to her eyes, as if looking for something.

"You were looking for something?"

Wendy nodded again and, reaching underneath her bed, she pulled out a book:

Insects, Bugs and Creepy-Crawlers:

A COMPANION FOR THE
YOUNG ENTOMOLOGIST

"You were looking for insects?" Erasmus asked.

Wendy nodded.

"Why?"

"She wants to be an en-entom…" Mitsy stuttered, "ent-om-ogo-list."

"An entomologist," Erasmus said and Wendy nodded.

Lifting her hand again, she made it flutter like a butterfly.

"Something came down from the sky?"

One hand picked up the other hand and flew off.

"And took you with it?"

She closed her eyes as if she was concentrating. But she shook her head.

"You can't remember?" asked Erasmus.

Wendy lay down on her bed and mimed waking up, then she pointed to her ear and tapped her finger on the bedside table.

"You woke up and heard a tapping noise?"

She cracked her finger.

"A clicking noise?"

She nodded. Then, to Poppy's horror, she mimed pulling something long and stringy out of her ear. Poppy couldn't guess what this was.

"How did you get away?"

Wendy looked around the room. She tucked her thumbs away and put her two hands together and made them crawl across the bedspread.

"A spider?"

Wendy lifted her finger as if to say, *Hold that thought*. Then she pointed to the dreamcatcher hanging above the corner where Mitsy sat.

"Spider's web?"

Wendy shook her head. She covered her face with both hands and played peekaboo.

"You hid?"

More spider hands.

"With the spiders?"

Wendy shook her head furiously.

"Oi! What's going on here?" came a voice from the

door. Mr Pocks entered, scratching his elbow manically.

Poppy shot up to standing position and grabbed her rat head.

"We were just…er…"

"No one is to come in here, you understand?" snapped Mr Pocks, standing aside and pointing in the direction of the annex. "She needs rest and quiet. You're disturbing her."

Mitsy slid off the trunk of toys and ghosted frumpily out of the room.

Poppy looked back to Wendy. Wendy was moving her hands like a butterfly and flapped them around her bedside lamp.

"Oh, look what you've done!" Mr Pocks scowled at Poppy, rushing over to Wendy's bedside table and opening the medicine bottle. "You've made her do those funny hand movements again!"

"She's trying to say something!" insisted Erasmus.

"Out!" Mr Pocks bellowed, and they obeyed.

"It's time for dares," Regina said loudly as Poppy, Erasmus and Mitsy rejoined the party.

"Yes!" Sid whooped, pumping the air.

Regina had written a whole bunch of dares and popped them into a shopping bag. The first few were surprisingly tame: Sid had to let a cockroach, that Regina had coerced out of the corner of the kitchen, crawl over his head. John Wharf was compelled to show everyone the top half of his pants. Eleanor, Poppy's ex lab partner, had to chew on some old chewing gum excavated from under a desk at school.

"I'm *bored* of this stupid game," Regina whined, after Sid had refused to kiss her as part of her dare. "Why don't we do something really scary?"

Poppy glanced over at Erasmus. He was squatted down beside the door with a pencil, writing something very carefully.

"Like what type of scary?" asked Eleanor, taking off her astronaut helmet.

Regina thought.

"Oh! I know!" she cackled. "I dare someone to go into Riddling Woods. Alone."

Poppy's chest fluttered. She got the impression Regina had come up with that dare so that she wouldn't have to do it herself.

"Pfft!" Sid snorted. "That's boring. Make it harder."

"Alright then," Regina said, still looking bitter from Sid's rejection. "You do it."

"Nah, not me." Sid coughed. "I strained my back scoring in football. Doctor said I'm not supposed to do anything...you know."

"My dad said that when he was little something came out of Riddling Woods and kidnapped a whole bunch of kids," Eleanor said, calmly fishing around in a nearby bowl for a packet of Quavers. "I bet you there's ghosts living in there."

"Ghosts are dead, how can they *live* anywhere?" asked John.

"I'll do it," said Erasmus, suddenly standing up. Poppy could see he was folding the piece of paper he'd been working on.

Regina doubled over with laughter. "What? You, Asparagus Boy!" she sneered. "Aren't you afraid you'll wet your pants?"

"What are you doing?" Poppy hissed into Erasmus's ear as Regina, Sid and the other kids from the party followed them to the woods with squeaks of excitement.

"I should have realized this ages ago," he muttered to himself.

"Realized what?"

At the very back of the group, Mitsy tried desperately to keep up, tripping every few steps on her ghost sheet.

Erasmus pulled out his camera. "Insects," he said. "Insects, bugs and creepy-crawlers."

They snuck around the back of the church and across the heath. Before long, the Riddling Woods leaned over them.

Regina folded her arms and Sid copied her.

"Go on then!" Regina jeered. "Let's see what you're made of."

Erasmus caught Poppy's glance for a moment.

"Don't go in!" Mitsy panted as she caught up with them and grabbed Erasmus's worm tail. "Don't go in!"

But Erasmus yanked himself free.

"Oooooh," Sid mocked. "Someone's got the hots for Asparagus Boy!"

Without so much as a shiver, Erasmus strode towards the woods. Poppy watched, her heart pounding, before the great gnarled limbs swallowed him up.

The group of them waited. And for a good minute, nothing happened.

"What if he hasn't really gone into the woods?" Sid wondered aloud. "And he's just hiding behind one of the trees and pretending to go in?"

"Well, go check," Regina said, shoving Sid.

"You go!"

"Do it yourself!"

"Look!" shrieked Mitsy.

A flash had come from between the trees. Not lightning, something smaller.

It flashed again.

"What the hell was that?" Regina asked worriedly, as she backed away.

"Ghosts," whispered Eleanor.

There was another flash, bigger this time.

"I'm outta here," Sid whimpered, and bolted back towards the church. Moments later, everyone else followed him in a clamour of terrified shrieks.

"Help him!" Mitsy called after them. "Help Erasmus!"

Poppy ran doggedly towards the woods, fighting against her costume. There was another flash. She followed it.

"Erasmus!" she called out.

But there was no response. She reached a clearing where she thought she'd last seen the light appear. Whipping her phone out, she used its torch to see by. Poppy froze.

On a branch above her, hanging like a bat, was Erasmus's satchel.

Her hands trembled as she unhooked it. The note she had seen Erasmus writing earlier was fastened to the buckle. His discarded camera flash lay at the roots of the tree pointing back in the direction she'd just run from. He'd put it there himself. She unfolded the note and read:

A RAG MAN: TEETHING VOLES LIMO
THRIVE PERU.
HOG A WEEKNIGHTS POWER.
TWO FOLD MELON.
THIS PIGS A MENAGERIES DREAM FROG.
WIRE HIM A TERMITES BED.
BOSS PARAGUAY

At 10 p.m., Dalia was on the phone in the darkened sunroom when Poppy parked herself at Gran's computer. *A RAG MAN*, she typed into the search engine.

Clunk…clunk…clunk went Gran's ancient computer.

Poppy had already knocked furiously at Erasmus's front door. No one had answered. His mum would be at work, but if Erasmus had been playing some kind of trick on everyone at Regina's party then surely he would be home by now. Poppy felt the wobbly stirs of panic tumbling through her stomach. He couldn't have been taken by the Peggs. How would they have found him so quickly?

The internet proved useless.

"Oh I love these!"

Poppy startled. Dalia had come up behind her and was leaning over her shoulder.

"Love what?"

"Word games!" Dalia said, settling in beside her.

"Your gran and I used to do the crosswords in all the magazines. I'm a *brilliant* speller, you see. There's nothing that makes my blood run quite as cold as a spelling mistake does."

Then you mustn't ever have spellchecked any of your own text messages, thought Poppy, then she frowned.

"Word games? What do you mean?"

"A RAG MAN," Dalia said, pointing to the words on the screen with her orange fingernail. "That's an anagram...of *anagram*!"

Poppy's temple began to pulse. Of course it was an anagram. Only Erasmus could jumble and rearrange letters at that sort of speed.

"I hope you're not cheating and using that computer to work it out!" Dalia chuckled, wandering off to the kitchen for a yoghurt. She snuffled about for a moment and then called out from the fridge:

"Did I tell you I had to get my hair coloured *again* today? I know! It was only a few weeks ago that my roots started poking through, and then this morning I saw a whitish sort of spot at the back! I tell you, girlfriend, I pegged it to the nearest salon and..."

But Poppy wasn't listening. She searched for an anagram solver in the browser, then typed in the message sentence by sentence, copying and pasting the results into a separate document.

I'VE GONE TO THE MILLS UP THE RIVER.

I KNOW WHO THE PEGGS ARE.
DON'T FOLLOW ME.
THERE IS A PAGE MISSING FROM EDGAR.
I REMEMBERED WHAT IT IS.
ASPARAGUS BOY.

The rain heckled the eaves as Poppy gazed out of the window in Gran's study. In the backyard, the wheelbarrow she used to collect the washing slowly filled with fat drops of rain. And on the swollen Suds River, a boy who couldn't swim, with powerful green eyes and skin as pale as fresh milk, steered his tiny dinghy towards the towering Mills.

Sixteen
CAMERA

Poppy spent the morning at school feeling sick. She excused herself twice to go to the loo during English so she could pass Erasmus's classroom to see if he'd shown up. Why had he told her not to follow him? Why hadn't he just spoken to her first instead of charging off like that? And then again, why hadn't she in turn charged off after him herself? She found herself unfolding Erasmus's note from her pocket. She'd jotted the rearranged letters beneath each line in frantic, scratchy handwriting that was unlike her own:

DON'T FOLLOW ME

In Poppy's experience Erasmus was, often regrettably, sometimes painfully, *always* right. What if she followed him and both of them were... She couldn't think it. She wouldn't allow it to enter her head. Even the smell of that thought made her heart pace furiously up and down the corridors of her ribcage.

When the last bell rang, she stuffed her textbooks into her backpack and power-walked out of class. She would walk home. She would make a plan.

A small police car had pulled up outside the school office. Mitsy was sat on the steps nearby, watching Poppy with worried eyes.

She felt sick again.

"Poppy!"

Ms Tall's dumpy cream sports car was parked next to it, at an angle.

"Miss Slub?"

Poppy turned.

It was Mr Hern. He was wearing a grim smile.

"Could you pop into the school office with me, Poppy?"

"She's a sensible woman," Constable Bunty said when he sat down at the desk opposite Poppy. Mr Hern had shown them into the office and closed the door very slowly, watching Poppy.

"Who is?"

"Eliza Crink," said Constable Bunty. He fished something out of a cardboard storage box beside him

256

and placed it on the desk. It was a see-through plastic evidence bag. Droplets of water fogged up the inside. Constable Bunty opened it up and dipping his hand inside, pulled out Erasmus's camera. Poppy felt her stomach turn sideways.

"Eliza Crink, the lady from that fabric shop, The Brindled Weave, found this camera caught in the weeds in the brook near her shop this morning," Constable Bunty went on. "As I said, she's a sensible woman, she thought it might be of some value to someone, and so she brought it to us down at the station. Turns out it's not valuable at all."

Poppy could feel her eyes becoming sandy dry.

"Now normally I wouldn't bother with this type of thing," Bunty said. "But it just so happens that this morning Dennis Wrist from the school office called a Ms *Tall* to tell her that her son...Er-aser...?"

"Erasmus," Poppy corrected him hoarsely.

"That's it, Elasmus, hadn't shown up to school," Bunty said grimly. "She was working last night, so she didn't know if he'd even come home. She called us, and told us rather forcefully that her son was missing. She said he was fifty-six inches tall, very fair hair, greeny eyes and always carried a camera with him. This camera, in fact."

Constable Bunty took a long sip of tea from a toucan mug.

"When did you last see Elasmus Tall?"

Poppy told Constable Bunty everything. Everything except the bit about Erasmus leaving a note, and why he'd left the note and why he'd gone off in the first place. Part of her wanted to tell him, to get it all out in the open, but she'd seen the way people treated Marley when he tried to warn them. So she told Bunty that she didn't know why Erasmus Tall had vanished. She told him that Erasmus was there one minute and gone the next.

Bunty must have felt sorry for Poppy, because after speaking with her he dropped her at the hospital and had a word with the ward staff, so that Poppy could see Gran outside of visiting hours.

Gran was tired. Poppy suspected that she'd been sleeping before she arrived. Dalia had driven ahead to the hospital and was waiting for Poppy beside Gran's bed.

She kept avoiding Poppy's gaze and eventually fished out her purse and asked softly, "Do you want a Coke, Poppy?"

Poppy shook her head and gave a half smile. Dalia didn't smile back, and drifted off down the hall to the vending machines. She and Gran had fallen very solemn after Bunty had a word with just the two of them in private. Afterwards, Poppy had noticed Dalia trying to catch Gran's eye every few moments, as if trying to remind her of something.

"Have you kept the sugar cubes hidden, Poppy?" asked Gran faintly.

Poppy nodded.

"Good girl," said Gran. "Bravo." She took a sip of water from the plastic cup beside her bed. Her lips were dry and chapped. "I think it's time to tell you something, Poppy."

Poppy listened.

"When your mother was your age and living with me here in Suds, she saw something that frightened the living daylights out of her. So much so that she tried to do anything she could to forget it. She made me promise never to tell anyone unless absolutely necessary. Now is that time."

Gran cleared her throat and took another sip.

"She was staying with her friend Macey Gunn over near Riddling. I think she was your age at the time. She was sleeping on the floor in Macey's room when a rattling noise woke her. The window was open, and there was something floating in mid-air outside. Standing over Macey was a great clicking shadow with blue, drilling eyes. She said the shadow looked as if it was…" Gran paused. "As if it was *combing Macey's hair*."

Gran's eye twinkled with a tear.

"I don't know how she managed it, but when the creature took her friend, your mum fought back. She bit one of its fingers. But she couldn't stop it taking Macey. Afterwards, Mrs Gunn said Macey had started acting strangely before she disappeared. Everyone thought Macey had run away because she wasn't happy at home, but your mum knew otherwise. She knew Macey, and she knew what she'd seen, and every spare moment she had she spent looking for her, piecing together clues, like you and Erasmus."

"Was Macey ever found?"

"*Macey* wasn't," Gran said, "but her nightgown was. A search team found it down the river." She sighed. "Your mum always refused to give up on Macey. It was in her nature. She was like you: she had a big heart."

Poppy scratched the side of Gran's bed with her fingernail.

"I hear her heart still," Poppy told Gran. "I hear it thumping all the time. What if she wasn't dead when they buried her?"

Gran sat up a bit, and Poppy felt her own heart drumming its way slowly up her throat.

"Be strong, Poppy," said Gran. "Be kind like your mum. Go and find your friend. Be brave for Erasmus. Be brave for me."

"I'm scared," said Poppy. "What if he's…what if he's dead?"

"You'll never forgive yourself unless you try, Poppy," whispered Gran. "There is something malignant out there, dear girl. Something wicked. Something… cunning. Find him for his mother, Poppy. I know what it's like to lose a child. It hurts like hell, petal."

Gran's eyelids folded, batted for a moment, and then she drifted off with a quiet snore. Dalia returned with her Coke.

"Come on, girlie," whispered Dalia. "Let's give her some peace and quiet for a bit. She's very ill, Poppy."

"I know," Poppy said. "I know."

Poppy knew what she had to do. She didn't know how long she had. She didn't know how long Gran had. But there were things she needed to find out first. The pounding began in her chest like a battle drum, warning her.

She didn't have a plan. She didn't even have the first clue as to how she would possibly get to the Mills. But go she must. Because that was what a friend should do.

Fairytales are always wrong, thought Poppy. *If you want to be truly brave, listen to your heart – then ignore it.*

Seventeen
PIG & DOG

It was 1 a.m. and Poppy was waiting for first light. At first light she'd head to the woods and follow the river. That was her best chance.

"YOU KNOW SOMETHING!"

Poppy pulled her pillow over her ears.

Ms Tall was drunk, and she'd been out in the street for an hour now.

Luckily Dalia wore earplugs to bed. Churchill, on the other hand, was very much awake. Poppy could hear his little hooves trotting around the kitchen.

"YOU'RE NOT TELLING THEM SOMETHING!" Ms Tall shouted up at Poppy's window. "YOU'RE A LITTLE WITCH!"

Poppy closed her eyes and clenched her teeth.

Breathe, she told herself. *Breathe.*

She could hear Ms Tall sobbing as the woman leaned on their creaking letter box.

"My boy," she wept. "Where's my boy?"

After half an hour of listening, Poppy heard a car pull up. She peered over the window sill. Ms Tall was clambering into a taxi, which waited for a few moments before rolling off into the night. When Poppy peered out between the curtains again a few minutes later, the street was empty.

"Shoo, boy! Shoo!" came a loud whisper from down the street, followed by little footsteps. "Go home!"

Poppy pressed her flushed cheek against the cold glass and squinted down the street.

"Go home, Marley!"

It was Mitsy disguised in what looked like her mother's coat. Marley the dog was following her, looking mournful. He whimpered.

Mitsy took a handful of dog biscuits from her pocket and let Marley sniff them before hurling them up the street. Whilst Marley was galloping after the biscuits, Mitsy pelted off at high speed. What on earth was she doing out at this hour?

Poppy put on her dressing gown and slippers. She tiptoed down the stairs and out the front door.

She felt Churchill slip past her leg and watched him trot up the garden path in front of her.

Poppy's breath poured out of her mouth in great plumes of vapour as she followed Mitsy to the end of the lane and over the stile. She kept shifting her gaze between the sky and Mitsy up ahead. Every flicker of movement around her made the skin on her back tighten.

Mitsy was halfway across the paddock when Poppy got to the fence. Marley must have abandoned his biscuits and was now in hot pursuit. After surveying the wire, Churchill snuffled his way underneath and charged after Marley.

The moon slid out from behind the clouds like a great searchlight over the paddock.

"Mitsy!" Poppy whispered loudly.

Mitsy heard her straight away, and when she realized it was Poppy she began to run again. Marley and Churchill joined her.

"Mitsy, come back here!" Poppy called out. "What are you doing?"

Mitsy ran faster, tripping every few steps on her mum's coat.

"He saved me," she said over and over. "*He* saved *me*, so I'm going to save him!"

Poppy tried to catch up, her woollen slippers sliding into the muddy dips the cows had made.

The river was still gushing and swollen from the rain the night before. Under the surge of water, the island where they'd buried the book had shrunk into a little tile of land and rocks in the middle of the surging torrent.

"How can you save him, Mitsy?" Poppy called out as she reached the river's edge.

Churchill was bathing in the mud. But Mitsy was nowhere to be seen. The dinghy was no longer moored by the trees.

There was a splash from upstream, and Poppy's blood ran cold.

A moment later, Poppy spotted the tiny girl floating down the river past her, clutching onto a branch.

"Mitsy!" Poppy shrieked. "Mitsy, get out of there! You'll drown!"

Mitsy struggled for a moment, angled the branch and caught it against a rock. She edged along it towards the island, gasping for breath in the icy murk.

There was another splash as Marley leaped in after her. Poppy flicked off her slippers.

"Go back, Marley!" Mitsy panted as she hauled herself onto the rocks surrounding the island. "Bad dog!"

Marley ignored her, paddling straight past her and over to the other side of the river.

Mitsy stood up, dripping, and glared over the river at Poppy.

"Y-you haven't even tried to help him!" Mitsy stammered angrily at Poppy. "He's your friend!"

Mitsy kneeled down on the ground. Poppy felt a sudden panic grip her.

"Mitsy. Mitsy, what are you doing?" she shouted across the whorls of water. "Mitsy get away from that thing!"

"I'm going to save him," the girl muttered through gritted teeth. "When I touch the book, they'll come and

265

get me. I heard what Erasmus said. It can track people. If I touch it they'll know where I am, and they'll take me to where he is. And I'll save him!"

Poppy began to wade into the swollen river. The icy water bit her legs before the pain faded to a numbing ache. She had to stop Mitsy. It didn't matter that she couldn't swim.

Mitsy began to dig furiously at the white chalk which had become white sludge.

Poppy felt Churchill paddling in behind her.

A cloud of white dust shot up from the island as Mitsy reached the dry earth. Within moments, the button jar which held the silk book was in her hands.

"Mitsy, drop it!" Poppy shrieked. The water reached her torso and she felt its grip suddenly take her as she lost her footing in the barrage of the current.

Churchill gave a hideous squeal and splashed after her.

Between mouthfuls of water, she sculled furiously with her cupped hands. Her head dipped beneath the surface and when she came up she saw Mitsy holding the silk book high in the air. The jar lay at her feet, and a cascade of glittering buttons was seeping into the river.

Poppy felt the wind change across the water like a ship correcting its course.

The anger drained from Mitsy's face and fear flooded in.

A rock suddenly met Poppy's chest as she struggled under the enormous weight of her soaking dressing gown.

A shadow coursed over the moon. Poppy coughed as the chalky dust filled her mouth, and looked up.

They were there, circling above Mitsy like great birds of prey. They had come. A rope strung with pegs descended from the basket. Mitsy grimaced and closed her eyes.

"Mitsy!" Poppy called out. "Get away from them! They'll take you!"

She gritted her teeth, and fought with the water. She was hurling angry thoughts at Mitsy: Mitsy was being stupid. Mitsy was going to get them all killed.

"Erasmus saved me," shouted Mitsy. Poppy finally hauled herself onto the rock and lunged towards the tiny girl, throwing herself at Mitsy's leg. But the basket swooped down and, with one clicking hand, the creatures swept the girl up.

Mitsy screamed as her body jolted. From beneath the folds of her enormous coat, something slipped and splashed into the river. Poppy dived into the water after it, grasping it awkwardly with one arm.

A sickening howl filled the sky, the sheetlike sail unfurled above the hamper and, like a hot-air balloon, it lifted effortlessly higher into the air.

Without warning, the branch Mitsy had used to float down the river swung away from the rocks. Poppy didn't see it coming until it smacked her in the chin.

The river dragged her under.

Twigs plummeted past her face as the water tumbled her head over heels downstream. Her hands met with mud, and she dug her nails in. She found footing, and kicked.

Air ricocheted through her lungs when she surfaced and, with her last threads of energy, she threw herself at the river's edge. She clawed at the tangle of weeds until she'd hauled herself onto the muddy bank.

By the time Poppy had staggered to her feet, the hamper was gliding over the distant woods, a tiny speck against the moon. And Churchill was nowhere to be seen. Churchill. Little warm-bellied, snuffling Churchill. Her waterlogged ears pounded. What would Gran say if he'd drowned? It would destroy her.

Poppy was halfway across the field before she looked down and saw what it was that had fallen out of Mitsy's coat. It was a book: FAIRYTALES OF THE ENGLISH SOUTH.

Eighteen
WHISKERS

Dalia was still asleep when Poppy collapsed through the front door. She was caked in mud and could taste blood in her mouth from where the branch had hit her. She didn't call the police. That would be about as helpful as wearing shoes on your hands. She needed to do something sensible.

Poppy hung Mitsy's fairy-tale book on the clothes horse in front of the fire to dry and made for the stairs. She needed to fetch her backpack and head straight off. First light could wait.

As her foot hit the first stair, a slip of dripping paper fell from the book onto the hearth. Poppy rescued it before the flames began to lick it, and even as she picked it up a whisper of steam escaped past her.

The page looked like a photocopy of a newspaper

obituaries section. Mitsy must have kept it since the day when Regina Pocks and Mean Sid had sent Erasmus's Edgar flying in the air, spreading the pages to the wind.

The newspaper was dated from March 1974.

> In memory of Geraldine Knip, aunty and best friend.
>
>
>
> Rest easy, Barnaby – a more handsome hound never lived.
>
>
>
> Please pray for the response of the soul of Gregorius Bard, devoted husband and glove-maker.
>
>
>
> Raise a glass to memories of Ada, Gerda and Hulda. Three friends and a very pretty yacht, lost tragically to the river. *Deine Freundein Deutschlandwerde dich nie vergessen.*

Poppy translated the German for herself: "Your friends in Germany will never forget you."

Falling back into Gran's Seat of Wisdom, she flipped the fairy-tale book over to dry the other side, and it fell open to the front page. Mitsy had written her name very carefully in purple felt-tip pen, and after the book's trip down the river, the violet ink had begun to run. But there was another name written in the book. A name which had been scribbled out many years earlier with a sharp ballpoint pen by someone at a charity shop:

Josie Herrison

That's my mum's name, Poppy thought. *This was Mum's book.*

She opened the book to the first page. HOW THE WHISKERED FISH CAME TO ENGLAND, Poppy read.

In that town, where the river cut deep and the trees grew black, there had always been four ugly sisters who were washerwomen. The sisters' names were Lye, Whipstitch, Huckaback and Claria. Their skin had become disfigured from the soaps, potions and woad powder they used in their trade, and their weary fingers had split at the ends like forks. As a result of their ugliness, the beautiful Queen Margaret banished them to live on the outskirts of town. It was said that before the sisters came to that town the cliffs were never white, but became so from the soap they tipped from their washing tubs each day.

One stormy night, a Norse sorcerer and his son were shipwrecked at the foot of the cliffs between the rocks where the sisters' house was. Answering their cries for help, the sisters lowered down their washing line, and rescued the sorcerer's son. Then they tipped their soapsuds down onto the ship and it slipped out from the rocky chasm and found safety in the harbour.

In return for their kindness the sorcerer told the sisters they could ask him for whatever they wanted.

The first sister, Lye, who liked to hear stories, asked the sorcerer for a way to listen to the dreams of anything she wished. So the sorcerer gave her a nearby seashell, through which the sister could hear the tiniest of sounds: the heartbeats of the ants, the song of the wheat and the bickering of the four winds.

The second sister, Whipstitch, who liked to weave and kept beetles to make silk, asked for a tool that would rake the colour from anything it touched. So, taking bones from the seashore, the sorcerer made her a comb, with which the sister could gather the colours from insects and wild beasts to use in her weaving.

The third sister, Huckaback, who liked to cook, asked for a device to remove and keep the flavour of anything she wanted. Finding a spoon from a long forgotten shipwreck which had been twisted by the tides, the sorcerer gave it to the sister, who delightedly used it to scoop the buttery sweetness from a yellow wild flower nearby.

There was a fourth and most ugly of the sisters, Claria, who was very poorly with a terrible illness that made her limbs shake and hair sprout from her face. In her youth she would swim like a fish, but now she hobbled from place to place with a wooden cane.

Being humbled by her misfortune, she asked the sorcerer for an easier way to take her foul-tasting medicine.

The sorcerer took pity on her and, gathering a handful of sugar, he squeezed the granules until they hardened and became like a cube. "Dip this cube in your medicine," the sorcerer told the frail sister, "and you will never taste bitterness again. Instead you will taste and know all the wondrous things of the world once more."

The other sisters sneered. "Stupid Claria!" they laughed when the sorcerer had gone. "Dimwit! You could have asked for anything and yet you settled for a lump of sugar."

Claria said nothing and quietly went about her chores.

The other three sisters, emboldened by their newfound powers, plotted to take revenge on Queen Margaret, who they hated for exiling them. So they disguised themselves. Using Whipstitch's comb they removed the colour from the carcass of a pig and wove a silk so like skin that it covered their warts and made them look beautiful.

At the Queen's court, they announced themselves as three travelling magicians who were there to entertain the Queen's young son, Prince Wilhelm. The Queen was delighted and sent them to the prince's chambers to show him their magic.

When they were alone with the prince, Huckaback sprinkled some of the blue woad powder, which the sisters used for dyeing their washing, around the prince's eyes to send him into a dizzying sleep. Then, taking her spoon, she drained the sweetness of his heart, leaving him sour and unfeeling. Whipstitch combed the colour from his eyes and hair, which rendered him grey like an old man. Lyc used her seashell to listen to the prince's dreams and pull them from his mind, so he was left empty and unable to speak.

Then, using a pulley and a washing hamper they had brought with them, they lowered themselves from the window of his room to the ground and escaped back to their home by the sea.

When the Queen saw her son, she was greatly distressed and sought for someone to cure him. But the three sisters were not content and decided to use what they had taken from the young prince to punish the Queen further. Huckaback, who had taken the sweetness from the prince's heart, made an elderberry jam, pouring the prince's sweetness into the batch. Whipstitch made a silken robe from the colour of his eyes and hair. Lye poured the prince's thoughts and dreams into a book. They sent these to the Queen and told her that only by their own magic would the prince ever return to the way he was.

The Queen wrote to her friend, the sorcerer whose

son the sisters had saved, and upon seeing the sisters' mischief he knew at once who was to blame. He went to the sisters' house and asked them why they had done this.

"We lived in fear," said Whipstitch, "and fear shall reign wherever we are so that all may know how it is to cower, how it is to be cast out, how it is to be forgotten."

Claria threw herself at the sorcerer's feet and pleaded with him to provide her with a cure for the prince. But the sorcerer shook his head. "Their power has grown greater than mine could ever hope to be. Only by the magic which dances through their fingers will they ever be undone. But the prince may yet be saved. Take him a grain of your sugar cube. I will try to contain their magic with a simple spell."

Reaching into the white cliffs on which the house sat, the sorcerer broke off a piece of rock, which had become like chalk from the sisters' soapsuds, and said, "Chalk be your curse. Wherever there is chalk, you shall not touch. For chalk is a very magic thing. Chalk can build houses. Chalk can conjure words. Chalk covers the faces of great ladies and fills the hands of lowly children."

The sorcerer started to draw a ring around them, but before he could contain them, the sisters leaped into their washing hamper and, tying it to a sheet, they cast themselves off the white cliffs. Unbeknownst to Claria, Huckaback had threaded their washing line around her leg, and as the hamper dropped over the cliff, she was pulled with it. Poor Claria was dashed to pieces.

Through their magic, the sisters' hamper lifted like a gull and sailed north on the Arctic gusts until they reached a town where no one knew their names. And they became faceless, weaving silks to cover their skin and working mischief amongst the townsfolk.

When kind Claria had fallen on the rocks, the sorcerer descended the cliffs to where she lay and held her broken body in his lap. "Take from my apron the sugar cube you gave me, and place it beneath my tongue so it doesn't melt in the salty water," Claria told the sorcerer. "It is our only hope to one day undo the damage of my sisters' mischief. For they drain sweetness and kindness, and yet this sugar cube could one day bring it back."

The sorcerer did as she told him and then, lifting her fractured body, he lowered it beneath the water, and a wonderful thing happened. Whiskers grew from Claria's face, scales pierced through her skin, her mouth grew wider and filled with needle-like teeth, and fins sprouted from where her arms and legs had been.

"You are not a fish of the sea," the sorcerer told the great catfish. "Swim into the rivers of this ancient land, find the cave in the deepest river, in that town where blossoms bloom as leaves fall, and wait there until that which points and is made of wood floats down the river to meet you."

Claria did as she was told, and the three sisters hunted for her day and night, looking for the powerful sugar cube. But she was never found, and to this day in some parts of England it is a wise tradition to hide the sugar.

Poppy's fingers trembled as the book fell into her lap. Everything was clear. Everything was illuminated. Everything except what she had to do. Erasmus was right. The Suds River *must* be the deepest in the country. Marley mustn't fully know what dwelled in the murky depths beneath his barge or else he would have told them. *"The cats need cat food,"* he'd said. Poppy felt like kicking herself, like *really* truly kicking herself – why hadn't either of them listened to Mitsy? None of this might ever have happened if they'd paid any attention to what she had to say, and, what was more, they might have discovered the truth. The *actual* truth about who the Peggs were – about *what* they were.

Gathering what she needed from her bedroom, she carefully filled her backpack:

1 x pair of Gran's tailor's scissors
1 x bag of baby cheeses
1 x sports cap bottle of spring water

6 x muesli bars
4 x nut bars
1 x apple
Mum's chalk (with note attached)
1 x pack of contact lenses (stolen from Dalia)

Easing the front door shut, she blew Gran a kiss high into the sky, as if hoping for it to be ricocheted back down to Gran's hospital bed by a satellite, and took off towards the churchyard.

Nineteen

TUNNEL

There were no lights on in Marley's barge when Poppy slipped down the bank towards the gangway. The only light for as far as she could see through the twisting trees was the glow from her phone torch as she guided herself between the piles of rusting junk.

She made quick work of the door, which had been padlocked from the outside. Safety pins weren't only made to safely pin. The inside of the barge no longer felt lived in, and the whole place was filled with the stench of cat food.

The trapdoor had been left open, and murky river water was sloshing in over the edge. Poppy found one of Marley's hurricane lamps and, lighting it with some damp matches, she kneeled down on the wet carpet beside the opening in the floor.

She didn't know quite what she was waiting for, so, holding her nose, she tipped a half-empty tin of cat food into the inky blackness. Poppy lay the tin on what she thought was a nearby blanket, but to her horror turned out to be a very wet dog – Marley.

She had to stop herself from shrieking. Marley gave her a sour pout, so Poppy gave his stomach a scratch by way of apology and asked him how he'd managed to get inside.

Marley tilted his head, got up and waddled over to the trapdoor, where the glistening, whiskered inhabitants of the river had started to appear. The dog dipped his snout into the water and then gazed encouragingly at Poppy.

She didn't know whether to call out to the fish, or simply try to pick one up and hope that it could be of some help. There weren't many scenarios in life when your friends' lives depended on speaking to a catfish. Somehow speaking to Marley or Churchill seemed ten times more reasonable than leaning on her elbows and making small talk with river fish.

She felt self-conscious with Marley watching her, and tried to send him over to his basket, but he started whimpering and kept dipping his snout in.

"Are any of you named Claria?" Poppy asked the lapping water.

Before she had the chance to clear her throat and ask again, something wet and furry bumped into her elbow as Marley threw himself gracelessly into the water. Poppy copped a mouthful of the muddy stuff and wiped her eyes on her coat sleeve.

Without thinking, her hand shot beneath the water and felt for the dog, even though she was already witness to the fact that Marley could swim. After a moment, there was a cartoonish gurgling of bubbles and Marley's head surfaced. He let out a few agitated barks, and ducked his head back beneath the water.

He wanted Poppy to follow him. *That's* what he was whimpering about. The idea of climbing into the inky darkness for the second time that night made Poppy feel physically sick. Whenever she tried to swim at school, her arms just flailed pathetically. Marley's head appeared again in the dim light and, giving another few yaps, he vanished.

Delaying the inevitable, she threw a tin of cat food into her backpack, along with her shoes. The mud on the edge of the trapdoor oozed between her toes as she teetered at the water's edge. She noticed that human Marley's purple goggles, which he'd used to look at the blue powder, had fallen between some upturned flower pots, so she pulled them on. They were a little too large for her, but better than nothing.

There was a split second where she thought she saw something glowing in the depths, but before she could decide if that was a good or a bad thing, she had jumped. Cold ricocheted through her body as she descended.

She tried to control the urge to flap her arms about in a panic.

There was a peculiarity to the water. It wasn't tumultuous and swelling, but she could feel its distinctive grip as it pulled her magnetically downwards. This had been her plan. To let the weight of the backpack help her to sink, however Poppy could feel herself pre-emptively gripping the strap with her hand in case she had to whip it off in a hurry and make and escape upwards. But either way – resistance to the water's draw was fruitless. She didn't open her eyes until she felt the first eel-like creature swooping past her leg. With her eyes open, she could just see the pale, whiskered beasts of the river gliding towards her. There was a yank on her backpack as one of the catfish pecked at the straps with its gaping mouth.

Without thinking, Poppy began to count as she held her breath, like she and Mum used to in the car when they passed through tunnels.

5, 6, 7, 8, 9, 10...

She dropped deeper into the river. She could almost feel the weedy water pulsing around her chest as her heart thumped viciously.

They knew the river was deep – Erasmus had measured it – but she still expected to feel the slimy bottom against her bare feet at any moment. Above her was blackness, and Poppy couldn't tell whether she was passing out, or whether she was too deep for the moon to reach.

Perhaps the lack of oxygen was finally getting to her, or perhaps for the first time since Mum died she was thinking clearly. Because at three hundred or so feet below the surface, Poppy realized she'd left her phone in her pocket. There were messages from Mum on there that she'd been keeping safe. Now gone. Lost at the bottom of a river which had perhaps already led one friend to his peril.

15, 16, 17, 18, 19, 20...

Before Poppy could push this thought any further, a set of sharp jaws sank into her hand. It was too dark to tell what had her in its grip, but whatever it was turned and dragged Poppy with it up towards what she hoped was the riverbank. Short whorls of water swooshed past her face as the creature churned through the dark ahead of her, and Poppy prepared herself for a painful death. Would she drown before she could be chewed up?

39, 40, 41, 42, 43, 44, 45, 46...

There was a sudden noise in her ears, and it took Poppy a moment to realize that her head was no longer beneath the water. She gasped as glorious lungfuls of air filled her aching chest.

The reason she hadn't seen the surface coming was the darkness. The thick, echoing darkness that now surrounded her. There was a panting in the water beside her. Poppy felt for an edge, and a slimy clump of weeds met her hand. Wherever she was smelled muddy and rotten, like a fishy compost heap. The creature beside her licked her face in the dark. It was Marley – Marley had saved her. She wrapped her arm around his neck in a grateful hug. Her arm stung, which made her think that perhaps Marley had gripped a little harder than he intended when he dragged her up to air.

The echoing of droplets and lapping water drew Poppy's attention to the fact that she must be in a cave, a vast one at that, but one that was deep below the banks of the river.

"What next?" she asked Marley while scratching his back.

CRACK!

There was a deep, bone-shaking rumble, and a powerful gust of warm, fishy breath caught Poppy off guard. From somewhere in front of them there was a slithering and a splashing, and then a dripping, ancient and terrible voice murmured from the bowels of the black cave: Marley's ears pricked as upright as they could go.

"ARE YOU FASHIONED FROM WOOD, SCALES OR FLESH?"

The force of the hot clumps of saliva and fetid air nearly knocked Poppy out.

"FLESH," boomed the voice, and Poppy heard its great mouth sloshing about in the dark. "ONLY FLESH MAKES A NOISE THAT BEATS LIKE A DRUM IN MY CAVE."

Poppy subconsciously clutched at her heart. Before the voice began to speak again, she hurriedly scrambled up onto the weedy clumps she could feel beside her.

"I-I can't see you," said Poppy.

"YET I CAN SEE YOU."

Poppy felt for Marley and wrapped her arm around his neck again. Her other hand rested on what she was sure felt like bones, slippery and caked in festering grime.

"I WISH TO TASTE YOU."

Poppy's finger stung as a shard of bone pierced her skin.

There was a groaning and a flopping noise as the great creature moved restlessly.

Poppy lowered herself back into the water, readying herself to make an escape.

A snap echoed beside her ear like the crack of a whip, and a thick muscled, tentacular *something* coiled around her ankle. With the slightest effort it whisked her off her feet, and Poppy felt the blood rush to her head as she hung limply, her hair pointing towards the ground. Her backpack tried to make an escape off her shoulders, but she somehow managed to cling onto it. The purple goggles were not so lucky, and became tangled messily in her hair before slipping off and vanishing with a plop into a nearby pool.

"STOP WRIGGLING," said the voice in the dark. "I WISH TO TASTE YOU."

"Don't eat me, please don't eat me!" Poppy managed. "I need your help! I want to stop your sisters!"

As the creature's mouth opened with a rotting gargle of decomposed breath, Poppy saw a faint, yellow light pulsing at the back of its throat. The light seemed to rise and fall with the creature's breathing, silhouetting its bones in a lantern of feathery gills and veins.

Around its lips and cavernous mouth was a spread of thick writhing whiskers, one of which Poppy realized had her in its grip. As the beast inhaled, the glow inside its belly swelled, filling up the cave, and Poppy got her first good look at the creature.

It lay in a shallow pool, with only its thick tail submerged. The rocks in the cave seemed to have cradled the catfish's body, giving Poppy the impression that it had been sleeping here for thousands of years and the geology of the cave had slowly shifted around it.

She felt the whisker sliding off her ankle and, before she knew what was happening, her face met the water and she was submerged again. She spluttered back up to the surface with the purple goggles somehow tangled around her wrist. She'd thought they were lost for good.

"Aren't you going to eat me?" Poppy asked, trying to sound brave.

"EAT YOU?" mused the catfish. "I ONLY WANTED TO TASTE YOU."

The catfish must have seen the confused look that spread across Poppy's face, because it went on.

"I CAN TASTE ANYTHING WITH MY WHISKERS. YOU TASTE OF WORRY. YOU TASTE

OF FEAR. YOU TASTE BROKEN AND SHAKEN. YOU TASTE OF QUESTIONS."

"Then you are..." began Poppy.

"CLARIA," finished the catfish. "I AM THE FOURTH SISTER WHO WAS BROKEN UPON THE ROCKS."

"Your sisters have taken my friends," Poppy told Claria.

The light swelled again, revealing the true size of the catfish, which was as high and wide as the school minibus.

"FOUL CREATURES," bellowed Claria, spraying Poppy from head to toe. "ALAS, MY MAGIC FADED THE DAY I WAS BROKEN TO PIECES ON THE WHITE ROCKS. IT SEEPED FROM MY BODY AND WAS WASHED AWAY ON THE TIDES."

"So you can't help me?" asked Poppy, finally beginning to shiver with cold as her bravado deflated.

"ALL I CAN OFFER IS THAT WHICH COMES FROM MY MOUTH," Claria sputtered. "WORDS AND SWEETNESS."

Sweetness, my left foot, Poppy thought quietly, as Claria's ancient breath descended on her like a stale mist.

She stepped forward, letting her eye wander around the cave. The ceiling was cathedral-like, peppered with jagged stalactites.

"Does anyone else live down here?"

"NO HUMAN HAS VISITED MY CAVE THESE SIX HUNDRED YEARS," Claria sighed.

At this point, Marley gave a short yap and waddled over to the catfish, curling up beside her gills, which were large enough to swallow him whole.

"ONLY MARLEY HAS COME TO VISIT ME," said Claria. "MARLEY IS MY ONE FRIEND."

With one whisker Claria scratched Marley's back, and with another, which snuck up behind Poppy, she lifted Poppy's backpack up into the air and shook its contents onto the ground.

"Oi!" Poppy bellowed, clambering up the rocks to where Claria lay as she attempted to catch the shower of soggy paper, chalk and food supplies.

The enormous whisker danced around Poppy, coming to rest on the tin of cat food. Claria made an unpleasantly satisfied grunt and, lifting the tin, she dropped it whole into her mouth and swallowed it like a rumbling bin-lorry.

There was a dry retching sound, Claria's yellow eyes flew open and, with a powerful cough that knocked Poppy off her feet, the box of chalk, note still attached, came barrelling out of the catfish's mouth and landed in the furthest corner of the cave.

Poppy climbed over the rocks to find Mum's gift crumpled and soaked in a thick, mucous-like gloop.

"HUMAN FLESH!" shrieked Claria, scraping her vast tongue with one of her whiskers. "YOU FED ME HUMAN FLESH! MARLEY WOULD NEVER DO SUCH A THING."

"It isn't human flesh," Poppy snapped angrily, shaking the mucous from the box. "It's chalk! And I didn't feed it to you, you quite clearly helped yourself."

Claria snatched the box of chalk from Poppy and laid it on the rocks in front of her. The whisker searched like a boa constrictor until it found what it was looking for and dropped it into Poppy's outstretched hand.

"NOT THE CHALK," hissed Claria. "THIS! THIS IS FLESH!"

Poppy wiped away the remaining mucous, revealing the wooden peg Mum had used to clip her note to the box of chalk.

"That's a clothes peg," Poppy told Claria, and as she said it a chill ran from her fingers to the back of her neck.

"IT IS A FINGER," Claria whispered to her, "BRIMMING WITH MAGIC. IT TASTED OF SOAP, DUST AND DEVILRY."

Poppy clipped the peg to her soaking sleeve and showed Claria.

"This is *definitely* a clothes peg," Poppy told her. "We use them for all sorts nowadays."

"IT IS THAT WHICH POINTS, AND IS MADE OF WOOD."

"I don't have time for this," said Poppy. "For all I know, those..things...your sisters have already done terrible things to my friends. I need your help."

"I WILL NOT BE HURRIED," said Claria. "I HAVE

WAITED A WITCH'S LIFETIME IN THIS CAVE. WHAT ARE A FEW MORE MINUTES?"

Poppy scanned the walls for an exit, a tunnel maybe, that might lead her above ground. She didn't know how long she had before the Peggs turned Erasmus and Mitsy into soulless, grey-eyed ghosts. She might have days, weeks even. Or perhaps she was too late already.

"I CAN'T SAVE YOUR FRIENDS FOR YOU," Claria began slowly, "BUT I WILL TELL YOU HOW *YOU* MIGHT."

Claria breathed out through her mossy gills.

"DEFEAT MY SISTERS AT THEIR OWN GAME," Claria told Poppy. "USE THEIR POWER AGAINST THEM. AND REMEMBER, MOST IMPORTANTLY OF ALL: THEY ARE FACELESS. TRUST NOTHING YOU CAN SEE."

"Did you ever save Prince Wilhelm?" Poppy asked Claria. "Were you ever able to return him to the way he was?"

"YOU THINK OF YOUR FRIENDS, YET YOU ASK ME ABOUT THE PRINCE?"

"Yes," said Poppy.

"THE PRINCE WITHERED LIKE AN AUTUMN LEAF. MY SISTERS PLUCKED AT HIS DREAMS, PICKLED HIS HEART AND BLED THE COLOUR FROM HIS EYES. I WAS NOT QUICK ENOUGH TO STOP THEM. BUT THE MAGIC YOU HOLD MIGHT BE ABLE TO."

"But I'm not magic," Poppy said.

"AND YET YOU HOLD MAGIC IN THAT FINGER," said Claria, pointing to Poppy's hand.

Claria's enormous eyes fluttered shut, and the light flickered faintly inside of her.

"MY TIME IS HERE," she hissed. The catfish's hulking body began to slowly shrink, as wrinkles and grooves formed over her shrivelled gills and glistening, fleshy plates. "I AM LEAVING YOU," she whispered.

Poppy scampered over and rested her hand on the slimy catfish, while Marley whimpered mournfully beside one of the great whiskers.

A sigh went up throughout the cave as Claria's skin began to sink to the ground and, like a bouncy castle at the end of a fete, she sagged into a pancake of skin and whiskers, before sinking slowly beneath the water. Poppy scratched her nails on the back of her hand to drag herself back into the reality of the cave. She was still miles away from helping Erasmus and Mitsy. Heaving her leg out of the weedy mulch, she waded cautiously over to where the catfish had vanished. Something was glowing, ever so faintly, beneath the lapping water. Her fingers searched around in the inky murk, and met with the glowing thing. She raised it above the water.

It was a sugar cube. A large sugar cube that gave off a faint pink glow.

Flitting through the scattered contents of her backpack, she found an empty Tupperware container, popped the sugar cube inside and stowed it safely.

Behind where Claria had been lying was an opening in the rock, large enough for Poppy to squeeze inside. Stuffing the rest of her things into the pockets of her still-damp dressing gown, she tried to coax Marley to follow her, but he gave a worried yap and bolted off into the shadowy corners of the cave.

The tunnel had to lead somewhere useful, Poppy reasoned, but at every jagged twist she expected to find a dead end, human remains or both. On either side of her was grey, untamed rock. At least that was what she could feel. It occurred to her that the sugar cube might still be glowing, so she dug it out of her backpack and held out the Tupperware container like a weird sort of lantern.

After a while the tunnel began to narrow and slope until she was met with nothing but a rugged sheet of rock. Her back ached from stooping, and she was shivering from the wet.

Poppy didn't have the energy to backtrack. Besides, even if she did, she was still faced with the prospect of finding her way out of Claria's cave. The water might not be so forgiving a second time.

Gazing around the tunnel, dimly lit by the glowing sugar cube, she got a distinctly surreal sensation.

Some of Claria's final words ran through her head:

Trust nothing you can see. Poppy assessed what she *could* see: a wall of plain old boring rock. Gran was better at playing this game than she was. Gran could see a strip of wire, and twist it into a pair of spectacles. Gran could take a chunk of sponge and turn it into a very convincing stone.

Poppy's fingers brushed the wall in front of her. It was soft. It was silky. Gran's scissors were at the bottom of her bag and, flicking them open, she pushed the blade deep into the rock. It cut like fabric. Working quickly, she cut a gaping hole in the wall. The circular piece of silk fell away and Poppy picked it up.

It was just like Gran had told her back when she first arrived in Suds. The Helligan Mills truly could make silk that looked like anything. It was bizarre, like holding a prop pillar from a school play which you would expect to be very heavy but was in fact feather-light. She pulled the box of chalk, Mum's note, the purple goggles and the peg from her pockets and hurriedly knotted them into a bundle using the stone-coloured piece of silk before tucking it out of sight at the bottom of her bag. Pocketing her scissors, she heaved herself through the hole.

Poppy found herself holding her breath to stop it echoing through her head. She was listening out for voices. Listening for Mitsy. Listening for Erasmus.

The air became suddenly close and quiet and velvety. Poppy felt a thick, suffocating terror filling her throat and lungs. Her thumbs slid under her fingers, and her fingers closed into two fists. Two fists hell-bent on saving her friends.

Twenty
MILL

Poppy knew she was in the Mills. From the moment she stepped through the hole in the silk and into the room, she could feel eyes. Only it wasn't just one pair of eyes. It was hundreds, and they were mounted on the walls.

The chamber that the tunnel opened into was how Poppy imagined an abandoned ballroom might look. A white skirting ran around the edge, with a high embossed ceiling fitted like a topping of musty cream on the pale pink walls.

From corner to corner, the walls were laden with simple black picture frames, each holding a macabre treasure: images of faces on strips of silk, like shrouds. Their skin was so lifelike that from a certain angle they looked as if they were looming out of the silk at her.

At the end of the room was an ordinary-looking door that seemed too small for a room of such size. Passing silently through it, she followed the corridor beyond to another door at the opposite end, which seemed to have rusted shut. Although she'd been trying to move quietly, there wasn't any alternative to using brute force.

After a few violent shoves, the door flung open onto a high landing at the top of a twisting staircase. As she descended Poppy could hear a fluttering sound, like the beat of thousands of tiny wings. The noise made her think of Wendy Pocks and her strange flapping hand movements; she was getting closer. The mossy steps led her into a cathedral-like workshop filled with machinery. There were lights on above her, so Poppy slipped the Tupperware container with the sugar cube into her chest pocket, where it was neatly obscured from view.

Clouds of furry brown moths filled the air, crawling sluggishly over each other and the contents of the room. There were looms still loaded with great warps and wefts of glimmering thread. Shelves lined the walls, stacked with grimy spools of silk, their brilliant colours still glinting through the cobwebs. Boxes and trays covered the floor, piled with rusting needles, hooks, ornate scissors, bobbins, spindles and shuttles. Brambles had grown through the windows, knitting themselves among the machines. The reek of rotting fruit filled the room, and it was only when she smelled it that Poppy noticed the festering mulberries drooping from the branches. A fat moth landed in her hair and she let it crawl across her forehead. This part of the Mills looked as though it was in complete disuse. The fabric for Miss Crink's shop must have been made in a different section of the rambling building.

In one corner was a strange sort of fenced-off pen. The floor of the pen was lined with round, woven baskets veiled in a fine webbing, almost like cobwebs but violet-coloured. The dried mulberry leaves scattered across the floor crunched beneath her feet as she walked over to take a closer look. Rain began to patter on the roof.

Poppy gripped one of the basket lids, and lifted it away. She peered inside. Soft white balls caked the inside of the basket, suspended in whorls of the purplish webbing.

They were eggs. And based on the creatures flitting about around them, Poppy realized they were moth eggs.

Poppy quivered. She'd never liked the idea of insects laying eggs.

There was a pitiful whimpering from the far end of the workshop. Poppy's heart quickened.

"Hello?" the whimper came again.

It was followed by a squeal, which Poppy recognized instantly.

"Churchill!" she cried, and bolted down the central aisle of the workshop.

The air was now thick with moths, swarming like angry locusts. Poppy covered her mouth as their dusty wings flapped against her face.

Mitsy was cowering between some upturned baskets, tears streaming down her face. Her arms were wrapped around Churchill, and he was desperately trying to make an escape.

"Poppy!" Mitsy trembled putting her arms out. "Poppy, they've flown away to look for you. We need to be quick. Come help me find him!"

Churchill trotted insistently after them.

Mitsy led Poppy down three flights of stairs until they reached a landing with a surprisingly modern door.

"I think they're keeping him in here," Mitsy whispered to Poppy. "I don't know what they've done to him yet. You go first. He'll want to see you."

Mitsy seemed changed from when Poppy had last seen her. She seemed to be fuller, as if she was occupying more of her body. Her movements seemed quicker, more decided, less shy.

Poppy didn't have time to think why this might be: her left arm was trembling out of control. Using her shoulder, she pushed against the centre of the wooden door while twisting the handle.

The room they entered was long and narrow with a low ceiling, and looked to have been built into the rocks beneath the Mills. The poisonous scent of acetone was thick in the air. A fumes hood hung on the wall to the left. From where Poppy, Mitsy and Churchill stood, each wall seemed to have its own dedicated purpose. On the left were shelves of narrow drawers with round knobs. One of the open drawers held white sachets, neatly organized with what seemed to be names and dates written on them. Below the drawers were benches piled with an assortment of long-necked conical flasks, spouted beakers and distillation equipment.

Built into the wall opposite was a long white workbench. A glass magnetic stirrer, like the one Miss Nnamani had in the school laboratory, was hard at work in the corner, stirring a batch of something that looked like red, human hair. Behind the other vials and pipettes was a wall decorated with thousands of tiny bottles filled with bright liquids that had been meticulously sorted into colours, like a musty rainbow stretching from one end of the room to the other. Stacked in the corner was a pile of wooden frames in a variety of faded colours.

There was no sign of Erasmus. But there was someone else in the room. The furthest wall housed what looked like a bulky typewriter to one side, and a glass display case to the other, featuring yellow typewriter ribbons pinned like preserved insects. And standing in front of it, with her back to Poppy, was a woman. She was dressed like a teacher, in a baggy pencil skirt, blouse and mustard cardigan. Mitsy, who was now holding

Churchill, backed herself onto a stool. Churchill gave a frightened wave of his trotters and wriggled free, scampering manically over to Poppy. Poppy picked him up and scratched behind his ears.

At that point, the woman turned, and Poppy felt a stabbing pain that started in her stomach and rose quickly to her throat.

"Mum?"

Mum smiled, and combed back her hair with her fingers. Poppy put Churchill down and let her backpack slip off her shoulders.

Mum kneeled down and opened her arms.

"Come to me, Poppy."

Poppy's throat was dry, and her words came out in a breathless choke: "How are you here?"

Mum frowned. "I've always been here, Poppy," she said. "You said so yourself. You still hear my heart even after all this time. You hear it on your pillow when you fall asleep. You hear it when you think. You hear it when you hold your breath."

"You're dead," said Poppy.

"Do I look dead to you, Poppy? Come over here," said Mum.

She was beautiful, and at that moment Poppy realized she'd forgotten a little of what Mum had really looked like.

"Don't be frightened, pet," said Mum. "It's over now."

"Am I dead?" asked Poppy.

"No, pet," said Mum. "You're just worrying too much. You always worried too much. You're just like me, aren't you?"

Poppy wanted to do something drastic. Like hit herself on the head with a nice big stick. Her vision felt dizzy and confused.

Mum smiled.

So did Poppy.

"Remember when we used to hold our breath going through tunnels in London?" asked Poppy.

Mum laughed. "Yes!"

"And we'd count who could hold their breath the longest?" said Poppy.

"Dad was always rubbish at that," said Mum.

"Do you remember that day on the beach in Cornwall when Dad found the jellyfish?" asked Poppy.

"I try to forget," said Mum, grimacing.

"And I lost my dinosaur on the beach, in the sand, and we never did find it," said Poppy.

"How *could* I forget?" laughed Mum. "Come here, my heart."

Poppy walked slowly forwards, stopping a few feet away from Mum.

Mum reached out to her.

"Go see your mother, Poppy," said Mitsy.

Poppy stared hard at Mitsy. Mitsy was grinning from ear to ear. She turned back to Mum.

"Why can't I hear your heart?" Poppy said slowly.

"Come here, Poppy."

"But I can always hear your heart."

Poppy lashed out and gripped Mum by the nose. The silk mask peeled away almost instantly, in a sickening slump of skin and hair.

"Dalia!" Poppy gasped.

"Perhaps," said Dalia, and pulled at her own nose. Her shoulders seemed to rise up out of her neck, and human Marley's great mossy beard spilled out over her chest.

"Marley?" Poppy croaked.

Marley's great big fingers pulled at his nose once more and the shoulders crumbled even lower than they were before. In a sweep, the silk slid to the ground and Eliza Crink from the fabric shop stood before Poppy.

She pulled at her nose one last time with her forefinger and thumb, the thimble still covering her stump. This time the silk just lifted a little from her face, but didn't come away.

"Dear pretty thing," said Eliza, taking a step towards Poppy. "This last face," she said, touching her cheek, "is stitched on. If I showed you what was under here, your nightmares would be filled for a lifetime. Shame you won't have one of those."

"You-you're one of the Peggs?" Poppy whispered, her throat desert-like.

"One of them, yes." Eliza sighed, but Poppy felt

someone else's breath on the back of her neck. She swivelled around.

Mitsy was still grinning from ear to ear. She already had her fingers clasped around her nose, and as she pulled at the skin of silk, her body seemed to swell and her neck elongated. Poppy recognized the dark liquorice-coloured hair almost immediately.

"Bon—" she began.

"Bonhilda Bonhoeffer, confectioner and purveyor of anything with a sweet disposition," Miss Bonhoeffer finished off.

"What have you done to Mitsy?" Poppy asked.

"Just combed a little colour from her, is all," said Eliza, pulling the bone comb from her sleeve and waving it in front of Poppy. "Remember this?"

"I don't understand," Poppy said, backing towards the workbench. She wanted to be facing both of them.

"It's simple," said Eliza. "We can be anyone we wish. Provided we comb their colour, I can weave a silk so lifelike, it would fool a customs officer. It fooled you, didn't it?"

Poppy felt an itchy surge spreading from the spot on her head. Marley had the same spot on the back of his head. Her head ticked. That was how they'd managed it.

"You pretended to be Marley," Poppy realized. "Bonhilda filmed *you* robbing her store!"

"Clever kitten!" said Bonhilda, stepping over to the

bench full of distillation equipment and examining a clipboard.

"Why?"

"You don't need to know that!" snapped Bonhilda, her mood shifting suddenly.

"Oh, her head will be empty soon," Eliza snorted. "What does it matter what we tell her? I pretended to be Marley because we needed to stop him dipping his finger in our plan," said Eliza. "He was giving away too much and, what's more, he stole the last of our riddling silk. Those other two didn't care much about it, but when you came along, it was decided that we needed that silk back, or at least to be in your hands, so we could keep a tab on you...for when the moment came. Riddling silk is the most intelligent silk I've ever made – the colour was combed from the green feathers of a homing pigeon's neck, to give it a tracking ability."

Eliza pulled a square of tatty green silk from her pocket, and Poppy recognized it immediately – the last time she'd seen it had been when Mitsy unearthed the book on the chalk island before being snatched away. Eliza must have peeled it off the book. Bringing the raggedy fabric to her nose, the creature breathed deeply.

"It's come back to me," she whispered feverishly. "The last of my riddling silk. We shan't be parted again. I never wanted to let you go in the first place."

She suddenly became herself again. "Behind bars was an ideal place to keep Marley. It would be a shame to kill him. We haven't had any orders for a rough, mossy fabric in years – but when we do, his colour will be perfect."

"That's disgusting," said Poppy.

"Did you ever wonder," asked Bonhilda, sliding the piece of silk with Mitsy's face into a frame, "why Dalia Terce, the laziest creature this side of the equator, suddenly took up spring-cleaning?"

"It was you," Poppy whispered. "You disguised yourself as Dalia and wiped the window sills in my room!"

Bonhilda held up the piece of silk with Dalia's face, and peeked out from one side. "Guilty!" She grinned. "Oh don't worry. It didn't do her any harm. Stealing just a drop of colour from an adult never does. We only put them to sleep with some woad powder for a few hours. When we drain children, it's an entirely different matter. The real Dalia knew that your grandmother would never wipe the cobwebs off the window sills, so we had to intervene."

"Cobwebs are dream-resistant," Eliza explained. "Cobwebs have the ability to catch dreams like flies. Your grandmother is a wise woman to keep spiders on her window sills. A child can easily be identified by which dreams slip from their windows. They're like fingerprints to the well-trained ear."

"So if *those* are not really your faces," Poppy asked, half-dreading the answer to her question, "whose are they?"

"It was all very opportune really, wasn't it, Whippy?" Bonhilda said to Eliza.

"They sailed straight to us, Huck!" Eliza agreed, then turned to Poppy.

"The three German women," Poppy realized. "The ones who died on the river. Ada, Hulda and Gerda. I read their obituary." *That was why Erasmus had the newspaper clipping about them that Mitsy had slipped into her fairy-tale book*, Poppy thought. *He'd suspected a connection.*

Eliza grinned. "They took their yacht a little too far down the river. When a storm blew in, they were capsized and came wandering into the Mills, looking for help."

"We each chose one of them," Bonhilda continued. "Knocked them off, wove silk masks from their skins, and Bonhilda, Eliza and Hetty were born."

"That was when we had the brilliant idea to close the Mills, send away our employees and go out into the town ourselves," Eliza picked up. "And open our own establishments to pursue our personal interests: a sweet shop, a bookshop and a fabric store."

"A bookshop?" asked Poppy.

"Oh!" Bonhilda exclaimed apologetically. "How stupid of us!"

"We should have introduced you," said Eliza.

"Poppy Slub," said Bonhilda, gesturing with her hand towards the corner behind her where Churchill had fallen asleep. "Meet our third sister, Miss Lye Pegg."

They grinned.

"There's no one else here," said Poppy.

Bonhilda shrieked with laughter. Using the bench to support the weight of her stout body, she leaned down and pinched at Churchill's skin – and like chewing gum the pig's flesh peeled away. The shape beneath leaped to its feet and curtsied.

Bonhilda and Eliza whooped and clapped.

"Mrs Hetty Gwynne?" Poppy rasped, her eyes widening to the size of eggs. "But you're the chairwoman of the Musical Society? You run the bookshop! Y-you were at our school for choir practice…"

"Selecting the finest minds with which to write my next book," said Hetty. "That was the day I found your friend."

"Erasmus?"

"Just so," said Hetty, fumbling in her pocket and producing her hearing trumpet. She pushed a pair of fingers inside the fanned end and made a twist as if she was unscrewing a light bulb. There was a click, and she produced a barnacled conch shell.

"The Norse sorcerer gave you that," said Poppy.

"And through it," said Hetty, "I listen to dreams. People thought your friend Erasmus was vacant and robotic. But if you could hear what I heard that day at the school, you would never stop listening. Every other child in the room sounded like a cacophony of lawnmowers and drowning cows compared to him. His head sings the song of stars and planets. Compared to him, every other child in the room sounded like sawdust and wet wool. I realized then that, using him, I could weave a story which would be so successful, whoever read it could never put it down."

"And that's what you did when you sucked the prince's dreams and thoughts from his head?" asked Poppy. "You made a book?"

"Exactly." Hetty sighed. "Your friend's was the most delicious mind I've discovered in a long time. I didn't expect such a cracking find when I was coming after you."

Poppy's lip trembled.

"Did you ever hear about Andrew Booker?" asked Hetty.

"He was the pianist," Poppy remembered. "The boy who liked running, the one who vanished from his bedroom."

"As you say," said Hetty. "Did you ever happen to read *Into Thin Air*, the novel by Brooke Warden? I sold it in my shop."

Poppy had seen the novel with Erasmus in the bookshop window. The one about the boy who could sprint lightning-quick.

"Not really my sort of literature," Poppy said, sounding braver than she felt. "I'm more of an Agatha Christie girl."

"Pity," sighed Hetty. "It was a solid read. How about *Bug Eyes* by Dewy Sponck?"

Perhaps some of Erasmus's constant cog-turning had rubbed off on her, or perhaps she'd just become shrewder.

"The author names are anagrams," Poppy said suddenly, ticking over the letters in her head. "Brooke Warden becomes Andrew Booker."

The three Peggs shrieked with joy.

"Th-the same as Dewy Sponck and Wendy Pocks," Poppy stammered in disbelief.

"Top marks!" Bonhilda congratulated her.

"A little joke of ours!" Eliza admitted.

"I couldn't *resist* signing my work!" Hetty told her.

"That clever little beetle Wendy Pocks managed to escape because she befriended our moths," Eliza snarled, flicking one of the insects nearby.

"I will say, however," Bonhilda noted thoughtfully, "neither Wendy Pocks nor Andrew Booker had much for me in terms of flavour."

"Aye," Eliza agreed.

"Andrew's flavour had a sort of mintiness about it, an indecision as to whether its key was major or minor, fruity or mentholic."

"He turned out an elegant, inky black silk," Eliza told them. "Nothing too special, but plenty of spring in it."

"That will be on account of all the running," Hetty explained, and the other two nodded.

"A few days after we got him," Eliza went on,

chuckling, "when the boy's mother, Alice Booker, came to the shop looking for a nice piece of black silk to drape over the empty coffin at Andrew's memorial service, I sold her two yards-worth of the same black silk! It still tickles me to think that they'd spent day and night looking for that boy, and yet days before I'd combed every drop of colour out of him, and dyed a hundred yards of silk with it. And now there that silk was, decorating his own coffin."

"Sugar," Poppy said suddenly.

"What was that, dear pretty thing?" asked Eliza.

"Sugar cubes," Poppy said, and the three of them flinched.

"Now why would you say something like that?" said Bonhilda, clenching her fist.

"Why do the people in Suds hide their sugar cubes?"

Bonhilda opened her mouth to say something, but Hetty leaned across and slapped her on the chin.

"Not a word," she said sternly, pointing her finger at Bonhilda and then Eliza. "Not a peep."

They hung their heads glumly. Poppy didn't like the moment of silence. She kept scanning the room as if expecting to catch sight of Erasmus, Mitsy or Churchill. What sort of state would she find them in? Would Eliza have combed them already?

"Where are my friends?" Poppy asked.

"Sleeping," said Hetty.

"And Churchill?"

"Is that the pig?" asked Bonhilda.

Poppy nodded.

"Sleeping," said Hetty.

Poppy lifted her backpack onto her shoulders again and felt for the scissors in her pocket. She didn't have a plan. From now until the end, whatever that would be, was going to be improvised.

Sugar, she thought, and the word ran through her head over and over and over, *Why do they want Claria's sugar cube?*

Her heart thumped electrically. In her pocket, she flicked open the scissors and let her fingers run across the pair of steel blades.

Then she brandished them, slicing open her pocket as she did so.

"Show me where they are," Poppy insisted, pointing her scissors at the three women and moving them from sister to sister. "Show me my friends."

Eliza threw her hands in the air and her thimble glinted in the dim light.

"All you had to do was ask," she scolded. "There's no need to spoil everything and flash those around. Follow us."

The Peggs harrumphed and filed out of the room one by one. Poppy suspected a trick. In fact, she *knew* there was a trick. But she needed to find Erasmus and Mitsy, and she wasn't going to do that by going back the way she came.

She kept the blades outstretched and edged towards the door the sisters had vanished though.

A pale green glow filled the domed chamber beyond. Pieces of turquoise silk were hung over lamps that lined the circular walls. In the centre of the room was a large round stone table, divided into sections like a pie by a series of shallow dips. On the table, filling a trio of the dips, were three bodies, each covered with a white sheet. A swarm of fat moths crawled lazily over the three bodies like ants on a neglected sandwich.

Along the edge of the stone table were urns filled with glistening blue powder, some of which spilled onto the exposed feet of the bodies. Beyond the table, tied down with enormous iron weights, was the Peggs's hamper. The sail sheet above it hung raggedly, as if at any moment it would fill with air and take to the skies.

Eliza skipped across the chamber and folded back the white sheets one by one. Poppy saw Churchill first. His trotters pointed upwards, and one of his ears had faded to white, from where the Peggs had combed his colour. The white spot on the back of her own head began to itch angrily.

Next was Mitsy. A streak of her hair had been bleached grey, and brown spots had formed around her mouth. Neither of them looked as if they were breathing. Their eyes were closed, and had been sprinkled with blue woad powder.

When the last sheet was folded neatly down, Erasmus

slipped into view. His body was frozen still, and his hair was white, as always. Unlike the other two, his eyes were open and seemed the same as usual – still wide, green and powerful.

Around each of their big toes or trotters was a paper tag, tied with string.

"We won't be able to use any of his flavour, or draw anything from his mind," Hetty reminded her two sisters, nodding towards Churchill. "Only a child's mind is worthy and elastic enough to be drawn out and massaged into words."

"Anything aged more than thirteen years tastes of moth eggs and dust," Bonhilda added.

"Churchill's only five," said Poppy.

"Pig years," explained Bonhilda, lifting the tag wrapped around Mitsy's toe to read:

"Clingy tannins. Custard and lemon notes, unwaveringly faithful colour hold. Gentle, buttery and affectionate swab of textures, coupled with a brave/ imaginative punch of rum."

Eliza had picked up Churchill's tag, and continued. As Eliza spoke, Hetty spooned some blue woad powder into her hearing trumpet.

"Dream patterns too bizarre for practical use, dull overtones creating an exhausted, flabby flavour symptomatic of domestication and being over-loved."

Hetty was beaming as she held up Erasmus's tag:

"Stubborn resistance to stretch, opening with

313

aggressive attacks to the tongue, humming with a sweetness known only to bees, peppered with the fire of stars, moulded by the wisdom of an ancient library, twisted with the cunning of snakes and the loneliness of the crippled swallow."

Hetty looked up at Poppy, smiling eerily. "I've been looking forward to writing yours for a long time, Miss Slub."

With a quick puff, Hetty blew hard through her hearing trumpet, and the last thing Poppy remembered before she closed her eyes was a cloud of glistening blue, sailing towards her.

Twenty-one
WOAD

Eliza and Bonhilda had wrapped Poppy's body in a white sheet and laid it out beside Erasmus. The white sheet was for Eliza's purposes, as she'd always said it gave her an objective canvas on which to assess their victim's true colour.

Mrs Hetty Gwynne was in the adjoining chamber, preparing a yellow ribbon for her hulking typewriter.

Bonhilda and Eliza emptied the contents of Poppy's backpack into one of the piece-of-pie-shaped dips on the circular table. They sorted through them excitedly.

"More muesli bars than is good for you," Bonhilda noted.

"And an apple," Eliza said, holding it up.

Bonhilda shook her head. "It's unnatural for a child to have an apple in their backpack. I don't like it one bit."

"*And* a rock," Eliza reminded her, pointing to the knobbly stone they'd found amongst Poppy's things.

"I used to collect rocks as a child," Bonhilda remembered fondly. "Do you remember? Clambering across the pebbles, the chalky cliffs on one side and the Channel on the other."

"Sister!" Eliza gasped, pointing a trembling finger at Erasmus's body. His hand had begun twitching, a sure sign that he was waking from the deep, dreamless sleep the woad powder induced.

"Oh, keep your hat on!" Bonhilda snorted, and seized an urn of powder. Moving along the bodies, she chucked handfuls of the woad powder over each of their faces, like a baker scattering flour over a worktop.

Eliza breathed a sigh of relief and went back to fishing through Poppy's belongings.

"Contact lenses, sister!" she exclaimed, holding up the box for Bonhilda to see.

"What about them?" asked Bonhilda.

"Weren't you just saying the other day how expensive your contact lenses are?"

"Yes, but they're custom-made," said Bonhilda dismissively. "I have to get them specially made, on account of my pointy eyes. Ah, well – waste not, want not."

She pocketed the contact lenses and went back to her preparations. "Shame there isn't something nice amongst those things for you, Eliza," she snorted. "Like a plastic finger for your stump."

Eliza paused and gave Poppy's body a wary look as she twisted the thimble on what remained of her knuckle.

"It was her mother that cut off my finger," she said darkly. "Do you remember?"

"How could I forget?" said Bonhilda. "Closest we ever got to catching her when she was trying to sniff us out and expose us. If I recall correctly, she bit it off, didn't she?"

"Little snake!" hissed Eliza. "She robbed me of a great deal of magic that day. That viper pilfered my comb too. And kept it and hid it for years! Thank the stars I had already learned to use my fingers to comb colours. But my fingers were never as powerful as the comb, especially after that little *swine* stole one of them. I vowed to get her back for it, and didn't we ever? A truckload of laundry hampers a few years later, and she was wiped out. Shame we couldn't knock off her husband as well, it would have been so much neater. I hate frayed ends. He was in the car too, you know? Walked away from the accident without a scratch."

Bonhilda raised her eyebrows with interest.

"The things my customers tell me, Bonny!"

"What happened to her after she left Suds, anyway?" asked Bonhilda. "Before we found her and finished her off, I mean."

"She made herself grow up very quickly, I imagine," Eliza told her. "Probably thinking that the faster she grew up, the less likely we'd be able to find her. But we did. All because of her mother's big mouth."

"She came into the fabric shop, didn't she?" remembered Bonhilda. "Telling you that she wanted to make a dress for her daughter?"

"Aye." Eliza grinned. "And I sold her a bolt of finest green riddling silk. From the moment her daughter put that dress on, her fate was woven. Best idea I've ever had, making that riddling silk. Never failed us once. Calls to us wherever it is."

"Are we ready yet?" asked Hetty Gwynne as she wheeled in her typewriter on a small trolley.

"I think so." Eliza breathed raggedly.

"Comb?" asked Hetty.

"Check!" Eliza replied, holding up her bone comb and kissing it.

"Spoon?"

"Present!" Bonhilda chimed, trying to hang the spoon off the end of her nose.

"And conch!" Hetty smiled proudly, tapping the conch shell on her trolley. "We've had our fun, now it's time to harvest the rest of the colour, flavour and dreams from this batch. Let's get down to it. Eliza, put on some music."

Eliza flicked a switch on a radio on a shelf and tuned in until she found a favourable frequency. An ethereal voice crackled across the airwaves and Bonhilda threw her hands skyward to shimmy across the floor.

"I love this one!" Hetty hissed with glee.

"Voice like a siren," Bonhilda agreed.

Eliza busied herself with a spritzer bottle, coating Mitsy's hair in a pungent chlorine solution until it hung dark and lank around her pale face. She readied a bath of acetone beside the girl's head, and fetched a fresh bolt of gleaming white silk from the cellars. There were many strange ways she used to dye and texture her fabric, but this was by far her favourite.

The bolt of silk was loaded onto a mangle with a spinning handle, so that it would pass through the bath and pick up the colour evenly. Then, taking her comb, Eliza raked its teeth through the girl's hair. When she had finished she dipped the tip of the comb into the acetone bath, and from it issued a ribbon of brilliant chestnut brown, the same colour as Mitsy's hair. The dye twisted through the acetone before rising to the surface and settling.

Eliza decided she liked the chestnut brown colour, and ran the bolt of cloth through the bath for seven or eight metres.

Hetty was working on Erasmus. The trouble with her conch was that it only coaxed dreams out of a child's head, but once they were out in the open it was difficult to know what to do with them. That was why she'd devised the typewriter.

Taking the loose end of the yellow ribbon, she stuffed it into Erasmus's right ear. Moving around to his opposite side, she took her conch shell and fitted the spout into his left ear. Hetty's finger began to glow as she inhaled.

There was a glimmer of a thousand different colours as dreams flooded into the conch shell, like angry little fish. She'd had dreams nip her on the finger before. This was why people's eyes moved so rapidly when they were in a dreaming state.

Common folk were under the false impression that dreams must look like pleasant little clouds – soft, warm and comforting. No, no, no. Dreams were vicious. They liked the dark, cosy cavity of a person's head and hated being drawn out into the light, which was where the typewriter ribbon came in. Like a sleepy tapeworm, the yellow ribbon poked out of Erasmus's other ear and Hetty caught it between her forefinger and thumb. She stretched it out and threaded the ribbon through the typewriter. Once it was loaded with paper, this bus practically drove itself.

There was a click as the typewriter keys began to tap and whirr, and the stories that had been squeezed from Erasmus's head filled the page as his green eyes faded to silver.

Bonhilda wasn't as industrious as the others. She didn't quite know where to start. She'd had one or two solid successes recently with her products. The dainty jasmine flavours she'd spooned from Wendy Pocks had gone into her upmarket range of dandelion flapjacks.

They were even selling them at Robespierre's, the posh deli in town. And then there was Andrew Booker, who'd produced a salt liquorice so moreish and rich it was sure to rot your teeth off in a single sitting. They'd snatched it off the shelves in Scandinavia. But this time she wanted to up her game, to concoct something sweet or syrupy that would make the masses fight tooth and nail.

She stared down at Poppy's limp body. Taking sweetness from a child's heart was easier said than done. The spoon, it turned out, wasn't exactly an elegant tool. It was a bit like separating an egg yolk from the whites using the eggshell itself. All going well, she would push the spoon firmly onto the point where she estimated the child's heart to be, and the scoop would fill slowly with a sweet-smelling syrup. The really unpleasant part was when you had to pour the syrup into a drying trunk, which was a large rectangular object with brass latches and two openings at either end for screwing in the pipes which the heat passed through. While the syrup was being dried into recipe-friendly granules, it made a ferocious noise and the drying trunk had been known to shake violently.

As Bonhilda remembered, Poppy was a brave young woman. There was a fear in her, yes, but there could never truly be bravery without fear. Perhaps her heart would render a bold flavour with plenty of punch, coupled with a souring aftertaste. That could work. Yes, she thought, it just might.

"What the Pegg is going on with this blasted machine?" Hetty snapped suddenly, slamming her fist against the typewriter.

"What is it, sister?" asked Bonhilda, dropping her spoon.

"It's not working! It's only typing out one word!" shrieked Hetty. "Come see for yourselves!"

Eliza and Bonhilda leaned over her shoulder, and read what the typewriter had written:

```
POPPY, POPPY, POPPY, POPPY,
POPPY, POPPY, POPPY, POPPY,
POPPY, POPPY, POPPY, POPPY,
POPPY, POPPY, POPPY, POPPY,
POPPY, POPPY, POPPY, POPPY,
POPPY, POPPY, POPPY, POPPY,
POPPY, POPPY, POPPY, POPPY,
POPPY, POPPY, POPPY, POPPY,
POPPY, POPPY, POPPY, POPPY,
POPPY, POPPY, POPPY, POPPY
```

"He's fighting it!" Hetty shrieked. "He's fighting the magic!"

"Give it time, Hetty," Bonhilda comforted her. "He can't fight for ever. Put your feet up while you're waiting, have a drink."

"It's that damned conch!" Hetty fumed, withdrawing

322

to an armchair beside the hamper. "I can't draw dreams like I used to. They're becoming more petulant by the minute."

Bonhilda rolled her eyes and lowered her spoon to Poppy's chest. She hadn't made Electric Sherbet in years. Perhaps she'd do a batch of that.

She tensed her arm to press the spoon and stopped.

Something had changed.

Something had been stirred.

Her stumpy foot brushed something on the floor, and she stooped to pick it up. It was a strange article: a circular piece of silk, an older example of their work, if she was any judge. But what was it doing here? It was dyed to resemble rock, and was very convincing, she had to admit. But she wouldn't bring it to the attention of her sisters. Oh, no.

Hetty would praise Eliza to the skies. Bonhilda was *bored* of Hetty. Why was it that the first place they bought was the Mills and not a charming sweet factory in Copenhagen? Hetty. Hetty had said so, and therefore it *was* so. Eliza and Hetty enjoyed discussing their work in great detail. Eliza was the youngest sister after Claria, and Hetty, being the eldest, always enjoyed pleasing her little sister. Bonhilda was just the piggy in the middle.

Bonhilda rolled up her sleeves and pressed the spoon onto Poppy's chest. She'd show them – she'd devise an Electric Sherbet so zappy it could run a light bulb for a year. She steadied her hand. The spoon twitched. She frowned. The spoon was leaping up and down now, hopping like a frog on a lily pad, faster and faster.

The next thing Bonhilda saw was a blinding flash, and a red-hot stab surged through her body at high voltage. With a gasp, she was thrown across the room like a bowling pin, colliding with a standing lamp.

In an instant, Poppy was up, Mum's wooden peg clipped to her finger; in the other hand the tailor's chalk. They'd been wrapped in the circular piece of silk which had lain beside her, fooling the sisters into thinking it was just a rock.

Hetty and Eliza swivelled around on the spot, their eyes wide.

Poppy snatched the comb from where Eliza had left it and pushed it into her pocket, along with her chalk.

"How did you evade the woad powder?" Hetty asked calmly.

"Contact lenses," Poppy told them. "I made sure to bring some of Dalia's with me. They're not a very strong prescription."

"Clever, clever, clever!" Hetty beamed.

There was a moment before Eliza realized what was going on. She looked from her own hand to the peg clipped on Poppy's.

"That's *my* finger!" she shrieked. "The little worm has my finger!"

"I didn't realize it at first," Poppy said, pointing the

clothes peg around the room like it was a pistol. "I even managed to blow up a rat with it."

"Who told you what it really was?" Hetty asked, with genuine interest.

"Claria," said Poppy proudly.

"She's lying!" screeched Eliza, but Hetty stopped her.

"You're making the same mistake your mother did." Hetty grinned. "She thought she could stop us, but how wrong she was. We found her, and we put an end to her. We squashed her like a beetle. But you still hear her heart, don't you, child? You hear it when you sleep, you hear it when you dream, you hear it when you wake."

Poppy tried to close her ears to the old creature's foul words. She held her breath, daring herself not to hear the insistent thumps of her heart. Of her mother's heart.

There was a moan from the corner as Bonhilda stumbled to her feet, smouldering. Across her face was a singed tear in the silk from where Poppy had zapped her with the finger, and through it peered a drilling eye, as blue as woad powder. Bonhilda cackled and, poking her finger through the slit, she tore the silk away.

As the material slumped to the ground, Bonhilda's real identity came swooping into view. Her head was warty and bald, save for a collection of randomly distributed curls across her dry scalp. Her teeth were long and furrowed, set inside a crumpled mouth. Poppy felt sick when she saw the hands, so wizened and desiccated they'd become like wood. Each finger was split at the ends, like a clothes peg, giving the impression that Bonhilda had twenty fingers instead of ten.

She gave a low squawk of laughter and began to approach Poppy with her drilling eyes and wiggling fingers. Her voice had changed. It was ancient and dry, like a burp and being punched in the stomach all at once.

"I'm going to eat your heart," Bonhilda smirked.

"I'll kill you first," Poppy whispered, biting her lip. There was no fear inside her. Only anger. It rammed itself into every cell of her body, squeezing out everything but a deep, suffocating hurt which coursed through her veins, humming furiously.

"Oh!" fumed Bonhilda. "You're a spiky little hedgehog, aren't you?"

"Play nicely, sister." Hetty tutted, then she turned to Poppy. "And how does Miss Poppy Slub propose she'll kill us? She only has one finger's worth of magic, and we are brimming to our baldy heads with the stuff."

Poppy hadn't thought about that. Her thoughts had been squeezed out too and replaced with nothing but a red hatred.

"Stop the typewriter," she said firmly, nodding towards Eliza, "and I'll give you back your finger."

Eliza leaped eagerly towards the typewriter.

"No!" bellowed Hetty, causing Eliza to come skidding back.

Hetty put her hands behind her head and began to unpick the stitching beneath her hair. Eliza followed suit. Their silk folded away and their forked fingers and penetrating eyes slid into view.

Poppy was surrounded.

Working as quickly as she could, she fumbled for the tailor's chalk in her pocket and drew a circle around herself.

"*Very* clever," Hetty admitted. "But you can't stay in there for ever."

She approached the typewriter and wound the knob on the side. With a clunk, the machine began to work faster, pulling the ribbon taut.

Poppy pointed the peg-finger at the machine and pushed from her chest, like she'd done before. The finger glowed like a coal for a moment, and then extinguished.

"You need a little more oomph than that to use magic," Hetty sniggered. "You can watch from there, trapped, as we extract the final components from your friends."

Poppy felt for the chalk in her pocket again. She must have clenched her fists at some point, because it was ground to a crumbly powder.

"Eliza," Hetty ordered, "open the hatch, we're going out tonight. I've been collecting some samples over in North Riddling that will blend perfectly with this batch."

Eliza obeyed, scampering over to a lever, which she lowered with effort.

There was a clanking of cogs above them, and part of the domed ceiling over the hamper glided away, opening the roof like an observatory.

"Ah!" Hetty sighed happily. "The night sky always makes for better magic."

She pointed to the typewriter. It had begun to type different words now. Erasmus's mind had given in. His head was slowly being drained.

Poppy's heart began to sink again. She could feel the anger starting to fray at the edges. Worry criss-crossed her brow and feathered through her fingers. She was trapped, but worst of all, she'd trapped herself. A chalk circle was a stupid choice, she thought to herself, and it was a blessing that Erasmus wasn't awake to see it. He would have given her ten geometric reasons why a circle was the worst choice of all.

Hetty found some spectacles on a nearby shelf and, pulling up her chair at the typewriter, she began to read.

"If I could pass on some advice to my dear Mr Buttocks in this time of trial, it would be this. Remember that even though the foxes blow their own trumpets and have many tricks, the lowly hedgehog has but one and that is the best of all."

Hetty frowned.

"What does it mean?" Eliza asked Hetty, stroking Mitsy's hair.

Hetty spun around like a great spider, clicking her forked fingers.

Poppy was holding the hearing trumpet.

She loaded the dusty, crumbled chalk from her pocket into the trumpet like a musket.

She breathed deeply, holding her breath in every recess of her chest as she did so, counting.

1, 2, 3, 4, 5, 6, 7, 8, 9, 10.

"It means you picked a fight with the wrong hedgehog," whispered Poppy.

With one short, foul puff, she blew, sending whorls of chalk dust billowing into the air.

Like mist descending on a lonely valley, the chalk gathered over the Peggs's warts and grooves. It caked their forked fingers, and nested in their patchy curls. Their tortured faces rearranged themselves. There was a hissing sound like cold water meeting a hot saucepan, and the Peggs were flung to either side of the room, as if stunned by an electric current.

Poppy didn't know how much time she had before the Peggs would begin to stir, but she jumped into action. As she expected, Mitsy was easier to move than Erasmus. Her breathing quickened as she hauled each of their floppy bodies off the table and into a pile beside the door. She had to work quickly.

Heaving an urn of blue woad powder from the edge of the table, she carefully sprinkled a handful into each of the sisters' eyes. Taking the Tupperware container from her chest pocket, she carefully prised it open and removed the still-glowing sugar cube.

The fairy-tale book had said a grain would suffice, so she scratched off a bit with her fingernail. She grimaced as she slid her finger under Erasmus's tongue. Without fumbling, she did the same for Mitsy and Churchill.

Then she waited.

Erasmus's eyes were still open. Poppy stared down at his cold, greyish skin.

"Come back, you stupid hedgehog," Poppy whispered under her breath.

"Mr Buttocks," came a faint rasp. She noticed a drip of colour in his eye, like a puddle of water expanding. Poppy's heart was thundering. But not a worried, sickening thundering: a brave, triumphant, fist-thumping thundering. Erasmus heaved himself up to a sitting position.

Mitsy stirred too and then coughed. Soon both of them were coughing and a cloud of recycled blue dust filled the air. Churchill took a little longer to stir, but soon he was wobbling about the room and sniffing at its contents.

Poppy collapsed onto both her friends and pulled them towards her.

"What are we going to do about them?" Erasmus asked, nodding towards the sleeping Peggs.

Poppy deliberately ignored him and turned to the

little girl. "I owe you an apology, Mitsy. We both do."

Erasmus frowned and so did Mitsy.

"Your fairy-tale book *did* have the answers we needed," she said, smiling.

There was a rotten-looking boat moored beside the river, with a puddle of rainwater gathered inside. Mitsy struggled under the weight of the last urn of blue powder, until she finally managed to plonk it at the water's edge. Erasmus had showed them a set of slippery stone steps that led from the bottom of the Mills down to this small dark cove where the river lapped at a muddy shore. Then he and Poppy had wrapped the sleeping creatures in long strips of their own silk, and hauled them down the slimy steps one by one. When the boat was filled with the three bundles, Poppy and Erasmus began to tip the urns of blue powder on top of them. Erasmus wore the purple goggles from Poppy's backpack to stop the powder from getting in his eyes. Mitsy stood at a distance, arms wrapped around the now silkless silk book. She'd found it tossed into a bin back in the workshop.

They emptied every last urn, until a blue powder pyramid shimmered in the fading moonlight. Poppy topped it off by grinding one of Mum's last pieces of chalk over the whole arrangement. There was no ceremony about it. Poppy unhooked the rope from the mooring post and kicked the boat out onto the river with her foot.

She dragged her muddy shoes up the steps to where Erasmus and Mitsy stood and the three of them watched as the current caught their consignment. From where they stood, Poppy could see Churchill was down the bottom of the steps still busy glorying in the muddy shoreline. When she looked up again, the boat had picked up pace and had began to rock to and fro as it made its way out to the middle of the swollen rapids. It gave one last giddy spin between the waves, raised itself up to the verge of tipping and, in a puff of glistening blue, vanished around the river bend, heading seaward.

Poppy's rusty hair danced across her face in the early morning breeze. Despite everything that had happened, despite all that she'd seen, she found herself thinking of her mum. Mum had been watching out for her, even after all this time, even though she wasn't here. And there was something new and promising in the air that Poppy never expected to be there. Running her fingers down her mud-flecked dress, she felt for Mum's wooden peg in her pocket to make sure she still had it. To make sure it was still there.

Shivering, she slid her backpack off and unbuckled it. Erasmus placed the comb, the spoon and the conch shell inside. Mitsy joined them, kneeling in the mud, as they gathered handfuls of small stones and packed them between the other items. Once the straps were secured around the backpack it formed a tight package.

Erasmus and Poppy shoved away the iron weights with their feet, and Mitsy and Churchill stowed themselves in the wicker hamper. The great dome above them had already been slid back to reveal the starry sky. Clambering aboard, they arranged themselves to distribute the weight evenly.

"How do we operate this thing?" Poppy wondered out loud, but she needn't have. Erasmus confessed he'd watched the Peggs on his journey to the Mills after they'd caught him on the Suds River, and remembered it all very clearly.

Once the hamper had creaked to life, and slipped out from the ceiling, Erasmus steered them over the river and tied off the sail. He lifted the bundle containing the conch shell, the spoon and the comb and placed it in Mitsy's muddy hands.

"You do it, Mitsy," he said, "you deserve to do it."

Mitsy gathered both of her tiny arms around the bundle and heaving it to the edge of the hamper, leaned out as far as she dared over the edge. Her eyes suddenly narrowed, and with a strength neither Erasmus nor Poppy knew she had, the little girl hurled the backpack out across the water. It soared for a split second before plummeting and with a *thwunk*, it slipped between the waves and sunk to the murky depths of the paint-water river.

Erasmus opened the sail, and before long, the hamper was lifted high above the crumbling Mills, and the four

of them watched as the cold sun began to open its great eyelid over the Suds River. Mitsy rested her head on Erasmus's shoulder and closed her eyes.

Twenty-two
DRAWING
TO A CLOSE

At first there was a scrape, then the tittering sound of twigs scraping the bottom of the hamper. Erasmus pulled the sail in and the great contraption skidded into a ropey landing, narrowly missing Gran's chimney.

When the hamper met the clothes line, Mitsy, Poppy, Erasmus and Churchill spilled out onto the early morning dew.

After extricating themselves from beneath the heavy sail they worked speedily, hauling the sheet in and stowing it in the hamper in the corner of the garden. Poppy re-erected the clothes line.

The real Dalia was nowhere to be seen. She was most probably still in bed, with her eye-mask skewed across her face.

Darting upstairs to her room, Poppy dropped

Marley's book on her bed, fetched her wallet and coat and emptied her pockets into her chest of drawers. Back downstairs she snatched a jar from underneath the sink and took it into the laundry. She scrunched up some tissue and wet it under the tap before rolling it into a little ball and popping it in the jar. Stabbing the jar lid with some scissors, she fashioned a few crude holes. Finally, she lowered the jar into the tangle of cobwebs on the window sill and coaxed one of its inhabitants inside.

It was only after she'd locked the front door that she noticed the snot-coloured rental car parked in the driveway. *Dad* was here. Dad was *here*. Poppy didn't want to imagine what his being here meant. All she knew was that she had to get to Gran.

There was a small police van parked outside Mitsy's house. As Poppy, Erasmus and Mitsy arrived at the end of the driveway there was a volley of yaps and barks from inside. Marley the dog's snout appeared at the window and he clawed excitedly at the glass. He'd obviously found his way home out of Claria's cave without too much trouble.

As Mitsy began to follow the path to the front door, Erasmus leaned forward and grabbed her wrist. He spun her around so she was facing him. Her big violet eyes looked up into his powerful green ones.

"You are not a nitwit," Erasmus told her. "And your book *isn't* stupid."

The tiny girl beamed and rocked giddily on her heels. She turned to Poppy as if expecting more praise.

The curtains in the house were suddenly flung open and Mrs Felt's pale, anxious face came into view. The front door swung open so violently that it upset a blue tit that had been luxuriating in a nearby birdbath. Mrs Felt's arms wrapped themselves like scarves around Mitsy's neck. Constable Bunty stepped out of the house, pulling on his custodian's helmet with a smile. He frowned when he spotted Poppy, Churchill and the until-very-recently-missing Erasmus lurking on the pavement, but they scooped up the pig and bolted before he had a chance to question them.

"She'll be at the pub still," Erasmus said of his mother. "She stays and cleans on a Monday night till Tuesday morning."

"I'll walk you," Poppy said hoarsely. "It's on the way to the hospital bus stop."

The Threader's Eye Inn was cold-windowed and as they walked in silence towards the front door, Poppy could smell bleach and hot water, and the sound of a mop slapping against floorboards echoed out of the open door.

She paused beneath the trees and Erasmus continued up the path.

"We'll speak," Poppy said and Erasmus swivelled round.

"But we're speaking now," he replied, frowning.

The mopping sounds stopped and Ms Tall appeared in the doorway. She leaned the mop against the wall and put her hands on her aching lower back. Fishing in her apron, she pulled out her cigarettes and lit one up, looking out across the misty pub garden.

Her cigarette landed, unsmoked, on the steps leading up to the pub.

There was a breath. Then a scramble of feet on the bleachy wooden stairs.

She stopped a few feet away from him.

Poppy edged away, hiding herself behind the trees.

Ms Tall put out her hand and ran her fingers through the boy's hair.

Her shoulders buckled first. Her chin trembled and she fell to her knees. Then, pulling her son towards her, she howled like a child.

It was the first time Poppy had seen Ms Tall without her sunglasses.

Her eyes were green. Green like his.

Poppy and Churchill stepped off the bus, which was the first of the morning, and crossed the almost deserted car park next to the hospital. She spotted Dalia's gold estate car near the entrance.

Poppy felt her heart speeding up as she passed the

little bit of garden beside the ambulance bay. Out of the corner of her eye, she noticed a familiar shape slumped on the bench, a disposable coffee cup in one hand and his head in the other.

Poppy approached the bench slowly, and sat down beside him. Dad looked up. His eyes were red and his thin hair nested in an untidy tangle on his head.

"The police let your friend Marley out of prison," he said hoarsely.

Poppy opened her mouth, but didn't speak.

"Apparently they didn't actually have any evidence against him at all in the end. Lost some of it, or so Dalia told me."

"I'm glad you're back," he said, nodding his head and swallowing. "The doctors think it's nearly time."

Poppy felt a lump in her throat. Churchill curled himself up beside Dad's shoe.

"Before we go in…" Dad said, putting his coffee cup on the ground. "Gosh, Poppy, I've come so close to telling you this so many times, but I…"

Poppy watched him.

"Your mother wasn't alone when she died, Poppy," he said and Poppy felt her mouth twitch.

"She wasn't even driving the car when she had her accident," Dad said. "I was. And I…I did everything I could to keep you from finding out."

Poppy's eyes welled, and hot tears bloomed above her numb cheeks.

"And I know you can never forgive me," he said, his voice breaking. "And I know I'll never replace her. But I want you to know that I wish I could...go back..."

His eyes filled, and his head fell into his hands as he wept.

"It wasn't your fault." Poppy trembled. "I promise you, it wasn't your fault."

He grabbed her arm and pulled her towards him.

"I'm sorry, Poppy," he wept. "I'm sorry for everything. I miss your mum."

Poppy sniffed. "Me too."

"I remember when she was pregnant with you," Dad said, wiping the corner of his eye. "She was having a scan. It was the first time we heard your tiny heartbeat thumping furiously away. And she said, 'Every beat my heart makes is going to be for this little girl.'"

"She's still here," Dalia whispered as they entered the silent ward.

Gran was in a room by herself this time. Poppy put Churchill on the end of her bed and he instinctively curled into a ball on her feet.

Poppy kneeled down beside Gran and pulled the jar from her coat pocket.

"I brought you a spider, Gran." She sniffed, undoing the lid and gently tipping the spider onto the frame. "For your window sill. So it feels a bit more like home in here until you can come back."

Gran swallowed. "Bravo, popsicle." She gestured to a plastic cup of water on her bedside table.

This was Poppy's chance. Slipping the Tupperware container out of her pocket, Poppy pinched a few grains of the glistening sugar cube in her fingernails.

Dropping the container back into her pocket, she brought the straw to Gran's mouth. But the water just seemed to dribble over her chapped lips.

"Is the sugar locked away?" she asked, closing her eyes.

"Uh-huh." Poppy nodded.

"Wonderful girl," said Gran. She breathed in raggedly. "I want to tell you one last thing, Pops."

Poppy held the old woman's wrist to her cheek and listened.

"I was sad for many years when your mum moved away with your dad. I suppose that's why I didn't like him very much to start off with," Gran began and Dad shifted awkwardly.

"But I remember the day my happiness came back. It was the day your mum told me she was expecting you. And then a few months later, there you were: a pink bundle that made us all so unimaginably happy."

Gran breathed a rattling breath.

"Off you all go now," she whispered. "I want to be alone for a bit."

Dalia and Dad said goodbye, and Poppy gave Gran's

papery forehead one last kiss. She let go of the old woman's knobbly wrist. Churchill had fallen asleep, so Poppy left him at Gran's feet.

The doors closed behind them, and for just a moment they swung gently back and forth as if waving farewell.

The last of the autumn leaves hurried down from the towering trees which surrounded the yard, as they groaned rheumatically in the breeze.

Erasmus rustled some lighter fluid from the garden shed and, using Gran's old gardening gloves, Poppy dropped the now naked silk book into the wheelbarrow atop a mound of dried leaves. The silk might be gone, but they'd both decided that they wanted to get rid of it, to be on the safe side. When it was dowsed with the fluid, Poppy struck a match and ceremonially lit it. There was a thunderous *whoof* as the pile ignited.

"You're going to have to do a lot of visits around here with that sugar cube of yours," Erasmus said to Poppy, mesmerized by the flames.

"Do you think Regina will be friends with us once Wendy comes back to her old self?" Poppy asked.

"Does it matter?"

"Not really, I suppose," Poppy muttered. "Although it would be nice if she laid off the terrifying persona just...just a smidge."

Erasmus smiled and then blinked.

"Back at the Mills," he said, "when Lye put that thing in my ear and was trying to get the stories out, my head was so full, it felt like I had another person inside there, sifting around in my thoughts. And for a moment, I thought that thing was going to suck everything out of my mind. And I was scared. And then I heard a name, just one name, and it made being scared go away. And I knew everything would be alright. Because it was my friend's name."

A flurry of autumn leaves drizzled down from the trees, and Poppy leaned over and kissed his soft cheek.

"She's here, guys!" Mitsy squeaked from the back window. "Poppy, she's here!"

Poppy and Erasmus hurried inside, and arranged themselves beside Dad at the kitchen table. Poppy had been up early baking bread. She'd let Erasmus knead. It was in the oven, with some knobs of butter melting into little pools, just the way Gran liked it.

The front door creaked open, and a huge figure stooped to get inside.

"Mindthe doorstep, MissuzHerisson!" Marley mumbled elegantly, as Gran steadied herself on his arm.

"I've walked through that front door a thousand and one times, Mr Marley. I'm not going to trip over it now," Gran told him, rolling her eyes at Poppy.

"Wellyer lookin' vury well, if I may say so, Missuz Herisson." He bowed.

"I look like the back end of a bus and you know it, Mr Marley."

The six of them sat down, and Gran was soon pouring hot water into fragrant pots of tea, just like she used to.

"When do you fly out?" Gran asked Dad.

"Tonight," Dad said in a muffled voice, as a few crumbs spilled out of his mouth. Churchill saw to those. "So I'm going to spend the afternoon with Pops. I won't see her again for a few months," he finished off, throwing Poppy a smile. "But I'll be back."

Poppy grinned. Her fingers dipped almost absent-mindedly into her pocket, where the wooden peg was now tucked safely away. It made her feel like Mum was keeping a close watch on her somehow. Out of the corner of her eye, she could see the flickering wheelbarrow in the back garden. As the fire caught the dry leaves falling from the trees above, it gave a greedy roar and the spine of the silk book twisted unnaturally in the heat.

Gran had built a mighty fire in the grate that night, and Poppy felt drowsy, red-cheeked and happy. It was stuffy when she went up to bed, so she opened the window and left it wide. A gust of icy wind rattled across the sill and the whorls of cobwebs jostled excitedly. Gran might still insist on abiding by her four rules, but Poppy could get away with this one. For now, things were as they

should be. And Suds was just like any other faded little
town, where the post didn't come any faster, and the
people weren't any meaner or kinder than they were
two towns over.

And yet that night, as she drifted off to sleep, Poppy
Slub still found herself feeling for the wooden peg
tucked beneath her pillow. Just so she knew it was
there. Just because. Just in case.

QUICKFIRE QUESTIONS WITH SAMUEL J. HALPIN

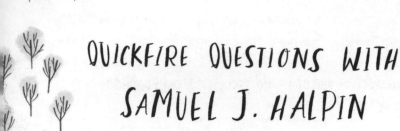

What inspired you to write The Peculiar Peggs of Riddling Woods?

My undying love for strange folklore, and of course my own indescribably wonderful grandmother.

Which book or fairytale gives you the shivers?

A favourite fairytale which always drove a chill through my spine was Pengersec and the Witch of Fraddom (spellings vary), where a malevolent witch is banished to float up and down on the seas in a tub.

Do you have a favourite anagram?

"Astronomer" when rearranged becomes "moon starer". Isn't that charming?

What sort of sweet would you pick from Bonhilda Bonhoeffer's shop?

Definitely a Dried Sourapple Skin. My tongue is tingling at the thought.

Have you ever met a miniature pig?

Never. I'm waiting for someone to introduce me.

What's the best costume you've ever dressed up in?

At school, I once dressed as the Mad Hatter and won a prize for my efforts. I've never felt prouder in all my life.

How do you come up with your ideas?

Sometimes they come out of nowhere, like cats in the night. Other times I might read a strange little quip and I start to boil and brew it in my head, until when I finally bottle the idea it's become something else entirely.

Acknowledgements

I was so afraid that I would miss someone off these words of thanks that I briefly considered throwing together a huge jumble of letters and telling people it was a thematic anagram. But rather bravely, as you now see, I've faced the thanking music and will now do my best to hurl my gratitude at everyone who has made it possible for *The Peculiar Peggs of Riddling Woods* to come gliding into the world in a wicker basket of its own:

To Emily Priestnall, for being a truly extraordinary human, for introducing me to my agent and for starting this book on its long journey along the river of publication.

To an exceptional agent, Silvia Molteni, for gripping my imagination with her ideas, dedication and belief in little old me.

To the publishing powerhouse that is Usborne. In the editorial team: Rebecca Hill, Becky Walker and Sarah Stewart. Rebecca and Becky your love for this book filled me with an air-pumping, heart-thumping fever from the moment I met you. Thank you for your laughter and your inexhaustible patience during my publishing novitiate. Sarah Stewart – the copy-editing plough that organiseth story magic. Thank you for your completely world-class comments and copy-editing. I still maintain that you are a genius.

The marketing folk – where would we be without your pure cunning? Anna Howorth, Joanna Olney, Stevie Hopwood, Jacob Dow and Katarina Jovanovic. Thank you for your inspired campaign and fist-clenchingly haunting build-up to the release of this book.

To the outstanding design team, Katharine Millichope and Sarah Cronin – the cover and inside design of this little book made me jitter with anticipation from the first moment I saw it. It is Tate-worthy.

And to sum up the Usbornites above, I'd like to say to *everyone* there: Thank you for your unfailing care for all the exquisite stories you produce. They are only made so by the way you sculpt, twist, design, pitch, sell, account and receive them.

To Hannah Peck – I have looked at your illustrations a hundred times and even now I still topple into each one of them and let my eyes take a swim between those wonderful tangles of lines. You're an artist in every sense of the word.

My wonderful family, to whom this book is dedicated, Mum and Dad: thank you for giving us your boundless imaginations and love of small things. The world remains yet to produce a pair of people so tirelessly devoted to enriching their children's minds. My siblings. Oh, you splendid creatures: Georgie, Jules, Micky, Mill, Xavie and Rem. You are my best friends and I love you all so very dearly. Thank you, Family, for your immeasurable love.

To Wojciech, for your unearthly ability to conjure cauldrons of the most delicious soups yet known to man. For your unwavering support, endless love, and for reading *The Peculiar Peggs* on the Underground to work, page by page, when this book was just an ink stained bundle that no one yet wanted and I was just a boy you'd met. I will never forget that.

My glorious nephew and nieces: Finn, Pip, Zuzu and little baby J & H Halpin who will be about to arrive when this book is released. I cannot wait until you're old enough to read this. I didn't know such an electric happiness existed until I met you all.

And finally, thank you, Sam. What...me? Yes, you, dearest. Thank you for not *completely* botching things up like you always do. You're welcome.